Dylan Petty
13450 Esperanza Rd
APT 224
Dallas, TX 75240

ISBN: 9781078355216
Imprint: Independently published

Toricane

First of the Aerilon Series

Cannington

Kingdom
of
Khan

Brimgan Mountains

Black Lake

Blackpool

Forraire

Hurricane

Tribes of Sin

Aexilon

Table of Contents

Introduction

"There are, it may be, many months of fiery trial and sacrifice ahead of us. It is a fearful thing to lead this great peaceful people into war, into the most terrible and disastrous of all wars. Civilization itself seeming to be in the balance." A suspended mass of contrasting colors levitated in front of the couch, taking the shape of a man in front of a podium, enthralling those nearby. A man with slicked, silver hair flicked his hand up. The noise resonating from the mass stopped.

This man's name was Darius Wagner. At first glance, he looked to be elderly, with deep wrinkles and a

cane at his side. He wore a deep frown beneath the
wrinkles and a knowing gaze that pierced the backs of
those sitting on the couch in front of him. The speed
and accuracy of his movements, however, did not give
way to the years behind them. This swiftness aligned
more so with his fitted three-piece suit, donned with
recently polished shoes.

The archway through which Darius entered was
much taller than any person could reach and wider than
seemed necessary for a room its size. It had a stone
perimeter that was met with mixtures of smooth wood
and metal textures, which encased the room in a bright
show of craftsmanship. The varying styles surrounding
the room seemed to show multiple artists from different
time periods collectively incorporating their minds into
one piece.

The room itself had very little inside of it, all of
which was being used. The balcony was shut off from the
room with a pane of glass that extended across its
entirety, showing two young women chatting in front of a
sunrise. They leaned against the railing which extended
from the exterior but lacked any support beneath it. Just
inside, a small couch sat an irritated couple. Darius, the
interruption to their morning routine, walked by the
couch, into the kitchen area, and looked in the fridge for
something worth eating.

Introduction

As he walked by, the noise stopped, followed quickly by the visual fading away and two heads swiveling to the culprit.

"What did you do that for?" asked the woman closest to him, who seemed more focused on her morning coffee than actually upset.

"It's all the same!" Darius exclaimed. "It's always the end of the world, the worst thing that has ever happened, or 'civilization itself seems to be in the balance,'" he mocked the words to which they were so intensely listening. The man continued to riffle through the fridge mumbling about everything always being the same.

He eventually gave up and started making eggs on the stove, which sat on an island between the kitchen countertops and the couch. Beside it was a half empty pot of coffee. The rest of the room looked bare without closer inspection. The walls didn't have decorations hanging on them or lights falling from the ceiling. Instead, the different textures surrounding the room seemed to mold into pieces of art that gave the room a lived-in feel. They trailed the ceiling with a glow that filled the space, compensating where the sunrise couldn't.

The young man on the couch, a slender fellow with matching plaid pajama tops and bottoms, interrupted Darius' rant. "They're saying this could be the war to end all wars," he stated simply. "It's not something you should brush off so easily."

Darius chuckled, "Come on, Ed. Didn't you live through the Napoleonic Wars? You know just as well as anybody, when you're in the thick of it, the fights will always seem more significant than they really are."

"Just like you know I don't like being called Ed," he replied, looking away, hurt at the thought of the war in his past. The woman beside him put her hand on his back, instinctively comforting him and gave Darius a sour look.

"Fine, *Edgar*. I shouldn't have brought that up. I know it's a sore subject, but the point still stands." Darius looked over apologetically, as he flipped his egg. "Back me up here, Chloe."

The woman, still glaring at Darius, had piercing green eyes with hair that flowed around them in heavy curls. She too wore a matching pajama set but seemed to do so with the intent of lounging with Edgar, rather than having just woken up. Her sharp features were usually softened with a smile, now being a rare exception. Nothing was more prominent upon seeing her, however, than her intelligence. The way she carried herself, spoke, and even laughed was a constant indication of a woman not to be trifled with.

She let go of the sour look after Darius' half apology and went back to her coffee. She took a big sip before replying, "It's already been a huge war for years, bigger than most. The fate of civilization might not rest in the balance. Still, having a little empathy for those who think so wouldn't hurt."

Chloe gestured toward the wall in front of her with purpose. Metal from the wall formed into a young man in uniform. The depiction allowed adjacent wood to flow into it, adding a scheme of finished colors that gave life to the shape. The man had a metallic grin on his face. He paraded across the wall in a cherry-finished uniform. A woman took shape off to the side, sadness etched into her eyes and a laugh formed on her lips.

"This is James Toggle, a random soldier, one of many. He will be shipping off to war soon because of the recent draft. James turns eighteen in three days. His plan was to marry this woman and work at the factory to support both of them. Instead, she'll be taking the job at the factory to replace the men being drafted, and he'll leave a couple days after their impromptu wedding. He's trying to cheer her up, but they both know what's about to happen. It's significant to them, whether it matters to the fate of the civilization or not."

The figures on the wall sat in place after Chloe stopped talking, but Darius motioned them away. The colors mixed into a portrait of himself sitting in a classroom. In the moving image, Chloe stood at the front of the classroom. "I get it. I get it," he said, cheerfully. "No need to lecture me. I'm not one of your pupils, Chloe." She wiped the image from the wall and let it revert back to the original artwork. "Can't I just be in a good mood?"

Edgar pipped up, "Of course, but a little empathy goes a long way." He looked at Chloe and got a nod in return. "Just because you've been here long enough to forget what it's like, doesn't mean we have. It's good to be able to connect with the recruits in that way, even somebody random like this." He gestured toward James.

Darius valued interacting with his pupils, and the thought of something creating distance in the interactions caused him to second-guess how willfully bliss his views seemed. It wasn't just anybody that could get to him like that. Chloe and Edgar were two of his more valued colleagues. He took the time to make his eggs that morning only due to the knowledge that they would be his company. If they were giving him advice, it was worth taking.

He put his eggs on a plate and went to sit with the couple. In the short walk to them, he pointed at the ground and waved upward. A chair that matched the couch's green cloth rose from the floor, along with a small, wooden table in front of it where he sat the eggs. "It could be a good thing to connect with the recruits more, especially first-years. They come here so bright and full of life, so to speak, with the responsibilities of their lives still weighing on them.

"How do you keep in mind the importance of everything happening on Earth with what's happening in your lives here? Things seem to move slower here but have that much more significance. They may call it *The Great War*, but it's just a squabble to us, a few civilizations at disagreement about who should be in charge. How do you put it in perspective?" It was unusual for Darius to ask for advice, which took both Edgar and Chloe by surprise.

Chloe took advantage of the situation before Darius could change his mind. She motioned the image of James Toggle back on the wall, a still-life of a soldier preparing to be shipped off. "It's all about focusing on the individual. This teenager is one of many, but it doesn't make his experience any more or less significant than what happens here."

"Plus," Edgar added, "it's been, what, a century now since there have been any commotions here? That's plenty of time to focus your attention on people like him," he pointed at the image for emphasis. "Just know what's going on with your recruits. You've been here a long time. Don't lose sight of why."

That last sentence seemed to especially resonate with Darius. He nodded, "You're right. It's still important to be present in their lives." He paused for a moment before realizing how rude it had been to interrupt their morning. "I'll let you get back to your coffee," he finished with a smile. Chloe and Edgar looked confused at the sudden change of heart but shrugged it off and relaxed back into the couch.

As Darius got up, the plate vanished into the table. The chair and table both dematerialized into the floor. He walked out of the room without a second thought. James' image dispersed, and the visual appeared back in front of the couch. He walked with purpose, as he always did, cane hitting the ground with every other step. His demeanor was exactly as it had been when he walked in the archway, only now his brow was one of a man in thought.

The walkway to his office had a granite floor that met walls with long spirals of interconnected rough green scales, smooth white brick, and variations of textures and colors where the two met. They formed a cylinder high above his head, only stopped by large windows throughout one side. He looked out into the courtyard to his right. There was an empty field where recruits would be out and about in an hour or so. Statues and trees were sprinkled throughout, the tops disappearing in the clouds, leaving a well-lit, but shaded, space below.

He walked through the corridor and whirled his index finger in the air for entertainment. A spectrum of colors emerged at his command. Spirals of gold and brown leapt out in concert with his finger, rippling down the long hallway. He flicked the air and created points of impact that caused waves of metalwork to echo. A few colleagues passed by without giving notice. They simply waved or said, 'Good morning.'

In the few minutes' walk to his office, Darius got bored of the ripples and started fusing granite from the floor with collections of gold and green pulled from the ceiling. They merged into a ball that moved through the hall alongside him. He did so without taking note of what was being created. His hand moved subconsciously, simply to bide time. Walking through the archway to his office, Darius found himself holding a figurine of a young man. He almost dematerialized the figure and let the granite settle back into his surroundings but took a moment of pause to look closer.

It was a figurine of James Toggle. A frown formed between his wrinkles momentarily before he sat the creation on his desk. Darius spent the next several minutes forming the figure more accurately, still unsure why. James, a soon-to-be soldier and husband, stared blankly back at Darius. *One of many*, he thought. *Maybe I focus on one for now.*

With the flick of a hand, liquid colors pulled out of the wall behind him and combined in the air. A miniaturized landscape of grass floated above Darius' desk. He shook his head. The green was replaced with sand and ocean. James' figurine liquified and floated to join the visual, forming back together as it walked across the beach.

Key points in James' life flickered quickly in and out. Darius looked on with interest, cane resting against the wall as James' father was sent off to war. From then, his father never showed up again, leaving most of the happier memories to stem from either his mother or uncle. He saw James meeting a young woman under a large oak tree after the sun had set. Every memory from then on had this woman in it.

Darius froze it. He wanted to explore in more detail, to feel what it was like to be there. He moved the images back in time, watching James' earliest memories. Darius spent the rest of the day getting into the mindset of James, attempting to understand what it was like to be of Earth in this day and age.

Eventually, he made it to the present and closed his eyes for a moment. When they opened, his eyes were a bright blue color, contrasting the dark brown they were before. His mind was with James now, watching a life play out that wasn't his own.

Post-Wedding Jitters

Alisa and James wanted to see each other, but it was tradition to separate the bride and groom until the ceremony. She needed him to get rid of that thought in the back of her mind, *we have two days.* He would be back in their new home eventually, but nobody knew how long. Her concentration shifted, instead, to putting on her dress. One step at a time. Just go through the motions, and they would be standing at the altar in no time.

The dress was a job for two, so James' mother offered to help. She was one of only a few people who could be there on such short notice. James' sister, his uncle and the preacher completed the party. Everybody had either been shipped off already or were too busy picking up the slack left in their family to join.

"You could always get married when he gets back," James' mother, Mariam, said for the tenth time today. She was a plump woman with a loving smile that never seemed to fade. "You know, when everybody can be here."

Alisa shook her head, "I couldn't ask for a better wedding. The one planned for next month was too big. I just want to marry him and ride off into the sunset," she said, before realizing it was two in the afternoon, "metaphorically. Nothing big and flashy. That's not us."

"What about your family?" Mariam unsuccessfully hid her curiosity.

With a slight half smile, Alisa sighed, "They don't approve anyway. It's amazing that you allowed James to get married before he turned eighteen, but, as of last month, I don't need their approval. Besides, they wouldn't have given it to me." She stopped for a moment but really felt the need to vent. "They are especially mad now."

"Why, dear?" Mariam looked up inquiringly.

"They would prefer me live with them than 'sully myself working at a factory.' I don't care. James and I would *prefer* to live together straight away and him take the factory job. That's not how life works. Things happen. He gets drafted. I need to work to pay for the house we just bought." Each reminder of the draft hurt a little. She looked down to see Mariam frowning at the thought of her son leaving.

"Don't worry Mariam, he'll be back in no time. Our life together may be postponed, but our marriage doesn't have to be."

Mariam finished adjusting the dress and stood up next to her. "Please dear, call me mom." She paused to give Alisa a loving glance, "I wouldn't approve of him marrying just anybody. My son is special but so are you. I wouldn't even need to meet you to know that. The way he talks about you, looks at you, everything you two do together: it's apparent you've both made the right choice."

Alisa turned around to give her a hug. "Thanks, mom," she managed through her closing throat. She would never admit it, but family approval meant a lot to her. It didn't cross her mind that the family is that much bigger now. One side of her family being wrong doesn't need to sour the other side. Her parents didn't agree with the marriage, but Mariam did. She would be seeing a lot of Mariam over the coming months.

Toricane

* * * * * *

James Toggle put on his suit for the first and last time before shipping out. Technically, it wasn't his suit. It belonged to his uncle, who offered it to him for the day. It didn't have quite the right fit, since his uncle was a few sizes bigger than him, but he still wore it well. The baggier portions slung down on his slight frame like a cape, revealing a slant in the shoulders that wouldn't otherwise be noticeable. His tie was pulled up just enough to fit the suit but not quite enough to meet his neck.

Alisa always told him that the life he possessed could energize the world. He was her battery, keeping her going through the hard times, when all else seemed to be falling apart. As he thought of her, a boyish grin spread from ear to ear, revealing a contagious smile. The smile ran up his face and into his sparkling blue eyes.

He adjusted the tie and started making his way to the altar. It's almost time. The nerves his uncle kept talking about were creeping into his stomach. *What if I forget my vows? What if I accidentally say, 'I don't?' Does that nullify the wedding? Is there a do-over?*

Deep in thought, with every possible worse-case scenario running through his head, he ran into his uncle. "Oh, sorry, Uncle Hugo. I didn't see you there," he said and continued walking.

14

"Woah! Woah! Hang on there, son." Hugo turned him around and saw the panicked look he expected. "Slow down. Take a deep breath. You're going to be great." Hugo took the few seconds he had to straighten his tie and fix the outfit as best he could. When Hugo had James' attention, he continued, "All you have to do is get up there and speak from the heart. Repeat what the pastor says and tell her how you feel."

Hugo had always been a sort-of father figure to James. Perhaps, James assumed, because he never had any kids of his own. It was a nice feeling to have somebody looking out for him, so he never questioned it too much, welcoming it instead. Due only to that connection, he felt close enough to share what was actually bothering him. "Uncle Hugo," James started, "what if I let her down?"

Hugo let out a billowing laugh that shook the wall he leaned against. "That's absolutely ridiculous. This girl loves you, James, and you're a good kid. What could you possibly do to let her down?"

James let the question hang in the air for a moment before answering, "I could not come back."

Hugo's laughter stopped. His face twisted like he was expecting a needle to puncture him at any second. That thought had crossed his mind, but he was attempting to let go of it for the day. The knowledge that James couldn't enjoy his wedding day because he was thinking about the war pained Hugo. Today was the day to be a rock, a role James usually took on.

"I'm going to be straight with you here. That's a real possibility." Hugo paused to collect his thoughts. "James, do you want to know the difference between you and all the other recruits?" Hugo always waited for an answer to his rhetorical questions. James nodded for him to continue, waiting for a reason to let go of the anxiety.

"The other recruits are thinking about surviving for the sake of surviving. When it gets tough--and it will get tougher than I, or anybody here, can imagine--they will cave into it. When dying becomes easier than living, they will die. There's nothing anybody can do to stop that. You, on the other hand, aren't surviving for your own sake. You're surviving for her," he pointed toward the wall Alisa was changing behind.

"When the going gets tough, when dying is the easiest option, you'll find a way to keep going. If your greatest fear is letting this girl down, then it's impossible for you to do just that. If you do everything in your power to get back to her, to be with her, you've done your duty. Screw the duty to your country. Millions die for their country. Fight tooth and nail to get back here and raise a family with Alisa. Do that and you will have made her proud.

16

"Not just that, you'll make me proud! When you get on that ship, it may very well be the last time I see you," Hugo's words were coming out slower as he fought back a tear, trying to get to his point before breaking down. "Purpose is the key to winning any fight. Your purpose is better than any I know. Even if you don't come back, you'll have made everybody here proud. It's not possible for you to let her down, son, as long as you fight."

At this point, there were only a few minutes left until the ceremony, and tears were making their way down Hugo's face. Once he thought of what could happen to James, they seemed to pour out. "I'm going to go clean up a bit before the ceremony," he motioned toward his face.

As he turned to leave, James pulled him back and gave Hugo a firm hug. "Thank you," he said, before releasing Hugo and heading to the altar.

James' sister, Cadence, was impatiently waiting at the steps with her arms crossed. "What took you so long?! We've been waiting!" she yelled across the room, motioning to the pastor beside her. "It's going to start any minute."

James rolled his eyes, "Okay, Cadence, there's only a few people here. We can start whenever we want."

The layout was that of a typical church, with enough benches to seat a hundred people. Each had a cloth ribbon from one end to the other. She had created an archway out of vines that extended over the center of the stage. On either side was a bouquet of similarly assorted primary colors, which seemed to be the leftover flowers after petals were placed throughout the entire walkway.

He looked around the room and was thoroughly impressed with the decorations. "Did you do all this in the last hour? It looks amazing." He was still reeling from the conversation with Hugo but found the surprise to be a good distraction from the metal butterflies floating around his stomach.

James expected Cadence to blow off her task and walk in at the last minute. He didn't realize until now she actually cared about making the scene look pleasant. The realization also came that she wasn't criticizing him for being late. Rather, she wanted the wedding to go as planned, something very unlike Cadence. *Maybe she needs a distraction as much as I do.*

"I love the arch, sis! I didn't expect anything this great." He made eye contact, so she understood the sincerity of it when he added, "Thank you."

She blushed, then abruptly changed the subject. "Come stand here! Alisa could walk out any second." Cadence motioned to the right side of the preacher, and

18

she went to stand a few feet behind where Alisa would be any second.

Hugo walked out of the bathroom and down the path Alisa would be on any minute. Seeing them standing at the ready, he took his position directly behind James. They hadn't actually discussed who would be standing where. It seemed to be an instinctive move on both of their parts. James looked around at the pastor and Cadence; everything was ready. It all panned out. How, he had no idea. Regardless, it looked better than he could've hoped.

As James looked around, his eyes flashed to a floor-length dress walking through the door. The dress was accompanied by an expression of excitement and eagerness. Mariam was almost transparent on the walkway, throwing out petals for the goddess behind her. James' mom quickly took her place in the front row, moving Alisa further into focus.

White dresses were rare in times like these, something only a few could afford. Instead, Alisa was wearing a sky-blue material that fit her frame closely and extended out toward the floor. It was beautiful by any standards. James' eyes flitted quickly from her dress, though. This was the first time he'd seen her truly smile since learning about the draft. He was going to cherish every moment of it.

He remembered the first time he saw her, like she was an optical illusion to him, discovered only to never be understood fully. A marvel to behold but not one to be taken in by a single glance. The enchanting presence she brought into every room carried over into his memories and filled it to the brim.

Before James could fully appreciate it, Alisa was standing in front of him. The preacher started to recite verses from the bible. The words were muffled slightly by a commotion outside, ignored by the family. One downside of a small town is having the church adjacent to the bar. People yelling was no rare occurrence.

The preacher spoke slowly, "We are gathered here today to join James Toggle and Alisa Moore in holy matrimony. In their time together, they have seen their love and understanding of each other grow and blossom and now have decided to live out the rest of their lives as one. I can say without a doubt, there is not a single person here that can show just cause why they may not be joined together."

The noise outside grew louder, but he continued unabated, "I believe you have made your own vows. You may read those now," he said, motioning toward James.

James struggled to pull out a piece of paper from Hugo's jacket pocket. He took a deep breath and looked down at the scribbles that had taken hours to manifest. He wanted it to be perfect, but the words he wrote down weren't. Shaking his head, James put the paper back into his pocket.

He looked into her eyes, "I love you, Alisa." There was a pause as he looked for the right words, "There's only one thing in this world I know for sure: my life is yours. It's impossible to know what's going to happen, but I do know I will cherish every day I have with you. When I'm not with you, I will fight to get back." He smiled, "Everybody has a purpose in life. I believe mine is to be with you." James slipped the ring on her finger.

The preacher gave a smile at the last sentence then turned to Alisa. She nodded through a tear forming in her eye. "People always look for *the one*," Alisa started. "They spend their whole lives thinking if they just find the right person, everything will be better. It could be anybody in the entire world for them.

"I know that to be untrue. It couldn't have just been anybody, only you. I will wait however long it takes for you, because there's not going to another one for me. You are my one." She finished with a slight nod, like the rehearsal she did the night before had been worth it. Alisa quickly grabbed the ring and slipped it on his finger.

The commotion outside became more distinct. Several voices could be heard yelling. Cadence shuffled uncomfortably but tried to refocus on the wedding. The preacher frowned at the interruption, "By the power vested in me, I now pronounce you husband and wife. You may now kiss the bride."

James leaned in to give one final kiss to his fiancé and the first kiss to his wife. It was soft and short. Alisa leaned in further to prolong the moment but was distracted by the yelling. It normally would have settled down by now but seemed to be getting worse. They both leaned back to hear the preacher say, "I present to you Mr. and Mrs. James and Alisa Toggle!"

Clapping ensued from Hugo, Cadence and Mariam. The preacher congratulated them. James leaned in for another kiss. On the other side of the wall a handful of people could be heard screaming. James wished they would stop. It was a perfect day, and the best part of it was being stained.

He leaned in further to the kiss, pushing the commotion out of his thoughts. The yells were impossibly loud. He heard a group gathering outside the church. He heard a gunshot. It shook the walls.

James took a step back, startled. He looked around to make sure everybody was okay. There was a small hole in the wall, light shining through. The preacher was still standing. Hugo was on his feet. Mariam and Cadence looked okay. *Where is Alisa?* She had just been right in front of James.

He looked down to find her kneeling on the ground. *What happened?* James looked for blood. There was none. He looked for life. She was alive. Not just alive, she was weeping. *What happened?* he asked himself again.

James followed her gaze and saw a young man lying there. His face was hard to make out through the blood. Overwise, he seemed like an average person, although somehow familiar. His suit was really baggy. *Baggy suit.* Something clicked in his brain. James looked down at himself to find the same baggy suit. He froze in place, unable to comfort the love of his life. *What is happening?*

"Hey there!" A voice came from the bullet-riddled wall. The enthusiasm of it momentarily took him by surprise. His head swiveled toward the voice. A man, looking directly at James, stepped through the wall. *Through the wall.* The wooden structure seems to mold its way around his body as he walked through it. Although, it didn't have to move far.

The man was small and skinny with greying hair and the most peculiarly square goatee. He walked toward James with a heavy limp and a large smile on his face. The smile was so out of place it caused James to look away. A frown appeared at the lack of attention. It was obvious this man expected more of a reaction.

It took a split second of seeing this inexplicably injured man to snap James out of his trance. He knelt down to comfort Alisa, telling her it would be okay. "I'm fine, Alisa. I'm right here!" He didn't get a response. "Look at me! I'm right here!" His entire family gathered around the body. Nobody looked at him. He put his hand out toward Alisa, but it went straight through her.

"They most definitely cannot hear you." The man was still walking toward James. Limping seemed to be slowing down his progress. The smile on his face never left as he said, "Unfortunately, you're dead. Your body is right there." He waved that thought off, "Oh, I'm sure you can see it. This must be difficult for you!"

At the last sentence, James turned toward this man, "Difficult?! Who are you?"

"Ah, yes. How rude!" The man extended his hand, "Daniel McClure, at your service!"

James stared at the hand. He looked back at Alisa. Daniel interrupted his moment of shock, "Aw, to be young and in love again. I still remember the first time I died, you know. Just glimpses, of course. I am an old man after all." James was frozen. Daniel's words went straight through him, incomprehensible in his state.

Daniel stared off into the distance, recalling what used to be. "I can remember beaches, sunsets and castles. Back then, of course, castles were all the rage! If you had the biggest castle, well, let's just say those kings were compensating for something. But, the beaches! Ah, the beaches! They were stunning. Seeing the sun coming up, reflecting off the ocean. Simply perfection."

What is happening? James thought, again attempting to comfort Alisa. He kneeled down and ignored this man behind him, giving Alisa his attention. His arm went straight through her. His words echoed vacantly off the wall.

"That was back before people could live long enough to really enjoy it! Life is such an adrenaline rush! It's like being in a train wreck next to all the people you love." Daniel gestated wildly throughout his explanation, "Some die sooner, some later, and you never really know the order of these things, but you do know it will eventually happen. That knowledge keeps you on the edge of your seat!"

He questioned that thought, "Or, maybe it's like watching a train wreck. You just can't look away, even though plenty of other things are happening. Oh! Or, it's just a regular train! Plenty of different tracks to go down. Wait, that's not right. There's no dying in that scenario. It's difficult to *track* down the right metaphor sometimes."

He waited for laughter from his one-man crowd, to no avail. James gave up getting Alisa's attention and sat back against the wedding arch. Daniel frowned in frustration, "Come on, James! That was hilarious. Track. Trains...You get it. Regardless, you can let go of whatever's going on here. We have much to discuss."

By this time, the family had started to carry him toward the clinic nearby. They were taking away his body. The love of his life went with it. "That's not me, Alisa. I'm right here," he mumbled, knowing she wouldn't respond. He was in a state of numbness, unable to understand what was happening. He realized the body they carried out was now just a shell. He knew this was the next step in whatever came after getting shot in the head. What he didn't know was why this man walked through the wall, acting like his death didn't matter.

Daniel perked up, "Don't worry about her! She'll eventually die too!"

Without comprehending his actions, James stood up and clocked Daniel, who saw it coming but let the punch connect. Some blood formed at the side of Daniel's mouth, which quickly retreated back to the wound. His face only moved slightly from the punch. The smile never left.

"I may be a little out of practice with this conversation stuff. Perhaps I said something I shouldn't have. Would you let me retry?" He held out his hand again, "I'm Daniel McClure, at your service."

James, defeated, shook his hand. He collected himself and tried to find the words. Alisa was gone, but he would find her. It would have to wait until after this man finished talking. There seemed to be no way to shut him up or get her back for now. After a moment, he asked, "Daniel, what is happening?"

"Well, James," he leaned in, as if to tell a secret, "you just died. That was your body they carried out of the room."

"Yes, I think I got that part." James turned away and started pacing, "In the thirty seconds you've given me to process that, I think I got it. Why are you here? Why did this happen? How did I just die?!" *Get it all out now, and let me go,* he wanted to say.

"Ah, yes," Daniel gave an exasperated sigh. "I forgot how much you don't know. I should've realized there would be questions. The last is easy enough! There was a bit of a squabble outside. Some drunk folks decided to get in a fight. As you can imagine, alcohol does not improve accuracy. Hence, you died. Rather elegant how simple and random it is, right?"

"Yes, *very elegant,*" James replied, to Daniel's delight. "Why me?"

Daniel pondered that question for a second before replying, "Like I said, random. Drunks get in fights. People have guns. Things escalate. You are really the most spectacularly random thing I've seen in a while!"

"Thank you?"

"Well, you're very welcome, good sir! As for your other question, I am here to guide you to the next step in this process." Daniel smiled, seeming to enjoy this responsibility.

James sat in silence for a moment. His family was gone, attempting to save him. They would be mourning him soon. One thought in particular invaded his mind. "Can I say bye to Alisa?" he pleaded for closure.

"Unfortunately, no. I'm in a bit of a hurry," Daniel waved it off, looking at a watch that wasn't there. "We need to move this along. She wouldn't even be able to say it back, which is not great closure. It'll just prolong the inevitable."

Slowly, the church liquefied into the ground. James tried to run out of the way of the ceiling. A hole opened up around him as it dematerialized, and the building disappeared into the ground. It was replaced with an endless field of green. James' town was gone. Grass stretched as far as he could see. His family had been right outside the door. He looked around for any sign of his family, town, anything. Nothing.

Daniel frowned at the scene in front of him. He waved his hand. The grass beneath their feet turned into sand. Water rose up from the ground to create an endless expanse of blue just in front of them. The sun unnaturally rose halfway above the water, reflecting off the surface. "That's better!" he said, with a smile. "Don't you think so?"

"Where are we? How did we get here?" James didn't understand where his town went. Alisa wasn't anywhere in sight. His panic heightened.

"We are still in the same place. I just changed it up a little." Daniel looked at his worried face. "Oh, don't fret. Your family can't see this. Only me and you can see the changes I made."

James had to admit, this was a beautiful scene, but it didn't feel real. Daniel basked it in for a moment. "I told you I liked watching the sun set over a beach. It's been so long since I've had the chance to truly see it." His eyes never left the reflection of the sun on the ocean, "Beautiful. Absolutely beautiful."

Regardless of beauty, James' mind was still on his wedding. Yes, he died, but who was this guy? Why is death watching the sunrise with a strange man. He was getting annoyed. "There's no time for me to say bye, but you have time to watch the sunrise?"

"It's actually a sunset, but okay. You make a good point. This train needs to pull into the station." He looked at James for a reaction to his callback. Nothing.

"Straight to business, then. First off, do you have any more questions we can get out of the way?"

"Are you serious?! I have so many questions. What—"

"Well, those are going to have to wait," he said, as a light appeared in front of James. "There's not much time before they start to get suspicious."

"Who—"

"They'll answer your questions, incorrectly but still answered. Just listen." Through the smile, his expression became serious for the first time. This got James' attention. "You're going to walk through that portal in a second. You're a newbie, so they'll explain everything you need to know. At least, everything they think you need to know.

"First off, don't tell them you saw me. You died. A portal appeared. You walked through. That's the extent of it. Second, don't trust Darius."

"Who's—" James started.

"No time!"

"No!" James yelled. "Why show yourself to me if it wasn't necessary?"

"That's point number three," he said, pretending not to be interrupted. "I need to establish a connection with you. Take this." Daniel pulled out a pen from his pocket and put it in James'. The force he pushed it into James caused a drop of blood to stain his shirt.

"Don't lose that! I'm going to contact you once you're on the other side, but you have to keep that with you. Now, go through. I'll explain more later, when I can establish the connection."

"Wait, but—"

"No, James. You've waited long enough. You need to appear with the others. Go now." His voice momentarily turned to anger.

James wanted more than anything to get away from this conversation, but he had to know, "Why me?"

"I told you, randomness is elegant," Daniel replied, before pushing James into the light.

Toricane

New Lease on Life

James was surrounded by nothing. The white light he was pushed into faded above as he fell from it. If the light wasn't fading, he wouldn't have been able to tell he was moving at all. There was no air or jolt of speed. His mind felt empty. He simply floated. Below, he was starting to make out a white void, one small thing to occupy his thoughts. It slowly got bigger until it surrounded him. He was suspended in unending whiteness. Somehow, he felt untroubled by the panicked despair leftover from moments before. James tried to remember where the despair came from, but he only saw white.

His feet touched something solid. There was a surface beneath him. Looking back, he noticed a chair and took a seat. There seemed to be nothing out of the ordinary to James, nothing to concern him in the world. When his gaze lifted from the chair, there were people surrounding him, all sitting and lined up in rows. They seemed to be having similar experiences, given by the confused looks.

James felt his heartbeat slow but couldn't remember why it had sped up. The panicked feelings left him completely. None of this concerned him. It was rather normal, really. He made eye contact with one of the others, a tall, lanky man with messy blonde hair and ripped pajamas. The man waved at him and got a wave from James in response. The man's clothes made him curious. Looking down, James saw a baggy suit. *Hmm, I wonder what the occasion was*, he asked himself. *I never wear a suit.*

No specific memories came to the surface. He was dead. There were people around him. *Oh well. I'm sure I'll think of why I'm here, eventually.* His mind moved to other things, like where he was and who all the people were.

Everybody looked to be around his age. For the most part, they all wore tattered clothes, with the exception of a couple pajamas. He started to look behind him when a woman appeared in front of them.

She had flowing brown hair and sharp features. The bright grey uniform she wore matched her demeanor. James could think of no explanation for how impeccably this uniform fit the woman. It fanned out and seemed to fade into the air before reaching the ground. He grew self-conscious while wondering if there would be any clothes for him.

"Hello there! Sorry I'm a little late," she started, even though nobody had seen her enter the room or knew what was supposed to be happening. They had no idea she was late. "I'm here to let you all know what's going on. To start off, don't be alarmed if you're having trouble remembering things. We have temporarily put a hold your long-term memory to allow for a peaceful transition."

While this would normally have been incredibly alarming news, everybody seemed to be nodding their heads. James' sense of calm was shared over the endless space. He understood why a group of newly dead people would need a bit of easing. *Wait, I'm dead? Strange.*

"You'll get your memory back just as soon as this introduction is over, I promise. Now, is there anybody here who doesn't know why they are here?" She paused for a moment before adding, "Don't be shy. Judge-free environment here. Just raise your hand. There are always a few."

James wasn't sure what the woman meant. He was dead. This was where the portal went. Was there more to know? *Maybe people didn't know this?* It seemed so obvious. His hand stayed down. Several others looked around before timidly putting their hands up, including the tall, lanky man who waved at James earlier.

"There we are. This is the not so fun part. The rest of orientation, however, should be very exciting!" She took in a deep breath, "I'm so sorry to tell you: you have died. This is the next step in your journey."

There was a quiet murmur from those who were just now realizing it. A woman behind James stood up, "Is this heaven?"

The speaker held her hand up, "I promise we will get to all of that. Please, in the future, if you have questions, raise your hand." It was apparent she dealt with this often. Her cheery attitude never left, allowing the woman to sit back down without feeling unheard. "To answer the question bluntly, no. This is not Heaven. This is also not Hell. This is simply the next step."

She took a moment to herself before continuing, "Ah! My colleague is almost here. We were both running a bit behind this morning. Back to basics, my name is Chloe Ruskin and I will be giving you a background on your experience here. My friend here," she pointed to her left just as a man in a suit appeared, cane at his side. James, again, felt outshined by his own baggy suit. "Is Darius Wagner. He will be showing you some of the differences between the place you came from and where you are now."

The woman sitting behind him shot her hand up. She was a young lady with brown eyes like two bronze coins, low cheekbones, and straight blonde hair. Her face matched the confusion James felt when people tried to teach him math. Before Chloe could call on her, she interrupted, "Where is that?"

Chloe laughed, but Wagner looked annoyed. Wagner answer, "It is here, young lady. That's where. No other information would make sense to you without context. So, we will give you that context, if you would let us. Also, please don't call me Darius. Professor Wagner is appropriate." His gaze surveyed the room as he talked, settling on James long enough to make him nervous. The woman behind James quickly sat back down.

Chloe finished chuckling and continued her speech, "You may call me Chloe. Don't mind Darius, he's been in a bad mood all day. So, where were we? Ah, yes! Right now, we are in a white-room. It's a place we reserve for orientations, so it won't overwhelm anybody. Let's just jump into it!"

Professor Wagner waved his hand. James saw black liquid seep from the wall to its surface, then solidify. It was a simple depiction of a line going between Earth and some place labeled Toricane. The image moved while they spoke. Chloe started, "All of you in this room have died for the first time and come to this place we call Toricane. It will not be the last time you die. On Earth, some religions assume you get one life, and some assume you get reincarnated forever. It's actually somewhere in the middle and not exactly reincarnation."

Wagner interrupted quietly, "I wouldn't call it reincarnation. That might just confuse them."

Chloe nodded, "Right. Okay, forget reincarnation. You aren't immediately born somewhere else when you die. Instead, you come here for one year." The bronze-eyed woman raised her hand again but was waved off. "I promise I will answer your question, dear. Just let me explain first.

"You are here for a year and sent back to Earth, born again with no memory of your occurrences here and, yes, born as a human person," she said, rolling her eyes. "You may have noticed, regardless of when you died in your life, you now appear around early adulthood." Most everybody was shocked at this and started looking at their hands. James noticed no difference. "As you die more and come to Toricane, you will get slightly older."

Wagner interjected, "This does not mean you are essentially immortal. First off, dying in Toricane prematurely is a one-way ticket back to Earth. You only have five lives. That fifth time in Toricane, you will be given the choice of staying here or moving on."

Chloe took the opportunity to cheer everybody up, "This means you have four more lives to live on Earth! That's exciting! Both of us have been through our Earth-time and moved on to permanent lives here. We age slower on Toricane, but the aging does still happen. It's only so long until you move to the next step in the journey."

Bronze-eyes stood up without being called on, "My name is Carissa Hart. If we die at different times, would we come back to our second year at different times?"

Chloe answered before Wagner had the chance, "Asking the hard questions today, Carissa! No, I think you'll find time works a little differently here. We actually have an entire training dedicated to time. It's not required, but possibly one you would be interested in taking."

A confident man with a bullet-ridden military uniform stood up. "What are you talking about? What is this Toricane? Why is there training? None of this makes sense!" He started to sit down then straightened up for a second to add, "The name's Gary Turnbull."

James saw Wagner step forward quickly before Chloe could speak. "The world here is not a peaceful place. At least, it wasn't until Toricane came about. We built this city from the ground up to give people the chance to live in a diplomatic community, separate from the rest of the barbaric world.

"All we ask of you is to be prepared in the case of an attack. That's why it's mandatory to enroll and take the programs here, to learn to harness abilities you would not have back on Earth, for the betterment of the community. Of course, you are free to leave anytime. You would simply not be welcomed back."

Wagner look satisfied with his speech and took a step back. Chloe, trying to soften the onslaught of information, added, "You'll find that the things we teach you in Toricane will help you become your best selves in the next life you live. Yes, it's for the city's protection, but I see that as a perk associated with the ocean of knowledge and abilities you will gain here."

A few other questions got answered as James sat there taking it all in. He would have to process whatever 'abilities' meant later, since his memories slowly flooded back. The suit he was wearing, his uncle's. He was at a wedding when he died. Somebody's wedding. It was Alisa's wedding. *Who's Alisa?* Why would he go to a wedding two days before being shipped off to who knows where. *It was my wedding.*

Memories poured into James' mind. Anguish came back. His family walking out of that church. He'll

40

never see them again. *How can I see them again? I need to get back.*

He remembered the beautifully decorated church. A tear welled up in his eye when he thought of Alisa's face just after the gunshot. She wanted him back, but now he was as far away as he could be. How could he get back?

"Okay, I think that concludes—"

James stood up, "What about loved ones? Will we ever see them again? How do we make that happen?"

Sadness infiltrated Chloe's gleam, mirroring several others in the group. Some perked up to hear the answer. Wagner made eye contact with James again, a look of pity in his eyes, "Unfortunately, that's not possible in the way you want it to be."

He took another step toward the group with a look of sadness, "My recommendation, after living five lives on Earth is to cherish the memories you have with your loved ones. In some lives you will have plenty of love and in others you will have none. Do not dwell too much on those times." He looked at James, "How old were you when you died?"

It seemed like a rhetorical question, but James still answered, "seventeen." A handful of people from the group turned to him and gave understanding looks, while a few snickered at his puppy love.

"Assuming your loved one was also seventeen, by the time you were reborn and again seventeen, they would be almost forty. It's a sad realization, but when you go back to Earth you will have no memory of them. You will not even know to look for them. You won't remember them until you die again."

James interrupted, "But, you said time works differently!"

Wagner allowed the rudeness, given the topic, "Yes, but not always in your favor, as Carissa may be able to tell you after her Time Study program.

"I do not recommend this, but you may *see* the person again by scrying them, another lesson. You can only physically see them and what they see. No talking. No interaction whatsoever. It can be painful seeing their lives without you in it, without being able to do anything. The process can also be physically painful if something were to happen to them during the scry." He winced at the thought.

"Your best bet is to allow them to live the rest of their lives and move on with yours." Several glares were immediately directed toward Wagner. "Yes, it's an unpopular thing, but I promise, you'll fall in love again.

42

The two most natural things in life are love and death. You've experienced them both and can do so again."

James sat down, not in defeat, but defiance. Everybody else murmured to each other as the session was wrapping up. Chloe quipped to Wagner about forgetting to include taxes in his list. The woman next to James put her hand on his knee, "It's going to be okay. I think it's been so long since they actually lived, it's hard for them to empathize."

James put on a half-smile before turning his head toward her, "Thanks." She had surprisingly long brown hair, parted in the middle. Her facial features were soft, along with her hand. James also noticed a wedding ring. He looked down to see a wedding ring on his own hand.

"I'm Azalea Spearing, 22 years old." She extended her hand out.

James shook it and replied, "James Toggle, young enough to deserve a snicker."

She rolled her eyes and sat back in the chair, "Ignore them! Seems like we all start in the same place here, regardless of how much *experience* you have." She laughed, and a snort came out. Azalea didn't acknowledge it, but several people around looked her way.

Chloe and Wagner finished up their conversation. James noticed that, when they were turned away from the group, a sense of urgency and panic were added into their hushed tones. Chloe faced the group and called out, "Are you ready to see Toricane?!" The murmurs heightened as she motioned everybody out of their seats. "Funny enough, we were right beside it the whole time. A fifth-year recruit created this amazing, seemingly endless, room to graduate Darius' final Create program."

"Actually," Wagner corrected, "he didn't pass the program. The boxes' illusion is stunning, but it lacks creativity. If you add any color to it, the illusion fades." He shook his head as he added some red around the sides and the walls seemed to immediately close in, "it's not all about mechanics. People need to be able to enjoy what you create in my program."

As they talked, the walls melted around them. It was a fast process, but Chloe purposefully slowed it down so they could take in their surroundings. The ceiling parted first, revealing trees directly above them. James noticed woven into the trees were different elemental creations. Swirls of fire and water decorated them, without falling or spreading. Some were form fitting the tree, while others hung from limbs like ornaments. One ornament hung low. It's elements turned from fire to water, ice to lava, pure to illusionary.

The whiteness lowered to reveal a wall in front of him like none James had ever seen with a small gap of empty expanse that took up the ground between him and the wall. It looked to be made of a smooth stone, with mixtures of metals that perfectly formed into the architecture like vines. Trees grew up on the other side. He strained his eyes trying to find their tops through the clouds. The walls continued as far to the left and right as he could see.

In front of them, a door appeared in the wall and started to lower into a bridge. He realized this door in front of him was actually the entrance to the fortress. James could see an entire city of different buildings and people through the entrance. It wasn't just some sort of training facility, this was Toricane. It went back farther than he could see, buildings increasing in height as it went. James could only see through a small opening between the door and wall as it opened. He moved closer to get a better look.

The door lowered slowly without a mechanism holding it. Landing on the ground, it seemed to meld into the grass. The door now seemed to be a wide, wooden bridge, which formed from the remains and ran over the pit surrounding this fortress. James had never seen anything like it. The door changed form right in front of his eyes.

The group started to make their way across, but James looked around in curiosity, attempting to find more structures like the one in front of him. They were standing in a clearing, sparse trees surrounding them.

Off in the distance behind them was a large, undecorated forest. It went on for as long as he could see. Above the trees, he could slightly made out a building in the background.

"What's that?" he asked, pointing toward the building as he caught up.

Without looking back, Wagner answered, "Those are some ruins that are currently unoccupied."

It was clear he didn't mean to elaborate on his explanation. Chloe continued for him, "Before our predecessors here in Toricane decided to start this warrior's academy, there were some small villages and tribes scattered throughout. It was much like Earth in the early days. People died and created the same world they came from.

"It wasn't until the founders decided to come together, for the betterment of their lives both here and on Earth, that the academy was made. Of course, it was necessary to protect themselves from attack and takeover, just like on Earth. Hence, we have Toricane, fortress for betterment." She gestured toward the opening in the wall, allowing recruits to walk through.

Lloyd, the tall, lanky man who was now standing near the back of the group with James and Carissa, spoke up, "So, this is the only civilization now?"

Wagner answered, "More or less. Anybody who doesn't want to participate in the laws of Toricane, which involve learning and contributing to society, have the option to live on their own. They can possibly find a tribe living out in the wilderness or just enjoy themselves in whatever way they wish. However, like I said before, they would not be welcomed back."

Azalea mumbled to the three of them near the back, "Seems super strict here." They all nodded in turn.

The group made its way down the bridge and through the doorway. Inside, the city was rife with people, all walking back and forth to shops. People chatted as they walked by, in no particular hurry. The shops lined every walkway, with little room to spare. Each building was a unique depiction of the owner's creation. The original look, however, was preserved in the smooth stonework. It was like a medieval artist's imagination come to life.

Some people wore the same bright grey uniform as Chloe. It was a form fitting robe that met perfectly in the middle and continued from the neck down to their much too similar shoes, fading from sight as it descended to the ground. The robe extended out at the bottom with a pattern unique to each individual. The rest, however, had varying outfits from every era. It created a scene of collective chaos. The slickness of the robes countering much more exotic or Victorian themes.

Taking in the scene around him, James still felt out of place in his baggy suit. They walked toward the inner part of this fortress. As he watched, the buildings got taller, turning into towers on each side of him. The road continued straight through Toricane.

Ahead, it ended at what he could only assume was a castle in its own right. The road stopped at a wall, much smaller than the one they passed through before but still taller than James could see over, with archways scattered along it. There seemed to be some barrier in the archways, sitting between James and the castle. It blurred his view of the castle, making it a mystery he needed solved.

Some people were asking Wagner and Chloe questions as they walked, but James wasn't paying much attention. The rest of the first-years were too preoccupied looking around at the sheer size and beauty of this place. James interrupted whatever they were currently discussing, "What's that building at the end of the road?"

Darius replied, "That, James, is where you will be taught. You'll have plenty of time to find your way around when lessons start. For now, you'll be staying here." He turned toward the building on his left and walked through the door. It looked similar to the other towers they had walked past. As Wagner walked through, he rubbed his hand across the wall and a label appeared above the door, '𝕱𝖎𝖗𝖘𝖙-𝖄𝖊𝖆𝖗𝖘.'

"For the next week, this will be your home!" Chloe exclaimed.

Everybody looked around at the interior in bewilderment. The tower was completely empty except for a single spiral staircase in the center. It led upwards to nothing. Carissa was the first to object, "Where exactly? There aren't any rooms!"

Wagner waved her off, "We'll get to that. A room will be ready when you get to it. First, we need to let you know exactly what to do this week, prior to your lessons."

Wagner had a serious expression on his face, which Chloe tried to interrupt and balance with joy, "Yes! The first thing you need to do is purchase a textbook for the year. This part tends to confuse people," she explained, before Carissa could throw any questions his way.

"We call this book 'The Book of Knowledge.' The pages inside aren't the same for any two people," she trailed off toward the end.

"You should also get some clothes," she added, looking around at the variety of different outfits. "Throughout the years, you will eventually learn to create your own things. For now, since you have nothing except for what was on your person when you died, Toricane will provide you with every you need."

Chloe finished and started making her way toward the door with Wagner. "Everything else will be explained to you when you have purchased your Book of Knowledge. Good luck!"

As she finished the speech, Wagner and Chloe started talking furiously amongst each other, not attempting to hide it this time, and ran out of the building. Several hands were raised, and everybody's eyes were on them. They left the tower in a frenzy, leaving the group to fend for themselves. There were twenty-one recruits standing around in the empty tower. Most looked around for a clue as to how to get in their room. Some huddled up in groups and started discussing how they died. James' thoughts were solely on getting that book. It had all the information he needed about the mysterious man he saw earlier and getting back to Alisa.

One for The Books

The recruits chatted for a few minutes amongst themselves about their various deaths. It started out as curiosity but ended up being a form of therapy, creating a bond of similar experiences. Gary didn't contribute how he died to the conversation, but several others did. A woman named Celia Simms, a short, blond athlete, was the first to divulge what felt like incredibly personal information. She was visibly upset at the thought but talking about it seemed to cheer her up.

"It's hard to remember the last few days," she started, "but I think it was the flu. I was training to be the first woman in the Olympic sprints. I pushed my body too far, I guess, and it couldn't fight against the illness."

There was no pity in the room around her. James, along with the rest of the first-years, contributed a feeling of empathy that could only be accompanied by similar experiences.

Carissa, always one to jump into a conversation, was next. "I remember mine vividly. I was walking down the street when a car came out of nowhere." She paused before adding, "I just remember the car right in front of me, then the white room."

James, who had been only half paying attention, was caught off guard by that comment. "Wait, you didn't have any sort of," he paused, looking for the right words, "out of body experience?"

Carissa thought for a second, "No. No out of body experience. Just splat, then here. What was that like?"

Gary stepped in, taking control of the room, "Did anybody else have an out of body experience? I didn't." He waited for somebody to speak. Nobody did. "Looks like it was just you. Strange." He gave James a suspicious look.

"It was probably just my imagination," he recoiled quickly.

Gary laughed, "Yeah, you're too young to have grown out of that. Was your imaginary friend there with you?" Laughs erupted from Celia and a few others.

Azalea tried to move the conversation back to light and cheerful. "I'm not sure how I died. Anybody else? I just went to sleep one night and bam, here I am!" A few nods came from around the group.

The group went back to discussions of their previous life as James thought back to his experience. In a way, his imaginary friend had been there. If, by imaginary friend, Gary meant an eccentric, weird fellow James couldn't think up in his wildest dreams.

Lloyd walked over to James and asked, "What was it like, the out of body experience?" He said it quietly enough that only the people directly around them could hear.

Carissa and Azalea turned to hear his response. "It was different. Stirring. Seeing your body just lying there...not something worth the experience."

Carissa chimed in, "So, how did you die?" Lloyd and Azalea looked at her like she'd just crossed the line, but they were also curious to know.

James figured there was no point in keeping it a secret. He wasn't trying to hide anything. "I was shot in the head," he bluntly stated.

They all three looked at his suit in confusion. Azalea, who had noticed his obviously new wedding ring already, put two and two together. "You were getting married," she realized with the matter-of-fact tone overshadowing any sympathy. James nodded. "An angry ex?"

"Honestly, I have no idea." He remembered what Daniel McClure told him and mocked the words, "Randomness isn't always elegant." They nodded in agreement.

Lloyd perked up, "But, we are here now, and it turns out we get four more chances!" James mostly shared in the enthusiasm. He wanted to look forward to the lives ahead but heard echoes of his uncle Hugo's words, *'If you do everything in your power to get back to her, to be with her, you've done your duty'*.

They turned back to the group, catching the tail end of a death story, before one person decided to try the stairway, since they still didn't know where their rooms were supposed to be. James recognized the volunteer from earlier, Gary. They were all dead for the first time, but he acted like he knew exactly what to do. The holes in his shirt only added to that effect, since they looked shockingly like bullet wounds, which led the rest of them to believe he died in the war. James assumed he was part of the war, something he would never get the chance to survive.

The four of them- James, Azalea, Carissa, and Lloyd- chatted while Gary walked up the staircase to nowhere. On his first step, the top floor of the tower lowered one floor, leaving a space for Gary to walk up the staircase. Realizing this is what Chloe meant by rooms being ready when they got to it, the rest of the group followed quickly. As each person stepped on the stairway, a new floor replaced the ceiling above them, getting closer and closer to the bottom.

Azalea spoke to the three of them as the larger group was thinning out, "We should probably get to our rooms. I'm not sure what time it is here, but I don't feel tired. Want to meet back here in a bit and figure out where to get our books?"

Almost immediately, James replied, "Yeah! Let's get our books," and started walking toward the stairwell. The other three followed, excited to see what the rooms were like. As James stepped on the stairway, the tower shuttered. Everybody grabbed the railing for support, unsure if this was some sort of earthquake. James froze in thought. *What did I do?*

After a few moments, the tower went back to normal and James' room appeared four flights up. He cautiously walked up the steps to his door. It said '𝕵𝖆𝖒𝖊𝖘 𝕿𝖔𝖌𝖌𝖑𝖊'𝖘 𝕳𝖔𝖒𝖊' in bright golden letters across the front. The other three in his group were just making it to their doors. Carissa shouted up from the second floor, "See you in a few!"

James found exactly what he didn't expect. The sign on the front of the door was speaking literally. The room was his bedroom. More specifically, the master bedroom in the house Alisa and he just bought. His first thought was that Wagner did not make this bedroom because this was not a good way to move on, like he had suggested earlier. It was a good way, however, to feel some normalcy, which is what he really wanted right now.

The bed was much cozier than the one it replicated from home, although that was nothing to complain about. James closed his eyes for a moment and soaked in the smell of home. The old wood and burnt smell he grew to love. Every broken board and piece of furniture was right. He could even make out the smell of Alisa's perfume that trailed behind her as she walked from room to room. It was perfection.

Before he could drift into the fantasy, he stopped himself. The room was rather bare. It contained only the look and furniture of his home, but none of his stuff. Irritated at the fact that he would be in this baggy suit for the foreseeable future, he walked out of the room.

Carissa and Lloyd were waiting at the bottom of the stairs, as he and Azalea, who also just stepped out of her room, made their way down. Other first-years filtered past. Some brave individuals made their way out alone, but most had found a group to meander with.

As soon as they stepped to the bottom floor, Carissa started talking, "My room was amazing! It had these gold stripes around it that had me mesmerized.

They were waving around me. I've never seen anything like it. It had a canopy bed! I can't wait to see the rest of this place."

Her enthusiasm was mirrored by Lloyd and Azalea. James didn't get as excited about the room, but his eagerness was piqued at the thought of getting his hands on that book. As they described it, this book gave any information you asked of it. All he had to do was ask how to see Alisa again. Of course, he expected obstacles, but there had to be a way.

The group made their way out of the tower. They looked back at it from the outside, expecting some difference due to the changes inside. It looked exactly identical as half an hour ago. James was getting used to not understanding and he let this one slide by without questioning it. The four of them wandered down the road, away from the academy and toward the shops they had seen on their entrance. On their way, they stopped the first stranger and James asked, "Where can we find The Book of Knowledge?" It felt strange to say, like he was a religious fanatic asking for the good word.

The man, who appeared to be middle aged, had a full, greying beard with a large smile underneath, "First-years, huh? You must be in all kinds of states! I was so scared my first day here. Couldn't quit thinking of everything I left behind. You get used to it, though."

Carissa responded, "It's exciting! I can't wait to have my book."

The stranger laughed and pointed further down the street, "You'll find all the stores you need closer to the gate. Toricane has a pretty simple layout. At the very center is the academy. In a circle out from the academy are all the living quarters and any further from that are the shops and fun places to hang out. You shouldn't really need to know this yet, but the head offices are underground, beneath the academy and spread out almost as far as Toricane."

Azalea spoke up, "Head offices of what?"

"Basically, anybody who doesn't own or work at a shop, works underground. They manage the laws and make sure everything goes smoothly here in Toricane. If you ask me, they don't really do much. We are pretty self-sustaining without an overseer. They don't interfere often."

He stood there for a second, trying to remember why this conversation started in the first place. James politely reminded him, "The Book of Knowledge?"

"Right! Keep going down the street and you'll see it on the right. A big sign out front says, '𝕭𝖆𝖗𝖑𝖊𝖞'𝖘 𝕭𝖔𝖔𝖐𝖘.' Nice guy, Barley. We play letchball every Sunday."

58

It was obvious he wanted to keep chatting, so James stopped it, "Thanks so much for the info!"

"Oh, of course!" He replied, coming out of his trance. "My name's Jerald. If you folks would like a drink tonight, feel free to come by my pub, 'Toricane's Trove.' You should be able to find it in your books, assuming you're getting along." He walked off, leaving the group to question what he meant by 'getting along.'

Azalea started walking down the street first. "I'm down to grab a drink after we figure out a little more about this place. Sounds like a good time."

The rest nodded in agreement. As they made their way to Barley's Books, conversation drifted to the crazy things that passed them. James saw a woman heating up food in the middle of the street with suspended fire. Lloyd noticed in one of the alleys was a cat seeming to wander with purpose, confirming that there were indeed animals in Toricane, a question that hadn't seemed particularly important but brought some small comfort. Carissa kept trying to stop and chat with strangers as they walked by, much to the rest of the groups chagrin. Azalea was the only one who was mostly quiet. She made comments about their findings but was otherwise deep in thought.

They walked almost the entire way back to the gate before reaching Barley's Books. Inside, they found a few of the other first-years in there as well. Gary, followed by Celia, had already purchased their books and were making their way back out of the store. Lloyd and Carissa waved at them but got no response.

As they walked in, and Barley, the owner, yelled to them from the other side of the store, "Hey there! First-years?" Barley looked to be the same age as Jerald, who they met earlier. Barley's voice hinted toward his age but was contrasted by sparkling eyes, excited to meet the newcomers.

The store was unexpected. It sold one item, The Book of Knowledge. There were stacks upon stacks of the book around the store, with no rhyme or reason for it. Some stacks acted as walls and others were just laying on desks. There were no bookshelves or any sort of organization.

Carissa replied, "Yeah, just looking to get our books."

He motioned them forward, into the store. When they got closer, he looked them over for a moment before asking, "Based on the previous group that came in, I'm guessing Chloe did not fill you in on how this works?"

"Well, we know the books show you what you ask it," James replied.

He smiled, "You've got it! Well, mostly. It's not a machine that spits out information at you." He grabbed a book off a stack next to him that went up nearly to his head. "I want to learn the history of Barley's Books," he said to the book.

He opened it to reveal a bullet pointed list of relevant facts. As he flipped through the pages, the list kept going. The items were as broad as 'Barley's Books is owned by Barley' to specifically giving a narrative of the hundred and first person to get a book at the store. "As you can see, it would be incredibly difficult for me to get anything useful out of this. To somebody this order and information might be very useful but not me."

Barley grabbed another book off the shelf. "I want to learn the history of Barley's Books." This book revealed a picture of Barley standing in front of a newly opened store. "Ah, that's a nice picture. I might get that framed. I didn't even know it existed! The things these books can find will astound you." He flipped to the next page to find a knock-knock joke.

'Knock-knock.

Who's there?

Barley.

Barley who?

Barley getting this business off the ground.'

Barley laughed hysterically at this joke. James couldn't help but chuckle at the idiocy of it. Carissa bent over in laughter as soon as she finished reading it and caught her glasses before they fell off her nose.

It took almost a full minute before Barley could gather himself enough to continue. "Sorry, it's just been a while since I've heard a joke so true. I like this book. However, I guarantee you that my Book of Knowledge would know exactly what I'm asking it to tell me. It just gets me. Do you get it?" he asked, looking at the four of them.

Lloyd attempted an answer, "So, it learns who you are the longer you have it?"

Barley looked at Lloyd with a face that said he wasn't completely wrong. "More or less. But...it's like finding a companion. Your connection will increase over time, but some people just click, and others don't. You need to find a book you click with."

Azalea laughed at this, "So, we're going to have a relationship with the book?"

"Precisely," he said, not picking up on the sarcasm, "because you and your book need to get along. If you don't get along with your book from the start, that's a red flag. A good book means a good experience here!" He paused for questions but didn't get any. "Great! So, go browse through some books. When you find yours, come up to the front and we'll get you all set."

All four of them exchanged strange looks. James broke the silence, "Okay, I'm going to go find a book I click with. Anybody want to join me?" Lloyd nodded and went with him. Azalea and Carissa went to a different stack to look.

Lloyd picked up his first book, "I think this has been the longest, strangest week of my life. Out of everything that's happened, this store is by far the weirdest." He opened the book and saw, '𝔚𝔢𝔦𝔯𝔡𝔢𝔰𝔱 𝔗𝔥𝔦𝔫𝔤𝔰 𝔗𝔥𝔞𝔱 𝔥𝔞𝔳𝔢 𝔈𝔳𝔢𝔯 𝔥𝔞𝔭𝔭𝔢𝔫𝔢𝔡.' Lloyd abruptly closed the book and sat it down.

James laughed, "I think you mean longest, strangest day of your death." They both smiled at the irony of that thought. James picked up a book, "Let's get crazy with this. Show me the future!" He opened it and found a handwritten inscription, '𝔑𝔬𝔱 𝔱𝔥𝔦𝔰 𝔬𝔫𝔢. -𝔇𝔞𝔫𝔦𝔢𝔩 𝔐𝔠𝔆𝔩𝔲𝔯𝔢.' He threw the book back on the shelf.

"Did it actually show you the future?" Lloyd asked, picking up the same book. He opened it and found the definition for psychic on the inside. "Aw, bummer. That would have been awesome."

Lloyd picked up a few more books and looked through them, while James reeled from what just happened. He picked up another book and found a handwritten note, '𝔗𝔯𝔶 𝔱𝔥𝔢 𝔟𝔬𝔬𝔨 𝔬𝔫 𝔱𝔥𝔢 𝔰𝔱𝔞𝔠𝔨 𝔟𝔢𝔥𝔦𝔫𝔡 𝔶𝔬𝔲, 𝔰𝔢𝔠𝔬𝔫𝔡 𝔣𝔯𝔬𝔪 𝔱𝔥𝔢 𝔱𝔬𝔭.' He contemplated ignoring the note but that didn't seem like it was an option. He picked up several more that just said, '𝔑ope.'

James cautiously grabbed the book behind him, second from the top. "Are you the right book?" he asked it. '𝔗hat's the one! 𝔥ave fun on your first day. - 𝔇aniel 𝔐cClure.'

Is this some sort of joke? he thought. He took the book to Lloyd, "Is your book doing this?"

"Doing what?" Lloyd looked down at the book to find a blank page. James looked down and noticed the writing had vanished.

He flipped the book closed and asked it, "Are you the right book?" Inside, he found a small description of The Book of Knowledge and what you should look for in finding your book, the same information Barley just shared with them. He walked away from Lloyd and the text faded, replaced again with the same inscription, '𝔗hat's the one! 𝔥ave fun on your first day. -𝔇aniel 𝔐cClure.'

Unsure why this was happening, James took the book to Barley. It didn't seem right, somebody controlling which book he could receive. James felt queasy at the idea that Daniel was taking his choices from him. "Did you find your book?" Barley asked with a smile as James plopped it on the counter.

"This is the one!" He said, a little too enthusiastically. Truthfully, the description he saw when he showed Lloyd was informative without being too detail-ridden. It seemed to fit his personality well, even if it was haunted with the presence of a mysterious man. To James, all of them seemed to carry that trait.

"Great. To make it yours, all you need to do is sign your name on the inside of the front cover. Do you happen to have a pen on you? I think I left mine in the back room."

Seriously? James thought, as he realized he did have one in his pocket. With a sigh, he took out the pen and signed. Barley was momentarily distracted with Lloyd's selection. Otherwise, he would have been bewildered by the signature.

When James' pen touched the book, the ink glowed a bright red color. The signature flashed a few times before fading to black. James would have no reason to find this concerning, except for the rush of adrenaline he got with each flash. He looked over at Lloyd signing his own book with no reaction. The adrenaline lasted only as long as the red ink, fading as the black color came forward. All of this was too much. He felt like he was being controlled.

He grabbed the book from the counter and retreated outside. For the first time since entering Toricane, James was scared. He was being watched. Not only that, Daniel was manipulating his decisions. He needed help. Before he could get it, James needed to find somebody he could trust. He also needed to find a place he couldn't be watched. He was jolted by the doorbell as, Lloyd came out of the store with his book, followed by Carissa and Azalea. James wondered if he could trust them. There needed to be somebody here he could confide in.

Lloyd's ripped pajamas fit him awkwardly as he walked. The awkwardness fit well with how uncomfortable he seemed in most situations. Carissa's constant pushing up of her glasses drew James' attention to them. She always looked like there were a million things on the tip of her tongue, and she was waiting for a lull in the conversation. Azalea gave off the impression of somebody who with a kind heart, if not a little naive, with her soft features and quiet, but firm, voice. Together, James felt good about them. He had an intuitive sense that if there was somebody who would be willing to help, it was them.

Carissa expectantly interrupted his train of thought, "I have an idea! We all need some new clothes. What if we each ask our book the same question and see what different answers we get?" James immediately got nervous. He really didn't want to see another inscription or use the book at all. Her excitement, one that seemed to overshadow his anxiety, made it impossible to refuse.

66

They agreed to each ask the book specifically, "What is a good clothing store for our group to go to?"

Azalea opened her book first. There was a simple map that indicated one clothing store a few shops away. It listed the name and owner of the store. She smiled at the page, enjoying this little experiment Carissa concocted.

"Let's go here!" she said, without needing to know anything more.

Carissa opened her book next. A list of ten stores in the surrounding area with addresses and hours appeared on the first page. She flipped to the next one and found a different ranking on each. The ten stores were ranked by quality, price, friendliness, cleanliness and popularity, each on separate pages. Behind that, a list of each store's current clothes and how busy they were right now. She kept flipping through the pages to a seemingly endless amount of information.

Lloyd grew bored of Carissa's and opened his book to find the name of the most popular custom clothing shop nearby. It had several pictures of men much taller than Lloyd getting nice, tailor-fit clothing. He immediately grew curious and started flipping pages, finding the clothes he would get there. Two of the outfits stood out to him, and he committed them to memory.

Carissa and Lloyd were busy with their books, but Azalea was waiting for James to open his. He took a deep breath and looked at the first page. A wave of relief washed over him at seeing the word '𝕮𝖑𝖔𝖙𝖍𝖎𝖓𝖌.' Reading the full title, it said, '𝕳𝖔𝖓𝖊𝖞𝖒𝖔𝖔𝖓 𝕮𝖑𝖔𝖙𝖍𝖎𝖓𝖌.' *Is this some kind of joke,* he thought?

Azalea's eyes grew large. "Try again, maybe," she encouraged.

James closed the book and said, "What is a *good* clothing store for the *group* to go to?" The new title was, '𝕮𝖑𝖔𝖙𝖍𝖊𝖘 𝖋𝖔𝖗 𝕾𝖆𝖘𝖘𝖞 𝕻𝖊𝖔𝖕𝖑𝖊.' There were two clothing stores listed, both of which came up in Carissa's top ten. One was the same shop Azalea's book recommended. He turned the page to see if any more information was given. The second page's title was, '𝕮𝖑𝖔𝖙𝖍𝖊𝖘 𝖋𝖔𝖗 𝕻𝖊𝖔𝖕𝖑𝖊 𝖂𝖍𝖔 𝕮𝖆𝖓'𝖙 𝕿𝖆𝖐𝖊 𝖆 𝕵𝖔𝖐𝖊.' The same two shops were listed.

"Maybe you'll have to get used to your book's sense of humor," Azalea said, while stifling a laugh. "I like it! And it gave you the same store as me." James knew he could've lightened up. He would have normally laughed it off and even enjoyed the playfulness. Daniel McClure was stopping him. This is the same kind of twisted humor James had endured in his out-of-body experience.

One for The Books

The four of them decided to go to the shop listed nearby in Azalea's book to pick up some new clothes. It didn't take long for James to start feeling better once the suit was off. The talk he needed to have with them got pushed back. He would do that tomorrow, after they had some drinks at Toricane's Trove, a well needed break.

"Really?" Azalea mocked as James stepped out of the changing room. "You're going with the grey uniform?"

James immediately became self-conscious. "I thought it looked cool. It fits perfectly!"

Lloyd came out from the adjacent room. "Everything fits perfectly. It doesn't look like it at first, but, as soon as I put it on..." he motioned down at his seemingly tailored button down and slacks.

James replied, "Wait. There aren't any clothes just a little too big or small?"

Carissa came around the corner, eyeing him, "You want clothes that don't fit right?"

He shrugged, "This uniform is great. I just think I'm going to get homesick. It would be nice to have something be the same, some similarity."

Azalea, who had yet to pick out anything, replied, "It's all too perfect. If everything fits just right and looks exactly how you want, then how can you have a favorite shirt?"

Lloyd looked down at his light blue button down, "I had my favorite shirt on when I died. There's no way I'm getting rid of that. It's just going to be put away for a while."

"You were wearing pajamas," James laughed.

"And?" he replied, offended.

Azalea spoke up, "And there's nothing wrong with that. A favorite shirt is a favorite shirt. But what if you pick out an even better shirt here?"

Carissa pulled out a grey uniform she was considering, "You're thinking too hard about it."

They all eyed her in disbelief, but she didn't notice, focusing instead on the uniform. James broke through her concentration, "*You* think we're overthinking it?" he laughed, followed by Lloyd and Azalea. "Azalea's right. I want something that reminds me of life. I can't just come here and magically forget about it. But that suit wasn't even mine, and there's nothing here that remind me of home."

Azalea looked him up and down then went to a rack of clothes nearby. She pulled out a pair of blue jeans. "Like this?" she said as her hands ripped a hole through one of the legs.

James couldn't tell if she was helping or teasing but it was exactly what he meant. "Yes!" he spoke too soon. The hole in the blue jeans repaired itself.

James face turned down. Azalea frowned, "Maybe we'll learn some trick to make our own clothes."

Lloyd pulled several slick pants out from a rack and walked back to the group. "I'm ready. Y'all ruined this for me," he glared. "I'm just going to wear these with my favorite shirt every day."

They all laughed and did the same, grabbing clothes in front of them, ready to be done with it. James ended up with several pairs of pants like Azalea gave him and a grey uniform. Azalea grabbed one shirt and pair of pants, saying they are most likely self-cleaning. Carissa walked almost all the way out of the store before rushing back in and changing her selection. They waited another half hour for her to decide.

Fishing in Troubled Waters

At Toricane's Trove, everybody exchanged stories and seemed more comfortable than earlier at the tower. It could've been getting out of their old clothes or the drinks, but James thought it was the atmosphere that really allowed them to let their hair down. It was like connecting with people through childhood stories because everybody's been there. Everybody here had lived their entire lives. They had all been there.

The only people James didn't see there were Gary and his posse. Nobody had seen them since Barley's, not that anybody paid much attention to them after just getting their Books of Knowledge. Carissa was the most interested. She kept asking her book question after question, always getting pages and pages of information.

James looked around at everybody's noses in their books while his sat closed in his lap. He was hesitant to use it, knowing his imaginary friend Daniel was involved somehow. Regardless, it was going to need to be used at some point. All the more reason to figure out what was going on.

The night went by quickly. James stayed out at Toricane's Trove until exhaustion forced him to fall asleep, knowing that was the only way he wouldn't obsess. Before long, the four of them were back at the tower. They decided to meet downstairs for breakfast the next morning.

He woke up feeling remarkably refreshed. James walked out and looked down the staircase to see a patiently waiting Lloyd and Carissa. No Azalea. "I'll see if she's almost ready," he called out to them.

He walked down to a door with a large golden label, '𝕬𝔷𝔞𝔩𝔢𝔞 𝕾𝔭𝔢𝔞𝔯𝔦𝔫𝔤'𝔰 𝕳𝔬𝔪𝔢.' He knocked and immediately heard a loud rustling behind the door. After a few seconds, the door opened slightly. James could see a room similar to his own inside, just before his view was blocked by Azalea peeking her head out with bloodshot eyes.

"You ready for breakfast?" he laughed, fully knowing she just woke up.

"Yeah, yeah. Almost ready. Two minutes!" She abruptly closed the door, but not before James saw her book lying open on the bed.

Lloyd and Carissa were talking about where to eat when he got downstairs. Instead of letting the book decide, they wanted to find their own way this morning, get some exploring in. They had only seen a small portion of the city so far and hadn't even set foot on the academy's grounds. Eventually, Azalea made her way downstairs, and they found a place that served Ancient Mesopotamian food. It was more of an experiential place, since none of them even knew what food Mesopotamians ate.

Turns out, they ate bread and fish. Not disgusting, but pretty bland with only the spices in the first civilization, which were basically none and not at all breakfast food. They picked at the food and chatted for a few minutes. James was working up the nerve to tell them all about Daniel and everything with his book, which he strategically left in his room.

Lloyd spoke up first, "So, aside from fish for breakfast, what are we going to do today?"

Carissa pulled her book out, which it seems she had already become dependent on, "Let's see. What do people normally do here their first week?"

They were all a little annoyed at the shortcut, wanting to just explore instead of having an itinerary. Still, curiosity pulled them in. Unsurprisingly, the book was filled to the brim with information on different places to go and things to do. The first page, however, had very little information. It simply stated, '𝕸𝖆𝖓𝖉𝖆𝖙𝖔𝖗𝖞 𝕬𝖈𝖙𝖎𝖛𝖎𝖙𝖎𝖊𝖘: 𝕮𝖍𝖔𝖔𝖘𝖊 𝖄𝖔𝖚𝖗 𝕿𝖗𝖆𝖎𝖓𝖎𝖓𝖌,' followed by a list of first-year programs available to them.

Compulsory:

- Create.
- Elemental Manipulation.
- Self-Manipulation.
- Sense-Enhancement.
- Toricane Fundamentals.
- World History.

Noncompulsory (Any 3):

- Luck
- Morals
- Music
- Particle Control
- Scrying
- Sports
- Telepathy
- Teleportation
- Time Study

Carissa read ahead, "'Based on the programs you choose, you will be categorized as either body, mind or soul.' What do you think that means?"

Azalea, the only one not reading, ignored the question and signaled toward a waitress, "Ma'am, can I get a coffee, please?"

The strikingly tan woman walked over and smiled at her. "I'm sorry, we only serve beverages from the Mesopotamian era."

"They survived without coffee, how? Okay, what else do you have?"

The waitress motioned her hand toward the table. In a rectangular shape, the top of the table in front of Azalea changed into a tan color and words inscribed it. The wooden table in that area separated. The woman grabbed the menu and handed it to Azalea, "We have water, milk, and sixty different varieties of beer."

Azalea laid her head in her hand, "I'll stick with my water, thanks." After the waitress walked away, she added, "How does this place still exist? Surely there are people here from eras with coffee and some better tasting food."

James laughed, "Don't worry, they still have sixty different types of beer." He looked back at Carissa's book, "If you want coffee that bad, maybe take Particle Control. Actually, it could be Elemental Manipulation or even Luck. Honestly, I don't know what any of these programs mean. There's one just labeled as 'Sports.'"

Carissa flipped through the book, "I'm really not sure. I don't understand most of the explanations for the programs. I think we're just going to have to decide based on the names. I'm more interested in these categories: body, mind and soul."

"Sounds ominous," James added. "They haven't told us anything about them. It can't be that important."

Lloyd joined in the conversation, "They also didn't tell us about the programs. We seem to be on our own here, at least until they start." He was anxious at the thought of it.

"Regardless," Carissa cut in, "we only have a few days to decide. I'll look up the categories. You all start looking up the lessons," she said excitedly, without looking up from her book.

The other three exchanged annoyed looks, but she didn't seem to notice. Azalea and Lloyd started to get out their books and flip through them. James sat there and finished his fish, looking on with Lloyd.

"Where's your book, James?" Azalea called him out, trying to find a reason not to follow Carissa's assignment.

"That's a long story. The short version is, it's in my room. It's going to stay there for as long as possible." They all looked up at him, curious.

Azalea got to it first, "We've been here for less than a full day. What could've happened?" They stared at him and waited for a response.

"Could we go somewhere else first? One of those programs is Scrying and I have a feeling that somebody is doing that to me."

Lloyd got visibly nervous, "Wouldn't they have seen you just say that? Are they listening to what I say?"

Carissa talked over him, "Did you get in trouble? I don't want to be an accomplice!"

As they spiraled, a smile appeared on Azalea's face. She anxiously threw her book closed and back open. "It says there's a barrier around Toricane's head offices!"

"Keep your voices down!" James whispered loudly, focusing on Azalea.

She ignored him and continued to close and open her book several more times. Her smile grew wider each time. "Got it! Follow me."

Azalea put her book away and stood up in one motion. They all followed abruptly, and James caught up just outside the restaurant. The streets were much more crowded than the previous night. People walked down the street in large groups, never in a hurry, just strolling. Azalea rushing down the street made several heads turn.

"You mind telling us what you're doing?" James asked when he caught her.

"Do you want your spy to hear the plan?" The way she eyed him made James back off immediately.

They walked toward the academy and took a left at the campus border. "We aren't allowed on campus until the first day of lessons," Azalea informed them.

"How do you know that?" Carissa asked, with a hint of envy in her voice.

"I did my research."

Lloyd interjected, "In the thirty seconds we were sitting at the table?" She didn't respond. James suspected that's what she was doing the night before.

The four of them continued around the circular border until they walked by a different looking building. The others they passed were all similar, towers with smooth stone and various artworks made out of a collection of materials and colors. This one was only as wide and tall as a single person. Its color was pure white, and it had no door. Every couple of minutes, a person would come along and walk confidently into the building. They motioned their hand and the walls materialized around them.

Azalea stopped abruptly, "Okay, so technically we aren't allowed to go in there, but we need to."

Lloyd and Carissa looked at each other nervously. James was the first to object, "How are we supposed to get in? None of us know how to..." He trailed off, unsure what to call it, and waved his hand in the air.

Azalea took a step back and pushed them against the campus wall, "One problem at a time." Just then, Professor Wagner stepped out from campus with another man and made his way to the white building. "Follow my lead."

The other three were in shock but followed after her as she walked toward him. Lloyd made sure to get as far in the back of the group as he could. They had to walk at a brisk pace to keep up, unusual for what James had seen of Toricane. He had no idea what Azalea's plan was, but, once she was on her mission, it seemed there was no stopping her.

The serious expression on her face, which had James following her without question, melted into a smile that complimented her soft features. She went from a librarian to a cheerleader in the blink of an eye. "Professor Wagner!" She shouted, as if just noticing him. "Professor, I didn't think we would see you until next week."

They both turned around, surprised, "Ah, first-years!" Wagner exclaimed. "What brings you out to this side of the city? Nothing exciting out here, especially if you can't get on campus." He paused in thought, "Remind me of your names. I try to learn them by the time the lessons start, but you've caught me off guard here."

James put a large smile on his face, following Azalea's lead, "I'm James, this is Azalea, Carissa and Lloyd. We're just trying to see as much of the city as we can!"

Wagner eyed James long enough to make him uncomfortable, "Oh, this is Professor Edgar Ruskin, he teaches teleportation."

Before they could acknowledge him, Azalea asked, "If you teach teleportation, why walk?"

Ruskin waited for Wagner, who was still staring at James, before answering, "Well, it's good to get a nice walk in once in a while. Right now, though, we're going to the head office," he pointed at the white building, "and you can't teleport there. No abilities whatsoever can cross between Toricane and its head offices. You'll learn all about it in the coming months, I'm sure!"

James tried to ignore the eyes on him. Unexpectedly, he felt anger boil to the surface of his mind. He suppressed it before speaking, "Any way you could let us in for a quick tour?"

Carissa spoke up, "Are we allowed in the main offices?"

Azalea's smile broke for a split second before returning. She laughed, "What could they possibly have to hide from a few first-years?"

Wagner responded sharply, "Students aren't allowed in the main offices. For this first week, you have free range of anywhere inside the walls, except the academy and main office. Just have fun in the city. We need to head out. We're in a bit of a hurry. I'm glad to see you're already making friends"

The two of them turned toward the building before Carissa stopped them, "Really quick, could you tell us what the classification is about? I can't find any information about it in my book."

Edgar turned back and said, "Don't worry about that. You're going to be fine. Just pick the programs you want to take, and it'll work out," before continuing on.

When they were out of earshot, James felt the tension leave his shoulders. He turned toward the group to see Azalea's scowl and Lloyd sweating. "A little warning next time would be nice," Lloyd said.

Carissa was off in her own thoughts, "Why so cryptic about the classification, do you think? I need to look some stuff up."

Azalea looked at the two of them, then over to James, "Do you still want a private place to talk?"

"Yeah, but I don't think we're getting there anytime soon."

"Did you notice they both had a medallion on their lapel? It had the same symbol as I saw in the book for the head office, golden with a hand holding a balancing scale." They all looked at her, confused. She waved them off, "Just give me a few minutes."

Carissa took out her book and started flipping through the pages. Azalea walked off toward the white building. James and Lloyd looked at each other in disbelief. "Who is this person?" James asked.

"I don't know who she is, but she's going to have to find me some barbiturates, if this is her on a daily basis," Lloyd said.

James laughed, "Based on what we've seen so far, I don't think it would be too hard for her to find."

Azalea had made her way to the building and stopped the first person that walked near. They couldn't hear what she said, but they could tell she was trying to charm her way in. Amazingly, the second person she stopped nodded and looked around to make sure the coast was clear. He grabbed her by the shoulder and walked them both into the building.

The three of them had no idea what to expect. After a few minutes, they gave in to Carissa's constant demands to look at programs. James found a few in particular to be interesting. Scrying was top on his list, his best chance of seeing Alisa. Luck seemed so interesting to him, also. *How would you even learn that,* James wondered. Lloyd favored Music, saying he was a great pianist during his time on Earth. Carissa couldn't decide on any one, but kept going back to Particle Control and Morals, a combination James found strange.

After almost half an hour, Azalea appeared back next to the group. Lloyd looked shocked, "Did you just teleport?!"

Azalea smirked, "No, how would I know how to do that? You just got too absorbed in your books." She pulled out several golden coins. "Each of you take one of these. I'm not sure how long it's going to take for them to realize they're gone."

She turned to walk toward the building, leaving the rest of them scrambling to catch up. Azalea paused, "Just try to act like you belong. We do look a little young, but they won't question it if you're confident."

"How do you know how to do this?" James asked.

She shrugged nonchalantly, "In my life, I was a spy. Follow me in quickly. The medallions should materialize the walls around you."

James attempted to take that in stride, but faltered, "Wait, you said you died at twenty-two."

"Yes, I did," was all she replied. *Does that mean you did say that, or you did die at twenty-two?* He didn't have time to ask since she stepped through the wall in front of him.

James looked back at the rest of the group. Both Lloyd and Carissa had the same panicked expression. In a different situation, seeing their faces would've been hilarious. Here, it was the opposite. With no time for comforting, he grabbed both of their arms and walked into the wall. He could feel the stone in the wall pull back around him. He never ran into it, but the rock hugged him all the way in. It felt like if he went any faster or slower the rock would crush them.

James expected to meet a surface inside. Instead, he felt himself falling. Darkness invaded his vision, and wind pushed up from beneath. As the wind calmed, a room filled with people walking in every direction came into view. The expectation of splatting on the floor after his fall was not met when he easily landed on his feet. The room was huge, with walls of different color grays, people speeding by and a receptionist area nearby. As he looked around, James noticed Azalea walking toward the nearest hallway.

Carissa and Lloyd followed his attempt to catch up to Azalea. She turned a corner and motioned them into a nearby room. There was, again, no door. James didn't like this setup. He wanted to be able to walk into an open space, not squeeze through stone. He, reluctantly, pulled the others into the room and immediately looked at Azalea, "Hey! We're not all spies here! You have to slow down a bit."

The room looked to be in some sort of conference area. The stone walls lightened with grout made from a small river of light. A circular wooden table took up the entirety of the room with ten chairs perfectly sat equidistant from each other around it.

"I know. I know," she said. "But I need to return these medallions before anybody notices. I'm not sure if you remember, but one of the programs is Telepathy, which means we can't give anybody a reason to suspect something is wrong."

James took a few deep breaths to calm down and grabbed a seat at the table. It was a basic room. The concrete-like walls and white décor extended into what James guessed to be a conference room. One window looked out into the hallway. Luckily, nobody walking by looked in. Carissa took a seat and opened her book: getting absorbed in it was a good distraction to what was going on. Lloyd looked like he was about to have a panic attack but took a few deep breaths like James and sat down.

Azalea looked at James, "So, what's going on?" She didn't try to contain her excitement. Having a new mission gave her purpose. She thrived off it.

"You know we're going to talk about the fact that you're a spy, right?" She nodded and egged him to go on. "I don't know much," he sighed. "You're sure that none of you had an out-of-body experience when you died?"

"Positive." "Absolutely." "Just remember waking up in the white room." Answers echoed around the room before a silence fell. They waited for the mystery to unravel.

James nodded, "Then, none of you met Daniel McClure." Everybody's head shook. "I got shot in the head, but my body stayed where it was, while my body fell. That's confusing." None of them interrupted him but sat with bewildered expressions. "I stayed where I was, while my body fell to the floor. Then, Daniel came through the wall just like we came into this office."

Azalea was in full spy mode, "What did he look like?"

Carissa asked, "Who is Daniel McClure?" It was a second before everybody realized she was talking to her book. James peaked at it and found blank pages. That's the first time anybody's book didn't have an answer.

"He was short. Walked with a limp. By far the most cheerful person I've ever met."

"What did he want?" Lloyd asked, surprising everybody at the table. Azalea gave him an encouraging nod.

"I have no idea," James said, honestly. "He was there for less than a minute before I went into light. All he said was I couldn't tell anybody I saw him. He also told me he would be in touch."

Carissa was still opening and closing her book furiously, trying to find any information. Azalea put her hand lightly on Carissa's book, forcing it closed, "Maybe we research this stuff later. For now, let's just concentrate on the story." She turned to James, "Well, James, has he been in touch?"

He took a deep breath before continuing, "Yes. I was going to just pretend it didn't happen, but, when I was picking out my book, all I saw on the inside of each book was a note written by him. He was leading me to a specific book."

"You got the book he wanted, didn't you?" Lloyd asked. At this point, James saw sweat coming through his shirt.

Maybe he does need some barbiturates, James thought. "I did. I panicked in the moment and didn't think straight. I don't know who he is or if anybody is helping him. I was stuck."

Azalea looked at him, trying to sniff out any lies, "What else?"

James reluctantly added, "I signed the book with a pen he gave me. He put it in my pocket when I died and told me not to lose it. Then, Barley didn't have a pen. The signature flashed red and I got this huge surge of energy."

"Wait," Lloyd interjected. "I signed my book right after you. Barley had a pen in his pocket. He gave me one. I'm positive I saw several of them. He even let me keep it, as a souvenir." Lloyd pulled out a pen that looked more like a quill than anything James had written with in his life. Azalea and Carissa nodded along with Lloyd.

Carissa, having her book temporarily put off limits, hastily asked, "Is there anything else?"

James shook his head, "That's all." He fidgeted with his fingers and reflected, "The way he was directing me with the book, though, it was like he could physically see me. That's why I'm trying to be discreet. I don't know if it was the book, scrying, or whatever else this place would allow him to do."

Azalea interrupted his rant, "Where is the pen?"

He thought for a second, "It's probably still in my suit, in my room."

"Don't get rid of it," she quickly commanded. "Keep it somewhere safe, but never on you. There's no way of knowing what it can do. Unfortunately, we may need evidence at some point." She looked through the window, "We need to hurry this up."

James looked down at the table, ashamed, "I'm sorry to drag you into this. I'm not even sure what I expected to get out of it. Something just doesn't feel right. I don't know...why me. He told me I couldn't trust anybody here."

James looked at each one of them before continuing. Carissa had her hand on her half opened book. Lloyd's gaze was shifting to the windows, making sure nobody saw them. Azalea eyes met his, unblinking and unmoving.

Azalea spoke up, "You can trust us. We need to find out this man's plan. Why is he using you? Who is he? Is there any way this could be some sort of test?"

"There's just no way," James said. "He was sadistic, laughing at me mourning my own death. There has to be a reason he contacted me, but I can't let you put yourself in danger. This place is essentially a training camp. That seems like the worst place to be keeping secrets and sniffing around."

"Think it through," Azalea countered. "If we're considering this a training academy, why would somebody want to infiltrate it? Any way you look at it, this affects all of us."

"Yeah, but—"

Lloyd stood up unexpectedly and all eyes went to him. "I know I'm not the greatest under pressure, and I'm not even really sure who all of you are."

"Great speech so far," Azalea said, with glares coming from James and Carissa.

Confidence seemed to grow in his voice as he spoke, "I loved my life. It was quiet and peaceful. It didn't have much of a disturbance in it. The sole reason for that is I never had a reason to stand up and fight.

"James," he said, looking directly at him, "I'm not sure exactly what's going on, but I believe you and you seem like a good person. So, I'll do what I can to help you." His voice seemed to become shakier, "Can we get out of here soon, though?"

Before anybody else could, James spoke, "Lloyd, I can't ask you to do that. I've known you for one day."

Carissa stood up, "Exactly. You've known us for one day and you trusted us with a secret that has consequences beyond what we might even know. I'm with Lloyd. Plus, I have to know who this guy is. I won't be able to sleep at night until I figure it out."

Azalea spoke from her chair, "Okay, this is all great, but we don't have a plan. Also, we need to leave within the next minute." She thought for a moment, "We can't come back here when we need to talk. For now, when you talk about Daniel just say Darius instead, got it? It's a real person here, so it will throw whoever's listening off. James, we can both use my book, at least until training lessons start. We'll need to figure everything else out as we go."

"What if we're talking about Professor Wagner?" Carissa asked.

"Say Professor Wagner," Azalea attempted to explain in the least sarcastic voice she could manage. "For now, try to figure out what you can on your own. It's the best we can do with the little information we have. Find out why Daniel's doing what he's doing."

The four of them left the room quietly. Some were content with their new purpose and others scared what this means for their future. They all felt a new sense of what Toricane was to them, a minefield. They quickly retreated to the entry spot and were sucked back up to the exit. As they left, an alarm sounded inside. Azalea quickly grabbed their medallions and dropped them at the entrance before walking casually away from the building. A few people ran by, but nobody stopped four young faces with no access to the head office.

Toricane

The Ivory Tower

The rest of the week passed by without much incident. James kept his book and pen in a safe Azalea, unsurprisingly, had in her room. It was difficult to get any information on Daniel without access to the academy, where they might pass off their curiosity as educational. Carissa, however, was able to do some investigating on the classifications. She asked some of the residents and eventually found somebody willing to open up at Toricane's Trove in the late hours of the night.

She found out each program is given a designation, body, mind or soul. recruits tend to favor a combination of courses in line with these, which makes living quarters easily divided up. Lloyd came up with a plan to get rooms close to each other: choose one of each. The chances that more recruits would go out of their way to choose one of each program was slim.

As an added bonus, this allowed them, as a group, to take each program. James took on Scrying, Telepathy and Luck. Carissa also wanted to learn scrying, so she registered for Scrying, Morals and Time Study. Lloyd was adamant about maintaining his musical abilities, choosing Music, Teleportation and Telepathy. Azalea, wanting to fill the rest of the programs, chose Sports, Particle Control, and Luck.

By the end of the week, the four of them felt almost at home in this new world. They were being pulled together by having unspoken knowledge about Toricane and unraveling it together. Their peers were pulled together by proximity alone, which put a barrier between them. Conspiracies and secrets were the foundation to their friendship.

They had developed a morning routine in the days leading up to seeing the academy. Lloyd and Carissa made their way downstairs and chatted, waiting on the other two. James walked out of his room a while later and knocked on Azalea's door. She was always already up but waiting for that knock to leave the room. Carissa would research places in Toricane to explore that day, then they would leave.

Other recruits would occasionally join them on these excursions, but none stuck around for long. Katie Key joined them for breakfast some days; Gary Turnbull for drinks at night; even Celia, who seemed more into herself than anybody else, wanted to explore the wall with them. They never really clicked with any of them, especially Gary, who seemed to butt heads with everybody.

But on Campus Day, it was just the four of them. James knocked on Azalea's door. Almost instantly, it opened, and she handed him the book and pen that had been locked in her safe. Chloe came to their tower a few days before and informed them there would be new living quarters for the first years on campus, and, as of today, these would disappear.

All the recruits shuffled toward the academy, excited to finally be able to step foot in it. Chloe and a few others were standing at the entrance when they approached, handing out medallions. On the medallion was a depiction of somebody James had yet seen, with the title, 'The Founder.'

"They're really into titles here," Lloyd remarked to James, sarcastically. "Everybody calls us first-years and now there's 'The Founder.' Next, they're going to have a savior."

A nearby professor, not understanding the inflections in his voice, responded, "No, there's no

Toricane Savior. This is the closest thing we have to that," he held up one of the medallions yet to be passed out.

Lloyd's face went bright red. "Aw, of course, sir," he said, before shuffling off toward through the entrance. James laughed, seeing how red Lloyd's face was. He had grown accustomed to Lloyd's nerves, still keeping an eye out for barbiturates if it ever came up in the lessons. James was distracted laughing when he stepped through the barrier between the city and academy. He was barely aware there was a barrier in front of him until he heard gasps and looked up.

The scene had completely changed in front of his eyes. From the outside, the academy looked like a basic castle, which was astonishing in its own right. Going through the barrier revealed a city which seemed to be a display of the powers the residents here possessed. They stretched buildings as tall and far as they could manage, with different art works climbing up the walls as he watched them.

Statues walked the grounds freely. Recruits graffitied the buildings with bright veins of light. Picture-perfect trees sprinkled the lawn with emerald green grass flowing like blankets around them. A recruit walked in front of them with a kite in his hands. James followed the string up into the sky and saw hundreds of feet up a giant bird of some kind flapping its wings as it slowly glided around the fields.

James looked behind him, where he had just come from. The city had disappeared. Instead, an open field stretched several hundred yards to the next closest building. Recruits walked on paths between the structures, chatting with each other and looking at the newcomers that were stepping into this world. As he looked back, James saw Carissa blink into existence a few feet away. He waited for her before following the path in front of him to the main building.

Around in all directions were open fields as far as he could see. On all paths, his vision was eventually hindered by a building, statue, or some other intricate artwork, whether mobile or not. It was difficult to tell what were buildings and what weren't. The only indication were the doors on nearby structures.

There was one edifice directly in front of him. James heard the professor behind him call it the main hall. It wasn't the size of this building that gave away its purpose but the sigil that shone bright on the tallest tower. It was a simple depiction of the book James had become familiar with, overlaid with a gigantic letter 'T'. The sigil gave him a sense of wonder as he looked at it.

"This is amazing," James mumbled to nobody in particular.

Lloyd stepped up next to him, "Eh, I've seen better."

He got several looks of disbelief. "Yeah, where's that?" James replied.

His eyes got wide, "Nowhere! Are you kidding me? This place is ridiculous!"

A statue twice the size of James waved at them as they walked by. A few of the recruits jerked back out of surprise. Azalea waved back, "It feels like too much. They stripped out all the humanity, the Earthliness."

"I'm sure that's not true," James replied, immediately backtracking when he saw the entrance. "Okay, the pearly gates are a bit on the nose. I think they're just being ironic."

The recruits continued through the field, past the pearly gates, and into the main hall. The four of them took a seat at one just past the entrance. It didn't take long for the room to fill. Shortly after the first-years settled in, the older recruits started making their way through the entrance.

There were just enough tables to fit everybody comfortably, with the professors sitting together at the far end of the room. After everybody settled, a professor got up and motioned for silence to fall. It didn't take long, most people had their attention focused on this strong jawed, bright eyed man from the moment he stood up.

He motioned toward the table in front of him. One portion of it broke off, spiking up to form a podium. "Hello recruits! For those who don't know me yet, I am the Provost here in Toricane, Flynn Castle. I'm excited to start a new year with all of you. Although, I was sorry to hear about your passing." Laughter echoed through the auditorium.

"I hope you all lived long lives full of love and laughter. There's no joy greater than waking up in Toricane, remembering back to all your previous lives, and knowing you lived each one to the greatest of your potential. This year is no different than any that have past, and yet it is remarkably different for each of you. The people surrounding you, your friends and loved ones, all have a plethora of new experiences to share with you.

"Only the professors and I sit still in our lives, waiting for the stories you bring us of the new workings of the world. There's a certain peace to the stillness here that we have come to cherish. However, that stillness has been stirred." Murmurs echoed around the room as older recruits questioned this claim.

Flynn put up his hand and silence fell once more. "There's been a mistake we have so far been unable to correct. One of you does not belong." Nobody in the entire building moved. "We received the new first-years a week ago today. We expected twenty new recruits but instead have twenty-one." James felt like every eye in the room was on him. Lloyd glanced at him out of the corner of his eye but quickly corrected himself.

"It's unclear how this mistake happened, but I assure you we will get to the bottom of it. We do not take security lightly, and this breach will be sorted out. If you have any information on this matter, come see me immediately. As for the rest of you, feel free to continue on as usual. For first-years, if you have nothing to hide, you have nothing to fear. Also, until we have this situation handled, first-years are not to leave the campus under any circumstances."

Flynn's expression, which had become rock solid during his lecture, softened. "Now, on to more pleasant topics. First-years, this is a lot to take in. I'm sure you're wondering why you have to go to take lessons and train after you have died. Death should be an escape from lively needs, after all."

He got several murmurs of agreement, "Over the millennia, it has been discovered that you can take things away from Toricane, not physical objects but subconscious talents. For instance, if I were to spend the entire year in Toricane teaching myself to juggle, I would have an innate ability to do that on Earth. You will have no memory of this place when you are born on Earth, but you will have hidden talents.

"When that was discovered, it opened up so many opportunities for people here. There was a discussion among the people of this world on how to use this information, a discussion that ended in bloodshed. It was an unpleasant time in our history, but one that blossomed into what you see today.

"From that point, it was necessary to protect what we had from outsiders who would seek to destroy it. We found a way to both benefit people and protect them. That's when the training academy opened, and we started creating programs people could take to learn from those who decided to stay after their Earth-time was up. Now we have a full system set up for people such as yourselves to do the best they can on Earth!"

Flynn held up his medallion, like the one James was handed earlier, "The medallions you received when you entered the academy grounds will allow you to reenter the city, if you wear them and walk toward the outer grounds. If you're not wearing the medallion, you'll simply continue on. There's not much of a reason to leave the grounds, but we don't restrict you to the grounds alone. The barrier will be shut off at sunset, for your own safety. Toricane is only as safe as we make it; there are many who would love to see us undone, so make sure you're back on the grounds by sunset.

"I'm sure you have all looked at the programs available to you. If you would open your Book of

Knowledge, you'll find a place to write in the three electives you have chosen to take. Based on these, the book will assign you living quarters, which are open to you as soon as breakfast has finished. Lessons start tomorrow, so get acquainted quick!"

With that, he waved both hands across the room. Plates materialized out of the tables. The centers of each table bubbled up and formed a serving platter with a cover. Underneath was a long strip of different foods. Everything from bacon and eggs to pancakes and omelets. Everybody dug in, eager to find out where they would be staying.

James' table was the only one not digging in. They all exchanged looks before slowly gathering food on their plates. Carissa got out her book and started writing programs down. "You should do this too! Let's figure out where we'll be staying." James was starting to think she was using her book as a defense mechanism.

They all signed their programs in the front page and watched it dissolve into a map of the grounds. The building just adjacent to them was marked with a star. Beside it said, '𝔙𝔬𝔩𝔦𝔱𝔦𝔬𝔫.' "Well, now we know what the fourth classification is," James said. "I wonder why it's called that."

Before his friends could answer, the map disappeared, and a note was scrawled across the page in handwriting he would recognize anywhere, '𝔍𝔱'𝔰 𝔠𝔞𝔩𝔩𝔢𝔡 that because you're still making the decision. Middle-grounding the system: waste of time.' The note would've freaked him out, if it wasn't so annoying.

"And what would you have chosen?" he said, out loud.

'Give away my presence to more people than your little friends and the decision to punish you will be swift. I will keep you undetected; you keep your mouth shut.' The note faded away almost as it was being written. He looked up to three sets of eyes on him. Only then did he realize his mistake.

"It's nothing," he quickly explained. "Just Darius playing a joke on me." The three of them nodded and put away their books. They pushed aside the rest of their food and followed James as he made his way out the door.

"Our little operation didn't work," James started as they passed the pearly gates. "He knows you all know. He said if I tell more people, I will get punished."

"Will we get punished?" Lloyd asked.

Azalea pushed into his arm, "That's not really important right now, is it?"

"Well...," he hesitated, "yeah, I guess it's not the most important thing. What else did he say?"

"He said he will keep me from being detected."

"That's great!" Carissa added. "You might not know who he is, but he's going to protect you, so it's not all bad."

Azalea shook her head, "No, Carissa. It's obvious James isn't supposed to be here. What's he being used for? Why does he need to be protected in the first place? It sounds like Daniel's protecting himself."

"They aren't mutually exclusive," Carissa shot back.

"Guys," Lloyd said, stopping them and looking back at James, "before we start saying James shouldn't be here, let's make it clear, we do like that he's here."

James waved him off, "It's okay. I understand. I don't like this any more than you do. I can't tell anybody because, while Flynn didn't say what exactly would happen to the person if they're found, it didn't sound great. But if I don't tell anybody, I'm being used by this person we know nothing about."

They all stared at him, knowing Daniel was listening in somehow. He continued, "There's no use hiding it between us, if he already knows. It's not like he could expect me to just take this in stride, like nothing's happening." They kept going back and forth on what he should do all the way to Volition Tower. It was eventually agreed, they needed to discreetly dig up dirt.

They got to the tower and found it, unlike the rest of the grounds, to be fairly similar to the first-year tower in town. The outside had more décor lining the walls, most likely put there by the recruits, but the inside was generally the same. It was much wider, with five spiral staircases sprouting up from the floor and the ground floor being set up like a common area. The staircase labeled 'First-Years' created a room for each of them as they walked up.

Azalea noticed there were only four levels for rooms up their staircase, meaning their plan had worked. They didn't have the entire tower to themselves, but it was better than expected. They split ways for a few hours, getting acquainted in their rooms.

James' wasn't what he expected. Last time his room matched the one he had in his life. This time it was updated. It still had the rustic feel, but the materials in the wall seemed to be almost liquified. They looked manipulatable. He touched the surface, and the walls rippled out like he just cast a rock into a lake.

The others were experiencing a similar, equally unpleasant room. It wasn't long before they grew tired of it and spent the rest of the day wandering around campus. James left his book and his worries back in the room. He found himself relieved to be free of it every time it left his person. The weight of it was akin to pressure pushing down on his shoulders, not giving him the chance to relax. For a moment, that weight was gone.

Burn That Bridge When We Come to It

James was nervous for his first lesson. Logically, it seemed like the least of his worries, but his hands got sweaty just thinking about it. It wasn't only that he had no idea what to expect. The professor put him on edge. All first-years' first lesson was Create with Professor Wagner, the same professor that kept eyeing him. Even during the Provost's introduction speech, he caught the Professor spying on him from across the room.

The classroom was already packed by the time they got to it. Carissa didn't mind because the front row was the only one left, forcing them to join her there. Lloyd, who was just as nervous as James, couldn't stop fidgeting in his seat, not unlike most of the rest of them. Everybody had their books and a pen sitting in front of them. Nobody was sure if that was necessary or required.

At the last possible moment, Wagner strode in, cane at his side. He was in the same three-piece suit, as always, but it didn't have the same 'just pressed' look that James had seen before. He didn't waste any time, materializing a chalkboard at the front of the room before he reached it.

"I am Professor Wagner. I was assisting at your first day here. Although, that tends to be a pretty wild day for you, so I wouldn't expect anybody to remember." He waved his hand deliberately across the room, "Please open your books to the first page."

James opened his book to a note from Daniel, '𝔉irst day of lessons! 𝔖o exciting. 𝔅reak a leg! 𝔥ope 𝔍 don't have to break it for you!' Just what he didn't want to see. The note quickly faded and was replaced with a moving picture of a hand gesturing through the air.

"You've seen people do this same gesture since arriving. Any ideas as to why?" Azalea raised her hand. "Yes?"

"It's a way of focusing your thoughts into one action."

"No," He paused for a moment in deliberation, "but close enough." Carissa looked disappointed she didn't get it first. "As you'll find in other programs, most, but not all, abilities we possess in Toricane, that we don't possess on Earth, are channeled through our senses.

"In a way, we focus our thoughts to create an action. More accurately, we use our sense of touch to feel the alterations we make to the world. If our other senses required that much movement, you would see those. To manipulate the world around you, it's necessary to feel it, see it, hear it, smell it, and even taste it."

As he spoke, Wagner dragged his hand in a circular motion. Within it, a small piece of ice appeared. He rotated the ice. Around it circled a flame. The two revolved each other until the ice melted, and a spinning ball of fire and water twisted through the air above his hand. He dragged his fingers around in the reversed direction, capturing the two in his fist. Wagner's palm opened, and a stone dropped out onto James' desk.

"Touch wasn't enough. I needed to visualize it. I smelled the two elements interacting. When I fully envisioned it, the image in my mind's eye came to life. What I just showed you will be the first test of your capabilities in my program this year. I estimate roughly half of you will achieve it."

Gary, sitting right behind James, spoke up, "Doesn't seem that hard. You just think it, and it happens."

Wagner laughed, "Yes, well, why don't you give it a go?"

He smirked and held his hand up. Gary poorly mimicked the movement of Wagner's hand. His wrist moved robotically in a circle several times, to no avail. He squinted his eyes at a point just above his fingers. Everybody sat in anticipation, waiting for the tiniest manifestation. Nothing.

"So, as you can see," Wagner continued, "it's a little harder than it looks. I think you will find your other programs to be simpler. Creating something from nothing is, in my opinion, the hardest skill to learn. Manipulating what's already there can be much easier, as some of you may have found with your rooms."

He seemed to be moving onto the next topic, but several hands went up. "Our rooms, sir?"

"Yes, I'm sure you noticed your walls to be more liquidly based than in your previous quarters. They have been specifically designed to be easier for you to manipulate. It's good practice, essentially. Now let's move on to the first lesson, vision."

"Sir," Celia spoke up from the back of the room, "why are you teaching us, if one of us isn't supposed to be here? They shouldn't get to learn this stuff."

Wagner faced Celia directly, "Why is that?"

"If they got here through some nefarious way, then they don't deserve to learn these abilities." She said, matter-of-factly.

"For all I know, Mrs. Simms, you could be that person."

James interrupted Celia's huff of frustration, "You don't have any suspects?"

"We have our suspicions. Those leads are being chased down as we speak," he said, making that unusually long eye contact with James. "Frankly, I don't see that it's your problem. Unless any of you hears something strange, you can continue on normally, on the academy grounds. I'm not so sure that person has any idea they shouldn't be here. Nonetheless, when they are found, they will be dealt with accordingly."

James couldn't help himself. He had to know, "Accordingly?"

"Yes, accordingly." Judging by Wagner's tone, the conversation was over. Murmurs spread throughout the room. The only part that stood silent was the front row.

Wagner silenced the room and continued with his lesson. Nobody really understood it, but they gathered that by the end of the week he expected them to manifest a pebble. He assigned reading, which he said they needed to only ask for. In response, Carissa asked for the assignment and was told to open her book. She left the room swiftly afterwards. James hoped the rest of his lessons didn't follow a similar pattern. Luckily, he and Azalea had a few hours of break before their next program, Luck.

The two of them went to the main tower to grab breakfast but noticed Gary following suspiciously close behind. They took a detour behind a statue to try and avoid him. He followed their every move.

"Where are you going?" Gary mocked.

Azalea was fast to respond, "Exploring this campus we've been at for one day. What's it to you?"

"You think you're so smart." He looked at James, "What's with the questions you were asking the professor? You know something you're not letting us in on?"

"I'm just as clueless as you, Gary," he sighed, really not wanting any trouble. "I was just curious what they're going to do to the person when they find them."

"The only people who care about the punishment are the ones who have something worth hiding," Gary, very accurately, stated.

Azalea stepped in, "If we were hiding something, I'm sure you'd be the first to know."

Gary ignored her sarcasm and kept after James, "What are you not telling everybody?" He pushed James against the wall. "Spit it out!"

Azalea, now pissed, pulled Gary off and clocked him right in the jaw. Immediately, metals jutted out from the wall and restrained all three of them. Chloe walked toward them.

"What's going on here?" she sighed.

Gary spoke first, "He knows something about the extra person."

James rolled his eyes, trying to act casual, "All I did was ask Professor Wagner a question about it during the lesson."

"That's a serious accusation," she said. "If you're standing by it, I'll take all three of you to Flynn right now. If not, I'll just count this as your first day jitters."

Gary was silent for a moment, "I stand by it."

Why is he so adamant about this? It was one question, James thought.

Chloe loosened the restraints and lead them into the main tower. She reintroduced herself to them as Chloe Ruskin, professor of self-manipulation. Even with the tense situation, she was lively, giving them a demonstration of what they can expect in her program later that week.

Her hand dragged over her face and Gary popped out the other end. It was a perfect replica, aside from the flowing hair and woman's body. Chloe put her face back to her own and talked excitedly about what they could expect to learn this year. The fight didn't seem to faze her much. She was simply doing her duty to escort them to Flynn, without trying to discipline in any way.

The way to his office was not as intuitive as one would think. James could have spent an entire day wandering around this collection of intertwining buildings and towers without finding a single office. It was like the recruits and faculty created their own individual pathways, regardless of physical layout or accessibility for others. One in particular stood out: a bridge that led from one recruit's room to the rooftop of a tower across the courtyard. As James stared at it, the bridge retracted back toward the bedroom.

They were led to the bottom of a particularly skinny tower that bubbled out at the top, like an upside-down raindrop. The staircase inside ran along its interior wall to a solid ceiling just as the building started to expand out. They expected Chloe to walk through the ceiling, as James had seen so many people do since coming here. Instead, she knocked three times.

"Couldn't we walk through?" James asked.

"Theoretically, yes, but this is Flynn's office. We want to be polite." She waited for a response on the other end of the ceiling. "Also, walking unexpectedly into the room of somebody who may be on the lookout for danger is a good way to get yourself hurt."

Just as she finished that thought, the ceiling directly above them melted away, inviting them inside. The room looked rather small in comparison to the view outside. This was due to the clutter of memorabilia and small statues that lined the room. Nothing in particular stood out. To James, it looked like a heap of junk. On the other side of the room Flynn stood rubbing his hand over one of the more detailed statues. It was impossible to tell if he was manipulating the material or petting the stone.

"How can I help you today, Chloe," he asked, turning toward the group of them, adding, "and friends?"

"I found these three getting in something of a kerfuffle. When I restrained them, Gary here had some accusations to throw that I felt would be best thrown your way." She smiled and gestured for Gary to step forward.

Flynn laughed, "Don't you love that word? Kerfuffle. It makes whatever you're saying sound as innocent as a pillow fight. Although, I'm sure this was not. Please, sit down." He motioned and four chairs appeared in front of him. Flynn took the statue that James now recognized as a mockingbird and sat in a chair of his own as it materialized around him.

He continued after they sat, "So tell me Gary, what are we accusing whom of today?" James should have been calm. Both Chloe and Flynn seemed to not be taking this seriously. They were going through the motions. Hearing out a complaint they didn't seem to be putting any heart into. This blasé attitude should've put him at ease, but it did the opposite. He felt that they knew something, something unspoken.

"James is the one you're looking for. He's the one who shouldn't be here." James looked for a reaction to Gary's accusation, but saw nothing. Either Flynn's poker face was impeccable, or he expected that.

"Really?" Flynn asked. "Why do you say that?"

Gary puffed his chest out, "I was something of a private investigator in my life. The questions he asked Professor Wagner were suspicious. It's not just that. It's a gut feeling! I've never been wrong about a gut feeling."

"Interesting," Flynn started. "I'm curious, do you have digestion issues? I sometimes get a feeling in my gut when I've eaten dairy, for instance. Perhaps we could call that a *gut feeling*. I get a gut feeling I shouldn't eat dairy. Although, it's difficult because ice cream was such a great invention, wasn't it? I blame dairy, but it's actually unfair to do that. It's my fault I still eat the ice cream."

"What?" Gary looked around at everybody, confused as to why he wasn't being taken seriously.

"I should be clearer." Flynn stood up and grabbed a different statue from the wall. This one was a small monkey. "James here is dairy. You are me. You accuse James of being the problem based on a question he asked in the lesson. In your words, a gut feeling. It's possible you are deflecting. You're looking for somebody to blame because you're afraid you are the problem."

"I'm not deflect-"

"James, do you have any defense to these claims?"

James was still trying to understand the ice cream metaphor. He focused up. "I'm not the problem," he sputtered.

"There we have it!" Flynn exclaimed.

Gary stood up, "You can't possibly take him at his word!"

Flynn laughed, "You expect me to take you at yours. Sit back down, Gary." Gary abruptly took his seat.

120

"I do want recruits to come to me with information. However, I would like you to have some proof. You were a private investigator and, I believe, a soldier, so you should know what that looks like. A gut feeling is not evidence." He turned to Azalea, "What was your part in this, Azalea?"

She paused, surprised he knew her name. "I was defending James. I threw a punch at Gary that got us restrained."

"A noble cause! There's no sense in having fists, if not to defend those around us. Am I missing anything, Chloe?"

She smiled, "Nope! I think that about sums it up."

"Then, you are free to go," he nodded. "Gary, Professor Wagner, which he insists I call him, is heading this investigation into the extra recruit. Since this happened during his lesson, he has all the information you do. I'm sure he will follow up, if he deems it necessary. If you have any information in the future, please feel free to come see me."

Gary stood up, unsatisfied, and stormed out. The other three stood up to follow before Flynn added, "James, could you stay for a moment?"

Azalea gave him a concerned look and said, "I'll be at lunch," before walking downstairs with Chloe.

Flynn dissolved the other three chairs. James expected a splat on the floor, but the fabric and wood vanished from view before he got a good look. Flynn waited for the ceiling to close behind them before continuing. "James, I'm sure you've had the opportunity to look through all the programs by now. You know one of the many skills available to the people of Toricane is telepathy." James' palms immediately started sweating. "You'll learn soon that telepathy is explicitly forbidden for people on campus, excluding learning purposes."

His adrenaline slowly subsided as Flynn continued, "It would be quite simple to read the minds of first-year recruits and find the culprit. Although, it's like reading your lovers diary, only to find they did nothing wrong. You cannot unread the diary, neither can you forget what you saw.

"Now, imagine twenty-one diaries. Your spouse is cheating. You had a spouse, right? Imagine she's cheating, and she has twenty-one potential friends she would tell. One of their diaries unknowingly holds secrets of an affair. The others are purely innocent. Do you forsake all twenty-one for the pleasure of knowing?"

James assumed it was a rhetorical question and waited for a response. None came. The stone monkey Flynn held started latching onto his arm like a branch. "Um...I would find out some other way. I would ask them directly."

Flynn gave him a look of disbelief. "You know she would never tell you, even if she did exist on this plane. The point stands. I cannot peek into your head, even if that would satisfy my curiosity."

"But, sir, why teach it, if you can't use it?"

"Do you know how to fire a gun?"

"Well, yes," James replied, partially understanding his point.

"You would never fire a weapon at somebody, unless it was to protect a loved one. That means, in a peaceful world, you would never need that skill. We both know there are people who learn to fire a weapon with the purpose of bringing harm to others. With telepathy, a unique circumstance happens. The more skilled you become, the more you can defend against an attack. Do you understand?"

"I understand warfare. I don't get your point," James simply stated.

"Ah, I forget sometimes people expect a point to my ramblings." Flynn put the monkey statue he was holding on the floor, and it walked back to its spot on the wall. "The world here I grew up in was much different. I figured out early on that telepathy was my specialty. I became so good in fact that it's impossible to completely turn off. I do not instinctively read thoughts, but I do read emotions."

James started to get nervous. Then, he got anxious knowing Flynn could read his nervousness. "Is that why you disregarded Gary? You knew I didn't do anything wrong."

"I disregarded Gary because he's a bully. He might be scared, but that's no defense for needless bullying." Flynn got up and walked to the other side of his office. He grabbed a Book of Knowledge and flipped it open. "I honestly don't know if you did anything wrong. Do me a favor, James. Take a look at this picture."

James took the book. Inside was a landscape painting of a gorgeous beach during sunset. The same beach Daniel materialized. A knife went through James' leg. His scream was halted. He looked down to find nothing. His leg looked perfectly fine. Intense pain radiated out from the initial jolt. The words *'break a leg'* flashed through his head. James looked up to see Flynn staring intensely into his eyes.

"The most peculiar thing has been happening lately. Since your group arrived, I haven't been able to pick up many emotions from people. The skill seems to have been dulled somehow. Out of nowhere, when Chloe brings three first-years into this office, my empathic ability completely disappeared.

"The only person I have ever met who can block me like this has been gone a very long time. So, tell me James, does this picture look familiar to you?"

"Who was it?" James asked. He immediately regretted asking the question, since he saw Flynn's eyes narrow.

"His name was Daniel and we spent years at this beach, staring at that sunset. So, do you recognize it?" He was uncomfortably close to James.

The pain in James' leg was becoming unbearable. It felt like the bone was about to snap. He curled his toes and felt a drop of sweat on his back. His teeth started to clench, but he relaxed his jaw before answering. "No, sir. It looks like a beach. I didn't go to the beach much during my life."

"What about that name, Daniel McClure?"

"No, sir. It doesn't ring a bell." The pain subsided, and James' shoulders relaxed at the relief.

Flynn was staring directly at him but seemed to be looking straight through to the other side. He broke concentration and took the book back. "Fair enough! You're free to go." Flynn turned around to fidget with a statue on the windowsill. James didn't second-guess this was his moment to leave and quickly made his way down the stairway.

After a few looks at the map in his book and assistance from some of the older recruits, James was able to make it back to the main hall. Azalea was waiting at lunch. She apparently thought he was a goner and was too nervous to eat. James assumed Lloyd and Carissa had eaten during the meeting. He sat down and they both grabbed sandwiches from the serving platter.

"You didn't need to wait on me," James said as he took a bite.

Azalea grabbed a sandwich, "I forgot to eat. I just assumed you would come back here. What happened?"

James finished his bite slowly, trying to comprehend what had just happened and how he was still in Toricane. "I don't know. I thought for sure I was a goner. He definitely knows Daniel is behind this." Azalea eyes got wide. "Oh, Darius. Right, code words."

"Anybody could be listening to this conversation, James." She looked sharply at him with authority in her voice.

"But we know they are, right? We know Daniel is listening. He can't expect me to just sit back and let him control my life."

Azalea's look softened. "Yes, that's true. It's a little too late for code words." She waited for a moment, "You still haven't told me what happened."

"Flynn interrogated me. He seems to believe me, for now, but he knows something is going on with Daniel. They knew each other a long time ago."

"How?" Azalea was on the edge of her seat, sandwich, once again, forgotten.

"I have no idea. I didn't really get the chance to ask questions. I could tell he was scared, or maybe angry. It's hard to read him with the cheery attitude covering everything up." James thought back to his interaction with Daniel and noted the parallels.

"I bet Professor Wagner knows, too," Azalea added. "From what I could tell, him and Flynn went way back."

"So, what, we get the information from them somehow?" James was skeptical.

"No. That's too risky. For now, just lay low. Daniel hasn't actually done anything yet. Until he does, we still have time to feel out the situation. Don't do anything that would get you 'dealt with accordingly.'"

Azalea finished and finally remembered her sandwich. James still felt the tension of his situation weighing on him, but she was right. They needed to play this carefully. It wasn't an option to go up and ask Professor Wagner about Daniel. They needed to wait for the right opportunity to present itself.

Rock-Paper-Run

After his encounter with Flynn, James tried his best to lay low. For him, the lessons started off with a bunch of lectures and introductory reading, so There wasn't much of an opportunity for anybody to stand out. He was worried about Telepathy being an issue, but, luckily, the professor hadn't picked on James for anything. He didn't even acknowledge James, really, which was fine with him.

Most of his programs- Elemental Manipulation, Sense-Enhancement, Scrying, and Self-Manipulation- all preached the same thing to begin with: use your senses to mold the world around you. It was a simple concept, but, as Professor Norwood explained, if it really was so easy, they would already be master manipulators.

One program James was excited to get into was World History, because he thought it would talk about the history of Toricane. Having been to the program, he thought it should be more aptly named Earth History. In all fairness, James had already learned a lot in that program. The abilities of Toricane allowed its inhabitants to see back into the past, through the memories of the older residents, giving them knowledge unlike what anybody has on Earth.

One of the programs that stood out was Luck. James didn't know what he expected, but it certainly wasn't anything he could've dreamed up. The professor, Hartmann, started each day by playing the lottery. The odds of winning were one in a trillion, as explained by Professor Hartmann. If any recruit wins, they get an automatic pass for the program. The rest of the days are spent playing various forms of poker without looking at the cards in your hand. It was a fun lesson, but nobody had figured out the point.

Most of the introductory lessons were a bore. Towards the end of his first week, however, Alicia Lucas, the professor for Toricane Fundamentals, caught their attention with a short introductory sentence.

"Today we'll be covering your battle training." This was the first James had heard of battle anything. His head swiveled quickly from his Book of Knowledge to Professor Lucas, along with the rest of them. Everybody waited for her to continue, not risking an interruption.

Professor Lucas was taken aback by the sudden attention. She laughed, "I'm guessing nobody has mentioned this yet. Usually it's come up with the older recruits by now. You all must be pretty secluded in your own cliques." James was slightly offended but couldn't deny it was true.

"Defending Toricane isn't just a matter of learning to use your powers. Anybody, with enough time, can figure out how to rip the ground apart or draw water from the ground. It's not until you're put in the battle situation that you can truly understand how to use your powers for good."

Carissa, expectedly, raised her hand, "What battle situation?" It looked like she was asking out of nervousness, instead of her usual curiosity.

"We have a fun tradition here in Toricane called 'The Labors of The Founder.'" A smile spread across her face as she talked. "Throughout the year we put on competitions between groups of a similar year. The twenty-one of you will compete for the opportunity to be part of our diplomatic team at the end of the year.

"Four of you, the winning team, will venture out of the city to find potential tribes to join us. It's an

130

important job and one that can quickly become dangerous. For that reason, the labors give us an opportunity to find the individuals with the best chance of surviving."

James' eyes went wide, and he looked around the room. Azalea was more attentive than he'd seen her in any lesson. She was one of the few not reeling from the 'survival' comment. Everybody was stunned. Until now, it felt like they were learning how to use these abilities for fun.

Azalea raised her hand, "What is the first labor, Professor Lucas?"

"Good question!" she started. "We are still working on developing the first labor. Professor Ruskin will announce it as soon as we're ready."

Murmurs circulated the room. James spoke up, "But when will we actually be learning how to use our abilities? I don't feel prepared for that."

"I've been here awhile. I've learned how the other teachers run their programs, and you do not have to wait long. Professor Norwood will be doing that next lesson. By lunchtime today you will have your first lesson in true manipulation."

The intense concentration Professor Lucas captured at the beginning of the lesson left immediately. For the rest of the lesson, recruits were chatting about

Elemental Manipulation with Professor Norwood. Their excitement escalated and peaked as Lucas let them go. They rushed out the door, ready to really learn.

James went to rush out with the rest. He started to close his book but noticed an inscription on the inside, '𝔅𝔯𝔦𝔫𝔤 𝔶𝔬𝔲𝔯 𝔭𝔢𝔫 𝔱𝔬 𝔱𝔥𝔢 𝔩𝔢𝔰𝔰𝔬𝔫 𝔱𝔬𝔡𝔞𝔶.' James instantly remembered the pain Daniel put him in before and hastily ran to his room to grab the pen from his nightstand. It was only a few minutes away, so he wasn't late, but he was still the last person to arrive.

As usual, Carissa had a seat for him in the front row when he arrived. "Where were you?" she asked.

"I just had to run to my room really quick. I forgot to bring a pen." It sounded like a lame excuse coming out of his mouth. Then, he remembered who he was talking to. Carissa, instead of questioning it, scolded him for forgetting as the professor walked in.

"I know you're all excited to get the lesson started today," Professor Norwood said when everybody settled down, "but we have one thing to do before we can. Everybody, open your books."

James opened his book, expecting a note from Daniel. Instead, a long contract appeared inside. It was too long to read, filling up the first half of the book. Carissa was avidly reading every line. The rest of them looked up, expecting an explanation.

132

"You're going to need to sign this before we can start the lesson. Your books have more power than you realize. They are connected to you and the things you do here in Toricane. For the first year you are here, you won't have great control over your abilities. Signing this gives professors a type of link that allows them to temporarily stop or reverse your abilities, in case of a security breach.

"There have been a few accidental catastrophes over the years this helped stop, but the contract is more than that. It's a way for us to teach you these powers without putting the academy at risk. Until you have been here long enough, it is a simple security precaution that we do every year."

Professor Norwood looked off into the distance, "Last year, we had a recruit accidentally make an earthquake that tore down most of campus. He wasn't able to stop or control it. The earthquake would've continued until he could gain control of it, but Flynn was able to temporarily put a halt on his manipulations."

The recruits murmured in excitement. It was thrilling they would be able to do something like that, even by accident. They all anxiously signed the book. James paused. He knew Daniel wanted this written with the special pen. He didn't know why. James' leg started to throb. *This is wrong,* he thought. The good guys don't hurt people to get what they want. The pain increased with his hesitation. He sighed, defeated and optionless, and wrote his name in the book. It glowed red and the writing vanished.

"Everybody done?" she asked, focusing back on the group. Nods came from around the room. "Great! Now partner up."

Carissa and Lloyd turned toward each other and started talking excitedly. James looked nervously at Azalea, "You ready?"

He caught her staring at his book with a worried expression. She looked up. Her scowl changed quickly to a smile. "Am I ready to make an earthquake that destroys campus? Never been more ready for anything in my death."

Each group had a rock and a piece of paper put in front of them. The rules were explained simply. The goal was to liquify the rock just enough to allow the paper to slice it in half. There was nothing special about either, but James felt intimidated by them. How was he supposed to cut a rock with paper? "All we need now are some scissors," he joked.

Azalea laughed, "Yeah, I think I know how to do this. We just wrap the paper around the rock. Paper beats rock."

Professor Norwood rolled her eyes, "People have been saying that the last few years. I had a recruit last year explain it to me and I can guarantee that's not how this is going to work." She settled at the front of the room and waited for attention to be on her. "You'll find that to manipulate objects, you must first change their state. Solid objects don't move as easily as liquid.

"One of you is going to concentrate on turning this rock into as much of a liquid state as you can. Remember to use your senses. Imagine how the rock should feel. Let the sound of splashing liquid fill your mind. See the rock giggle with surface tension." Norwood closed her eyes and demonstrated how that looks. The rock in front of her started to move as if it was trying to burst out in laughter.

"As you're imagining this, your partner will cut the rock with the edge of the paper. When you are able to do this, you'll be one step closer to true elemental manipulation." She sliced her rock with a piece of paper and the two halves once again became solid objects, separated by a thin slice of air. Norwood stopped the demonstration and sat at her desk, allowing the first-years to start.

James grabbed the piece of paper, "You go first?"

"Sure," Azalea said, already glaring at the rock pensively. She brought her hands up to the rock and swirled them around it. Nothing happened. Around the room, everybody was trying something different. Lloyd was just nervously sweating at the rock. After a few minutes, some recruits started pleading with it.

Azalea's face grew stern in concentration. She focused her mind solely on the rock. James waited, paper at the ready. He saw emotion leave her face and purpose flow into it. This was her mission. It was one of the few times he really saw how she could throw everything else out of her mind and plow forward into her goal. There was one thing she needed to do and one thing only.

When Azalea was fully concentrated on the rock, James picked up the piece of paper and slid the edge as hard as he could against the rock. They heard a scratch of paper on solid rock. There was no dent. Azalea huffed, "You messed up my concentration! Give me another go." Without waiting for James to point out how much of a sore loser she was being, she put her hands over the rock and closed her eyes. "I got this."

The other recruits were having just as much success. Gary, in the back, was actually holding his rock up to his forehead. Lloyd had given up and was letting Carissa have a chance. Azalea's hands slowly came off the rock and she nodded toward James. He took the paper and slid it as hard as he could into the rock. It went a couple millimeters in, and Azalea stood up from her chair, "Yes! Got it!"

Professor Norwood walked over to the desk, "Nice job, Ms. Spearing. Impressive work." Her words were of encouragement, but the tone she used never changed. She handed the paper to Azalea and reformed the split. "Let's see which one of you can get further today."

Azalea smirked at James and motioned toward the rock, "Go ahead."

"I will," he smirked back at her. "Just keep the edge of the paper on top of the rock. It'll slide right through," he added confidently.

James looked at the rock and imagined the paper sliding through it. He pictured two halves of the rock sliding apart. The image in his minds' eye showed two pieces of perfectly sliced stone. As he put his hand up, the rock completely liquified. The paper smacked onto the desk and liquified stone poured over the table. Azalea and James both jumped back, scared to get any on themselves. As soon as the rock hit the ground, it solidified into a puddle.

Professor Norwood jumped out of her chair, "What's going on here?" She saw the puddle of rock on the ground and looked at James, concern on her face. "You did this?"

"I didn't mean to. I wanted the rock to separate and it just...," he trailed off in his explanation, not sure what he was trying to explain away.

She pulled the rock back into its original form and set it on the table. "It's okay, James. Your job in this program just may be less of learning to use your abilities and more about learning to control them. After all, the assignment was to cut the rock, not make it a puddle. For now, let Azalea give it another go." Her tone stayed consistent, but she kept her eye on James.

"How did you do that?" Azalea asked. Her curiosity didn't stem from a desire to replicate it. She was concerned for him. Nobody else in the room could come close, yet he outperformed his own expectations on the first try. Impossible.

He shrugged his shoulders, "I just imagined what I wanted to happen."

"And, it just happened?"

"Kind of. That wasn't what I pictured happening. But it was the same idea." He gave her a half smile, "Give it a try."

Azalea spent the rest of the lesson focusing on the tiny, recently solidified rock, not talking to him much. Other than James, she advanced furthest in the group, getting the paper halfway through the rock. Lloyd couldn't get anything to happen and Carissa kept partially liquifying the sides, causing a jelly-like rock to ripple against the paper's edge. Everybody was exhausted when the lesson ended. The little rock took it out of them. Professor Norwood dismissed them. Everybody sulked out.

"Lunch?" Lloyd suggested as they walked out.

"After that, I'm going to need five lunches," Carissa sighed.

James nodded along. He looked at Azalea, who had stopped a few feet back, "Something wrong?"

"No, nothing wrong. I'm just supposed to go see Professor Wagner." She started walking in the opposite direction, "I forgot to turn in my homework last night and he doesn't have a lesson right now. I'll see you after lunch!" She left them in confusion, not giving a second glance back.

* * * * * *

"Come in!" Professor Wagner called from inside his office.

Azalea walked in and took a seat. She didn't speak, instead internally questioning if it was a good idea to come in the first place. Maybe she should just leave, come up with some excuse like she did with the group. She could go have lunch peacefully by herself and none would be the wiser. Still, with a world worth of options open to her, she stayed planted in the chair. James

needed help that a group of newcomers couldn't give.
She needed information.

"Can I help you, Mrs. Spearing?" He looked
slightly annoyed that she was silently sitting there. "I do
have work I should be getting to," he said, looking at the
stack of papers in front of him.

"I need to talk to you about James." The only way
to give information is to give it, Azalea thought. No going
back now.

Wagner pushed his papers to the side and fully
engaged himself in the conversation. "Go on."

"I don't want anything bad to happen to him. He's
a good person."

"Neither do I," Wagner added. Azalea was going
to need more than that before she would open up.
Darius seemed to realize that. "Given the life you've
lived, I'm assuming you're fairly good at keeping a
secret?" He must've come to the realization about truth.

"I wouldn't be here otherwise," she stated.

"Would you like to hear one?" Azalea nodded.
He continued, "I've known James is the problem all
along, since the first second I saw him."

Azalea kept a straight face, "I never said he was
the problem."

"Before James died, Chloe and Edgar, you know them both as Professor Ruskin, gave me a piece of advice I took to heart. They said I wasn't engaged enough in the lives of my pupils. They told me it had been too long since I died, and I needed to empathize more with what happens to recruits on Earth."

"So, you have empathy for us? That's not exactly comforting. Empathy only gets you so far. Self-preservation tends to trump empathy." She was starting to think twice about coming here.

He continued like there was no interruption, "I took it upon myself to observe somebody on Earth. I performed a type of scrying that allowed me to see them, their past, their present, even feel what they feel. I chose a completely random person. Twenty recruits a year come here. The chances I would scry somebody here was truly small. Impossible, really.

"So small, in fact, I decided to look into their past, to get a real feel for the person. I wanted to get in their head, to understand the human experience on Earth." Wagner sat back in his chair, remembering the occasion. "That was two days before you arrived."

"So, the impossible happened. That was James?"

"Impossible things don't happen, but, yes, that was James." He traced the desk with his finger, creating tiny ripples as a distraction from the memory. "For that one day, I observed James. It took twenty-four hours from the time I started watching him for a stray bullet to hit him directly in the head. The same bullet I felt go through my own head. It was, of course, just through the scry but it felt real, nonetheless. I quit the scry immediately."

Darius took too long to get to his point. Azalea got restless. "You've died five times. A bullet through the head is probably one of the least painful ways you could go. Not the worst thing in the world."

He shook his head, "That wasn't the hard part. He died in one day and came straight into this world. The person I grew attached to. I saw him in the white room and immediately knew it wasn't a coincidence. The only explanation is that, somehow, somebody killed him and sent him here because I was watching him. So, no, Mrs. Spearing, I don't want anything bad to happen to him. And, yes, I do know how good of a person he is."

They sat in silence for a moment. Azalea looked him over for any clue of a trick or deceit. He looked guilty. It was a remorseful look that didn't fit the stern attitude she was used to seeing from him. As far as she could tell, he was being genuine. "James is the problem," she said.

He nodded solemnly, "You knowing must mean he's told you, correct?"

142

"Yes, the second day here. He knew almost immediately."

"So, why come here?"

She avoided the question, "Why have you not done anything? First-years are still not allowed to leave campus. Is that just a scare tactic? Were you waiting for him to come forward?"

"That doesn't matter now." There was a knock at the door. It immediately opened.

Chloe stepped in, "We need you now, Darius. There's been an incident." She turned to leave, not waiting for them to follow.

"Tomorrow, we are going to meet and talk about this. I'll send you a note in your book telling you when and where." He rushed out, leaving her sitting in the office.

Azalea sighed. *Back to old habits*, she thought. Spying was never the job she wanted. There was always somebody who needed help, somebody who couldn't help themselves. Other people could live their whole lives without sabotaging the ones they care for. She just started her second life and was already playing double agent against the person who showed her the most compassion. Azalea sighed again and stood up. She heard the noise of something large breaking in the direction of the main hall and walked that way.

* * * * * *

James, Lloyd and Carissa sat at lunch talking about what they had labeled, 'The Meltdown.' Not a particularly clever name for a small rock liquifying. Nevertheless, the gossip had gotten around to the whole academy. Several older recruits came by to ask him what happened. They couldn't believe it.

Brenda Garza, an obviously jealous fifth year, wanted to get the full story, probably hoping it wasn't true. Dwight Lawson, a stout man who James heard had caused the earthquake the previous year, hoped his incident was worse so people would stop talking about The Meltdown. He became famous in the first five minutes of lunch. The attention was different for James, but he didn't hate it.

Halfway through lunch, Celia stormed over to him, obviously wanting the attention for herself. She slammed a rock on the table in front of him. "I bet you can't even do it again. You just lost control, which is really worse than not doing it at all." The nearby tables looked toward them. Everybody within ear shot was watching intensely.

The attention James felt was now closing in on him. He didn't have a response. It really was an accident, and he didn't know if he could do it again.

Carissa chimed in, "He has nothing to prove to you, Celia." Carissa rolled her eyes. Celia huffed and walked away in a rage, leaving the rock.

Lloyd looked at it, "Can you do it again? You should show us how. I couldn't even get it to budge."

"I really don't know how I did—"

Carissa interrupted, "I have to know how you did it, James. Please!"

James looked at the rock and realized he had no idea what he was doing. "Okay, I'll try. But no promises!" He eyed the rock for a moment and thought back to the same images as before. *Split the rock in two. Slice the rock down the middle.* He imagined exactly what Professor Norwood explained: a liquified rock standing upright. He wanted to do it right this time, not just make a puddle of stone. In his mind, he saw the rock slicing in two.

As soon as he pictured slicing the rock, it started melting. He looked at the two of them, "It worked!" James couldn't believe he actually managed to do it again.

They were still looking at the rock, mortified. James looked down and saw the rock melting through the table. The table started melting and spreading quickly. All three of them stood up and stepped back a few paces.

"Make it stop!" Lloyd yelled, getting the attention of everybody in the lunch tower.

"I'm not doing anything!" he yelled back.

The melting spread to the chairs, floor and even started making its way to the wall. Chloe, who was eating lunch on the other side of the tower, threw her fork down and ran their way. She held her hand out toward the spreading pit in the floor. Nothing happened. Her hand twitched and she focused her concentration on it. Still, nothing.

"Everybody out of the tower!" she yelled. People immediately ran for the nearest exit, barely taking enough time to grab their books. Everything else could be remade. The four of them stood in horror as the floor melted into the ground. "You too! Get out! I'm going to get help."

She sprinted out of the lunch tower. The three of them came out of their trances and followed their classmates. Even recruits who were just passing by stopped to gather in the crowd that formed outside. To those gathered, it was something of a spectacle; to James, it was a horror show. Whatever chain reaction James started was accelerating. The bottoms of the walls surrounding the building started to dissolve. He saw the building slowly shrink and the puddle turn into a small lake. The sinkhole underneath etched toward them ever so slowly. He saw several older recruits attempting to stop the liquifying. None succeeded.

Chloe appeared in front of them with her hands raised. The sinkhole stopped in front of her. It wasn't spreading, but the tower continued to fall. The few stories it had left were fading. Professor Wagner appeared beside her, hands at the ready. The tower, which was now melting faster than it could fall, stopped in midair. The lower part of the building dematerialized away, revealing a large, dark hole in the ground beneath it.

"Were any recruits in there?" Wagner asked, in a calm voice.

Professor Atkins, the telepathy teacher, appeared a few feet from him. "All recruits accounted for," he said.

"Give me some ground to put this building on," Wagner commanded.

Chloe and Atkins walked toward the sinkhole and it retreated away from them. The grounds slowly became rebuilt, although not quite as gloriously as they were before. When the sinkhole was filled in, Wagner sat what was left of the building on top of it.

He released his grip on the tower and turned to the group of recruits. "Spread the word: all fifth-years are excused from lessons this week. Your assignment is to rebuild this tower exactly as it was, the surrounding area and all, by Friday. Your assignment starts now.

"Everybody who is not a fifth-year, the main hall is closed this week. A temporary building will be made by dinner time just south of here." He finished the speech and started talking furiously with Chloe. The recruits started to filter out slowly, all murmuring with excitement. James couldn't help but be impressed by the speed Wagner recovered and solved the situation. Less than fifteen seconds ago Wagner wasn't even here. Now the chaos was gone, and plans were underway to fix it.

After a moment, Chloe walked south and started the construction of a small tower. There were no frills or décor, just the necessary building blocks. Wagner walked swiftly toward the group, forgetting to use his cane, as James had sometimes seen him do. Wagner didn't look mad but worried. James expected mad. This was something of a relief.

"Come with me, James," Wagner instructed, walking past him and ignoring the rest of the group.

"Where are we going?" he asked.

"I'm taking you to Flynn. He'll figure out what to do with you." As they were walking off, James heard a voice in his head say, '*Having fun yet?*'

Rock-Paper-Run

Calling a Spade a Shovel

James sat in Flynn's office, waiting for him and Wagner to finish talking downstairs. He didn't know what to expect, but it couldn't be anything good. He was already a suspect, and, somehow, Flynn knew about Daniel. James heard the talking below turn into yelling. Still, he couldn't make out what they were saying.

The last time James was in this office he didn't have the chance to actually look around. He took the time to wander, calming his nerves. The room was one big pile of clutter. While it was a cramped area, each object seemed well taken care of, most being in their own cases. Every statue had its own shelf. Each trophy

150

with its own embroidery. Not a speck of dust on any of it.

One glass case in particular stuck out to him. It was as tall and wide as James. Inside was a cape with a plaque that read, 'The Founder.' It looked like a ruby had been melted down and woven together like cotton to be threaded, creating a smooth, flowing piece of impenetrable armor. The cape gleamed off the light coming through the window, while its ruby structure hung naturally down to the floor.

James' eyes followed its ripples to the bottom of the case. He saw a helmet with the label, 'His Castle.' At first, there wasn't anything about the helmet that stood out. It resembled what James remembered to be a Roman helmet, with red plumes that looked similar to the cape's material. The golden material that encompassed the rest of it didn't stand out as extraordinary, except for the crest resting at the top. It was the same symbol he saw on many other artifacts around the office, a castle's tower with a griffon perched on top of it.

James made his way around the room, searching for this symbol. There was a suit of armor to match the helmet, a shield, and many bronze-age weapons, which still looked sharp to the touch. His eyes scanned the assortment of items, and he noticed the shield had a

particularly dark shadow which drew in the light
surrounding it.

He stepped forward to examine the shadow more
closely. James moved the shield to the side. As it shifted,
he heard the clank and clatter of other metalwork fall.
He looked back, no Flynn. With raised voiced muffled
in the distance, he turned back to the clutter.

The shield moved to the side, and he noticed the
light around him diminish. It was being sucked into a
singularity of darkness. A small marble of nothingness
seemed to float on the shelf. Without light, surfaces
below it faded to nothing.

James reached out to it. His hand disappeared
within a few inches of the singularity. The marble was in
his hand. He was mesmerized by the emptiness of it.
Without considering what he was doing, James put the
emptiness into his pocket. It floated down as if only
slightly affected by gravity. The darkening effect was
diminished by the confined space.

He heard the talking below stop and quickly
moved the shield back. He looked at the windowsill for
something to feign concentration on. He saw that same
Roman symbol from before on a small, stone statue,
which resembled a griffin. It was incredibly detailed and
only a few inches tall.

There were indentions in the wings smaller than any knife could've made. Cracks in the talons showed wear from years of use. Attempting to sell his act, James reached up to feel the griffin. Flynn's voice came from the stairwell, "Marvelous isn't it?" James, expecting Flynn to interrupt, pulled his hand back as if taken by surprise. "You wouldn't believe what that little statue has done for me."

"What is this symbol?" he asked, still curious about the relics and unable to ask about the marble.

Flynn smirked assuming James was attempting to delay the inevitable conversation, "I think that's a story for another time. Have a seat." His voice seemed much more relaxed than how James heard it downstairs, just a few moments ago.

"Sir, am I getting kicked out?" James asked. His mind snapped from the empty marble to the incident he just caused. Whatever mesmerizing effect was present now faded. He stood by the griffin, not wanting to look directly at Flynn for the answer.

Flynn motioned for a chair to come up under James, knocking him off his feet. The chair moved in front of Flynn's desk. James barely held on as it skittered across the floor. His hand gripped the side for a few moments after, bracing himself for another unexpected movement.

"No, James. You're not being kicked out. It's quite obvious at this point that you are the problem. Although, neither me nor Professor Wagner knows why. So, I'm going to ask you one time, do you know why? Are you aware of anything going on that I should know about?"

In James' head, he screamed at Flynn, '*Yes! I absolutely do! Please help me!*' He told Flynn everything that happened since the moment of his death. All the things Daniel asked him to do and the consequences for not following his orders flooded out. He told Flynn that Daniel was monitoring them, listening to their conversation. He said he had no answers and needed them badly.

"No," James said. "I have no idea." A warm waterfall ran down his spine, calming his nerves, perhaps a reward for his loyalty.

Flynn laid back into his chair and said, "I believe you. Professor Wagner has told me to take you at your word. He has some kind of trust in you. I'm not sure why, but I owe that man more than my life. So, if he says to trust you, then I trust you."

"Thank you, sir." James paused, "If I'm the problem, what will happen to me?"

"That's an interesting question. Having an extra recruit isn't really a big deal. The issue is security. Why and how were you put here? Could it happen again? The why has been partially answered today. To destroy the campus." He glared aimlessly at the thought.

"I did sign something today. Didn't that give the professors some sort of power over the things I can and can't do?"

"Normally, yes. Frustratingly, it didn't work for you. Chloe attempted to undo the damage, but nothing happened. That reminds me, hand your book over for a moment."

James took the book out of his bag and gave it to Flynn. He hoped there would be some inscription from Daniel on the inside that would solve all his problems without him actually having to say anything. It wouldn't be his fault, just coincidence. Unfortunately, his Luck lessons were not paying off. Flynn flipped through the pages and handed it back, disappointed.

"Nothing weird." Flynn pondered that for a moment, then remembered, "So what happens to you? First off, you will stop using your abilities unless you are in this office. I will be replacing your core teachers. You can still do your electives; those should be fine. As of this moment, you are explicitly forbidden to use any creation or manipulation outside of this office. Understand?"

James nodded firmly. Flynn continued, "That should solve the immediate problems, but we still need to figure out how you got here. Professor Wagner assured me he is working on that. You still need to come to me with any information you get."

"Yes, sir."

"I want you to understand. If you break either of these rules, I will kick you out. There are plenty of forests beyond the borders of Toricane that you can live out your time here. And if I find out you were less than forthcoming, getting banished will be the least of your worries." His face was stern, leaving no room for interpretation. He didn't require an answer from James, only understanding. "Aside from that, you are free to live as a recruit here."

"Does that mean the city will now be open for recruits?"

He laughed, mien fading back to his normal carefree gleam, "That's your first thought? Yes, the city is open for recruits again. However, I recommend you stay within campus borders. I want to keep an eye on you." For the first time since this meeting started, a twinkle came into his eye. "Plus, if you go into the city, I won't be able to tell you about my crest," he said, pointing toward the Roman helmet behind him.

"*Your* crest?" James asked, now fully enthralled.

156

"For another time," he smiled toward James, both looking eager for that time to come quick. "For now, go back to the main hall. Chloe's about to make an announcement you won't want to miss." James was reminded of a boyish mischief not akin to the other professors. "Come back tomorrow, and we'll start your lessons."

James walked out of the office feeling incredibly lucky. He'll keep his secrets and, at least for now, be safe. No getting kicked out of the academy. No pretending he has no idea what's going on, or relatively no idea. He just has to stay on campus. As he walked through an alley between two intricately decorated towers, that thought didn't seem so bad.

When James came out the other side, he picked his friends out of a crowd that had gathered since The Meltdown. Recruits of all years were assembled. Lloyd and Carissa were walking up to the group, and Azalea was standing in the midst of the recruits waiting for an announcement. She smiled and waved at him to come over.

"Chloe is supposed to announce some big thing they've been keeping from us. The older recruits know about it, but I haven't gotten any info out of them!" she said as he arrived.

He laughed, "You seem awfully chipper after what happened earlier."

Azalea shrugged, "I just had an epiphany. We're here, in this wonderful place, there's no reason to get hung up on the little things. We can just enjoy the good parts of it."

"I was just thinking the same thing," James said. She smiled at him for a second longer before Lloyd and Carissa made their way over.

"Oh!" Azalea started to say, "What happened at—"

"Recruits! I know you're all excited but settle down." Chloe's smile stretched from ear to ear. She was unmistakably ecstatic about the news. The crowd slowly quieted down. "It's time for the announcement of this year's Labors of The Founder!" Clapping erupted from the crowd.

"For those who don't know, The Labors of the Founder are four competitions completed throughout the year. There is a week dedicated to each one, with each year going one day of the week. You will split up in groups of four and compete against your classmates." Another cheer erupted from the crowd.

She waited for the recruits to settle down before continuing. "The winning group of each group will be awarded at the end of the year with a trophy and a mission." Her voice got low as she continued, "As the Founder would have done, the best of the best get to roam the forest by themselves in search of ancient artifacts and other tribes, using your newly acquired skills out in the open wilderness." There were several "ohs," and "ahs," from the crowd. "Only the winning groups get this highest of honors."

The experience reminded James of when he was drafted. There was a big production of soldiers showing up in town. They paraded down the street, showing everybody the glory and splendor of the military. They had to. If they wanted to mitigate a revolt, it was necessary to show a good cause behind the draft.

The propaganda wasn't what drew James to sign, though. On the day he signed his contract, there were two soldiers talking not too far away from the booth where he was eating. They had a long discussion of what being in the military means.

The memory was accompanied with one of the soldier's voices. "It's about protecting those around you from having to do it. It's about giving loved ones the life they deserve, even if you can't be in it." They talked about how being there for people wasn't enough, not always. Sometimes it took a sacrifice.

That's when he decided to sign up. It was still a week until his birthday, so James could've waited and hoped the draft miraculously ended. He didn't. Unlike the theatrical production of a parade through town, the idea that he could be there for Alisa got to him. James knew he would do what it takes to give Alisa a good life, even if that meant a sacrifice.

Alisa, James thought. It had been a couple weeks since showing up in Toricane, and thoughts of Alisa had been forced to a minimum. He was so focused on not getting caught, on surviving here, thoughts of how to get back were put to the side. Even if there was a way back, there was no way to know what he was going back to.

A loud cheer jolted James back into the present moment. The four of them joined in the festivities as Chloe continued her announcement. Letting themselves get wrapped up in it really allowed James to feel like a part of the academy. It was different but good. "The first labor," she paused theatrically to build suspense before continuing, "is a hunt." Murmurs ran through the crowd like fire. "For this labor, we will be in the forest. Of course, you will be supervised by the professors. We are in the process of creating an animal for each group. You will simply have to be the first team to either capture or kill the animal."

She smiled at the simplicity being portrayed. "It will happen in two weeks. There will be some hidden elements. Be prepared for anything," she finished slowly.

James looked at Azalea, a smile on her face, anxiously awaiting the competition she craved. On his other side were Lloyd and Carissa exchanging whispers about what the surprises could be. These were his friends. He belonged here, but Alisa was not with him. It was the dichotomous uncertainty of belonging in two, mutually exclusive worlds.

He should be looking for a way to get back to her. But if his accidental misfire of a killing on Earth could be considered a sacrifice on par with protecting Alisa from enemies beyond the border, then he fulfilled his duty. There's no final authority that rests on these things. It was up to him to decide if he'd fulfilled his earthly duties or if he should be doing everything he could to get back. He wasn't ready to make that decision.

In the moment, right now, he was just excited for the labors, excited to learn to harness abilities he never thought possible with Flynn; he was excited for the opportunity to stay. There was no better feeling to James than making a difference. Here, with abilities to learn and a conspiracy surrounding him, he felt needed. He looked at Azalea again. She was staring back at him, a questioning gleam in her eye. In that moment, he decided to be here, in this moment.

A Fair-Weather Friend

The next day, when James left to have his first lesson with Flynn, Azalea had her first official meeting with Professor Wagner. She planned to demand that it wouldn't just be her sharing. She needed information from Wagner. If something dangerous was headed James' way, she wanted to know about it, regardless of her ability to tell him.

Azalea waited for James to wander out of sight before heading toward the meeting spot. She started off in the direction of Wagner's office and took a detour just before the entrance of the tower. She walked around the perimeter of the tower, looking for a notch in the wall. Three knocks then she stepped toward the wall, confident it would open up around her as Wagner said in the note earlier. Azalea ran straight into the stone.

"Sorry," she heard mumbled through the wall, "I wasn't quite ready. Go ahead and come in."

She waited a second, expecting to hit stone again, before stepping through. It was a dimly lit, bare room. It looked as if nobody had touched the space in decades, and for sure none of the recruits had fixed it up. In comparison to the rest of campus, this room was desolate.

Azalea looked around for the usual décor of Toricane, veins of light and fire reflecting off pools of ice. Instead, she saw cobwebs lining the corners of the room. There was one desk on the far end with a chair on each side. They looked freshly made, the only part of the room that was.

"Why can't we just meet in your office?" Azalea asked, sitting at the desk.

"We would be more easily overheard—"

"So, we can be overhead here?" Azalea asked.

"Nothing is impossible, but not only does nobody know about this room, nobody can enter it without my permission. If anybody were to come through that wall, they would enter the back wall of my office."

She didn't quite understand how but let it go. "So, I told you about James. It's time you tell me what's going on."

"You've told me nothing." Wagner waited, calling her bluff.

She stewed for a moment, not wanting to give away every detail of what James had shared with her. It wasn't her information to share. The longer she sat though, the more she thought about the need to build trust. Azalea wanted all the information Wagner had. It had to start somewhere.

"Okay," she started. "Daniel was there when James died. It was a sort of out-of-body experience, he said. Daniel told him to trust nobody and he would be in contact."

"And he has been in contact, I'm assuming?" Wagner probed without worry, knowing Azalea wouldn't lie when her information directly fed into how much she could help her friend.

"Yes. For one, I took us into the main offices when James told us, hoping for some protection from being spied on, but I think he was still able to hear. Daniel knows that Carissa, Lloyd, and I know he's a part of this.

"As an added bonus, I do know he's been in contact since then. Daniel forced James to buy a certain

Book of Knowledge. Then, Daniel forced him to sign the contract in it with a pen given to James by Daniel."

"He gave James a pen?" Wagner look genuinely confused.

"A pen, yeah. Do you know what that means?"

"I have no idea. Is there anything else?" Wagner leaned in from his chair, hoping for more information.

Azalea sighed, "No, that's all I know. I couldn't get anything from the books, so I'm lacking in information here. That's why I came to you. I saw James struggling to control some sort of inner power and knew it couldn't end well."

Wagner sat back, disappointed. "Well, I'm assuming you have questions. This information stays between me and you, though. Not even your two other friends can know. It's too risky. Got it?" Azalea nodded. "What questions do you have?"

She paused, looking for the right one to ask, "James told me about Flynn and his last meeting. Why did you keep what I told you from him?"

"That's a tricky question. The short answer, he's too close to the situation. Flynn holds a hatred for Daniel that I've not seen in anybody. When your best friend betrays you... They were as close as two people can get. That relationship is long gone now. My fear is that his hatred toward Daniel would be redirected against James. He would do anything to rid the world of Daniel, including, but not limited to, getting rid of James."

"'Getting rid of,' meaning?" He gave her a knowing look, and she moved on. "Why does he hate Daniel so much? Who is Daniel?"

Wagner stood up and motioned toward the center of the room. "Let me show you," he said.

Liquid seeped up through the floor as Azalea stood from her chair. Texture-less blobs of color, shapes that moved as if in zero-gravity, formed into balls of spiraling images that expanded across the floor. The colors merged and created boundaries, expertly drawing a scene in front of her. The flat shapes expanded, creating dirt and grass at their feet. The life-size depiction of a man rose from the recently animated ground in Roman armor, holding a dented shield and the hilt of a disfigured sword.

Azalea stood smaller than the man. She was in a field, face to face with him. It looked so real. She knew it was simply a manifestation of Wagner's, but one she could reach out and touch.

The scene before them seemed to zoom out, separating Azalea's perception of it from herself, to show a battlefield in the forest. She stood over the field. The Roman was one of many in a horrific battle. Several

166

bodies flooded the ground. The trees nearby had been cleared out and shards of them were scattered throughout the field. Mounds of earth shot up as Wagner allowed the image to move forward in time, adding an unpredictable chaos to the battlefield. The scene had swirls of the trees and rocks being thrown by invisible forces. All at once, Wagner froze it in place.

It was truly a battle as Azalea would have imagined two sides facing off would look like, a chaotic mess of death and destruction. She thought back to the violence faced every day back on Earth, and it didn't compare. She was never in the heat of battle, but, somehow, Wagner had shown her what that was like. He placed her on the battlefield, in the midst of confusion, beside the elemental manipulations she saw swirling by, the only thing that compared to her size on the shrunken field.

The original Roman man wasn't the only one in that uniform, but she saw various different kinds of armor and attire on almost every person. There was no uniform to distinguish one side from the other. These men knew each other. That would be the only way to distinguish them.

One man flew above the original Roman soldier with a gleaming red cape, looking more like an ill-tempered cartoon than real life. He stared toward the ground in a concentrated glare, hands pointed out at the debris below. A woman stood against the cartoon and his soldier wearing a robe and holding an ornate stick. The eruption of earth disappeared in a circle around her, like a bubble of protection. A small, leprechaun-looking man stood beside her holding a cane, with a knife at his waist.

Azalea looked back and forth between Wagner and the leprechaun man. "Professor, is that your cane?"

Wagner held it up, "It's not actually mine. This cane belongs to Daniel McClure."

"Explain."

He nodded as the scene stood frozen in front of them, "It might help you to understand, I'm not showing you something from a history lecture. This is a memory. It's been a long time, so some of the details may be blurry or altered by perception. Regardless, this is how it happened."

Azalea tried to sit patiently, but the more information he gave, the more confused she became. "What happened? There's a huge hole I'm missing in this story. Who is fighting? Why are they fighting?"

He nodded, "We call this The Great Calamity. It was the culmination of a schism between those of us set on spreading knowledge and those bent on ruling by fear." He pointed first to the man flying in a red cape then to the woman in the robe. "That is The Founder and The Destroyer. They both died in this battle. The

168

remains of their mission were left to each of their second-in-command."

"The Founder and The Destroyer? Is this one of those 'the winners write the history books' things?" she asked rhetorically, knowing the answer had to be yes. "And what was this mission?"

"The mission was to win. No survivors. This was the final battle. The winner would define what become of the world here, what the newly dead would be introduced to. It's easy to rule over the weak. It's harder to give them the opportunity to become strong. That's what this war was about."

The memory shifted. Azalea quickly traced The Founder and Destroyer as Wagner accelerated the scene. Unable to make out details, she saw the two of them fall, killed by a mess of debris Azalea couldn't trace back to any origin. Leveled sections of the forest expanded beyond sight. Soldiers died off in troves of armor that were reformed into weapons, leaving bodies scattered. Wagner flicked his wrist and the colors changed, shifting perspective and zooming toward the Roman soldier and Daniel, a few soldiers still battling off to the side.

"Is that you?" Azalea asked.

"No. That is Flynn. My part comes in soon," he said slowly.

Azalea saw a fight break out between Daniel, the cane and dagger wielding second-in-command to The Destroyer, and Flynn, the Roman second-in-command to The Founder. Daniel pulled a sword from his cane and charged. Flynn raised his shield. They seemed evenly matched. Neither was gaining ground. Every blow of a sword pulled solid forms of light and darkness toward their enemy. Manifestations of pure darkness parried attacks of bright, sharp light rays.

Azalea took a step back and covered her face as one clash of swords sent a blinding light through the room. When she opened them, the two had been blasted apart and were charging back for more. The swords clashed; darkness replaced the light; Azalea's pupils strained. Each blow was swift and solid but frightening, as if the dance had been practiced but neither knew what result the true performance would yield.

As if by instinct, the two of them collectively created swirls of elements around the fight, ready to enter at a moment's notice. Air, fire, wind, earth, metal, light, and dark all swirled together without mixing, devastating anything in their path. It was clear these two had battled before, instinctively creating a sway of predicted moves.

Flynn's sword broke under the pressure of a particularly intense light-fueled blow from Daniel's cane.

170

Flynn impulsively created twenty more swords from the metal in the swirl nearby, all hurling toward Daniel. Daniel threw the dagger at his waist. It sped through the air, breaking every weapon in its path and landing in a close soldier's back, turning him to dust. Daniel lifted a finger and the earth shot up from under Flynn, throwing him to the ground. Ice shards and darkness erupted from the elemental swirl, taking advantage of Flynn's prone position.

On the ground, Flynn raised his shield, which acted like a magnet to the darkness, catching the attack. One ice shard escaped the shield's pull and dug deep into Flynn's leg. He cried out in pain. Light rushed toward the wound but not quick enough. Daniel jabbed his sword through the ice and further into Flynn's leg causing darkness to spread. Daniel slapped the shield out of the way. He grabbed the end of Flynn's sword, and what remained of it turned to ash.

A knowledge that the end was near flooded into Flynn. In his last moment, a burst of light erupted from Flynn as he passed out, knocking all the soldiers nearby to their knees. Daniel split the light burst around him with a flick of his wrist and lifted his sword. It came down toward an unconscious Flynn. Parts of the elemental swirl fell around them as the ability to concentrate left Flynn.

A man cloaked in darkness appeared behind Daniel. The dagger, which had been imbedded in a nearby soldier, was now in its owner's back. Daniel fell. His sword dropped to the side.

The complete elemental chaos surrounding them stopped abruptly and fell. The light and darkness melded together and faded out of sight. Soldiers continued to battle on. The cloaked figure rushed to Flynn's side, carrying him off of the battlefield. As he left, the memory faded to nothing. The colors mixed back into the ground beneath them. Darius and Azalea both stood in silence for a moment.

"That cloaked figure, was it you?" She was still attempting to reconcile with the horrifying battle Wagner just showed her. The almost cartoonish nature of the manifestations and abilities didn't give her comfort. Having the battle rage around her, a battle like Azalea had always imagined but never actually been a part of, causing her to feel as if she was there. Her shock, however, would have to wait. More important things were at stake.

"Yes," Wagner stated. "I killed Daniel, but not before he defeated Flynn. If this is really him, then that melting act we saw yesterday was just a practical joke. He always had such a twisted sense of humor."

"Pride is a powerful thing," Azalea said, as she sat back in the chair, focusing on the issue in front of her instead of the battle she saw.

"Pride? Whose pride?"

"Flynn's. I understand why he hates Daniel so much. He was the second-in-command. He took charge and lost, which he sees as Daniel's fault." Wagner didn't confirm but let her continue. "Why battle in the first place? You make Toricane seem like heaven. It's an academy to learn the types of things people wish they could do on Earth. What's to hate about that? I know the whole tribe thing, but nobody's ever really said why they fought."

"Well, that part is pretty simple. Two of the tribal leaders wanted to work together, creating advancements and technologies like none you could find on Earth. They did exactly that. They created the Book of Knowledge, only it wasn't called that.

"There were two versions: The Book of Knowledge and The Book of Destruction. One tribe wanted to control the knowledge its people saw in the book. The other wanted to give knowledge without restriction."

Azalea interrupted, "A story as old as time. Good versus evil. Rule with compassion or manipulation. If you control knowledge, you control people. The problem with this story is the compassionate don't have the stomach to eradicate the terrible. Once the battle is won, what happens to the soldiers who fight for the other side?"

"Flynn took care of them. He woke up the next day. We had everybody, including Daniel, captured. He told us true compassion takes strength. He also said, 'when true compassion doesn't work, it takes a strong will to do what needs to be done.' We left him to deal with the prisoners. I always assumed he killed them."

"We now know that's not true," Azalea tested her boundaries with Wagner.

"I'm sure he had his reasons," Wagner shot back.

"They always do. Compassion."

He leaned back, "What would you have done differently? Sided with evil?"

"Of course not. There's always a grey area, like what you're going to ask me to do." Azalea had been here before. She knew the only way to play double agent was to get close to your target. She hated thinking about James as a target, but it was true.

Darius' face darkened. "We both know how being a spy works. It forces you to do the one thing you don't want, gather information on those closest to you. So, yes, you need to work in that grey area. Get close to James.

174

Become more than his confidant and friend; be the one person he comes to when things get worse."

Azalea mentally kicked herself. If she had thought this through from the beginning, obviously it was always heading here. She could've avoided this by not coming to Wagner. *Maybe that's why I didn't think it through,* she thought. *There's no sense in dreading the necessary, the inevitable.*

Wagner gave her a moment to contemplate. Azalea thought back to the day of her death, reflecting on the parallels between her life and what came after. Her life, back then, was a grey area. She liked to think coming to Wagner was her learning from past mistakes. The first time she had tried to do it all herself, there was no Wagner to lean on.

When she failed her mission, when her husband died, it marked what would be the anniversary of her death. For that last year, she was on the run. A different place every night. Always finding a small job to just scrape by, small enough to not draw attention when she left. Azalea didn't enjoy the scouting and stealing that was her life. It was the simple necessity of being double-crossed. When you play spy, that's what you come to expect from people. When the people who double cross you can kill you and get away with it, you find ways to hide.

175

She eventually grew tired of that life. Always on the run. Always scrounging for food. So, she got sloppy. It wasn't long after when the cops found her. They didn't hesitate. She ran straight for the back window. She wasn't fast enough. Azalea was shot before her second step. Once again, Azalea was put in a tough spot: succeed in the mission or let the people she cared for suffer.

Wagner interrupted her train of thought, "If you don't get close to him, I'm not sure how this is going to work. I don't know how else to help James and find out Daniel's plan."

"I don't feel right about it. It's not compassionate." She evaded eye contact with him, understanding the double standard she measured Flynn with.

"You're right. It's strong willed." Darius waited for her to speak, leaving a silent tension in the air.

"Yes, I'll do it," she conceded. "You're right. It's the only way." She stood up to leave after the defeat, but he stayed. "Just tell me you'll figure out Daniel's plan. Nothing can happen to James."

"When I have an update, you'll be the first, and only, to know. I expect the same from you. I'll see you next week, same time and place." Azalea walked out with the answers she wanted but felt no different about the situation.

* * * * * *

As Azalea made her way across the grounds, James was in the process of learning to control his powers. Flynn and James started out in his office. It seemed like the most obvious meeting place, but the flaw became immediately apparent. Flynn's first demand was for James to lift up a rock and chunk it out the window, from across the room. James had no trouble picking up the rock, but it went straight through the wall behind him.

After that nearly catastrophic attempt in Flynn's office, they ended up training in a remote field on the edge of the grounds. Nobody and nothing were nearby for him to destroy.

Flynn said he was being trained like the soldiers back in his day. It was a tough process, but the hardship sounded worth it in the end. Instead of asking James to cut a pebble in half, a tree was thrown at him. It was up to him to decide how to not get hit by the tree. His protection came through creation, manipulation, sense enhancement or any number of other abilities available to the people of Toricane 'if they truly dig,' as Flynn said.

"Your turn!" Flynn taunted as a rock he threw at James was split around him.

"My turn to what?" James asked, bewildered and breathless.

"I've been throwing stuff at you all day. You're really good at melting whatever it is, but I haven't seen you do anything else. It's your turn to attack me." Flynn stood completely still and defenseless in front of James.

"What if I hurt you?"

Flynn laughed, "I haven't been worried about hurting you, have I? Don't get soft on me."

James closed his eyes for a moment and focused on how to attack, something he had never done before. He felt an instinct come forward from somewhere distant. As his eyes opened, a pile of rocks exploded out of the ground about ten feet behind Flynn. The debris headed toward him. Flynn swiped his hand through the air. Wind pushed the dirt and rock back.

"That was close, and quite powerful, but we're learning control. Part of that control is aim. If you were to have that same accuracy walking through a wall, you would get stuck in the middle, waiting for somebody to come through behind you." Flynn didn't move an inch. He waited for another attempt.

James closed his eyes and envisioned a more focused attack. He felt the air around him slightly raise the hair on his arm. He heard a bird in the distance calling out. The rocks below his feet shuttered as he worked his mind through the ground. Heat beat down on him from the sun above. Cold came up from the ground below. It was all too much to concentrate on. His hand pushed forward, toward Flynn. A small whirlwind formed just outside of his grasp.

The wind propelled itself across the field. On the other side of it, he saw a similar whirlwind created, flowing in the opposite direction. They met in the middle and, after a moment of chaos, the small tornado dispersed.

"That was better! You'll find wind to be the easiest element to control but the hardest to use effectively. Again."

Each attack became more and more focused. The ground in the field was pulled like a rug. Flynn floated in the air to avoid it, something James didn't know was possible. A ball was conjured and thrown at Flynn, what was later called a lazy attempt. There was even a fire created in the field, which burned the grass between them, where it was accidentally manifested it.

With each attempt, each deflection of an attack, Flynn's smile grew. The amusement he received from James failure put a fire in James' belly. James reacted instantly after the last deflection and pushed his hand forward, like he was throwing a dart. Needle-sized icicles flew discreetly, covering the distance quick, and hit Flynn in the shoulder.

"Bravo!" he yelled, grabbing at his injury. "I did not see that coming. What was it?" Flynn pulled out the icicle and his smile faded. A stern expression came over him. The ice melted in his hand, steam billowing around him. Flynn looked through James, with no sign of actually seeing him.

When the shard had completely boiled, James interrupted, "Is everything okay?" He had never seen this before.

Flynn's eyes came back into focus and his voice became level, "A shard of ice? Is this a joke? Who told you to do this?"

"Told me to? You did! You told me to bring everything I had."

His expression lightened, as if through some effort, "I apologize. Ice shards are a bit of a sore memory for me." He paused, wondering if he should say why, before continuing, "Daniel almost killed me with an ice shard."

James saw this as an opening, "So, you two were enemies?"

"Only in the end. We were friends for a long time, always playing practical jokes on each other. He was particularly good at them. Neither of us would have

180

guessed I would get the last laugh." Flynn cleared his throat, "That's good for today. You made great progress. Perhaps this soldier training is the right way to go! Just remember, no using your abilities anywhere else. It will be very easy for you to lose control."

"Of course, sir."

Before James could continue, Flynn interrupted, "Unfortunately, you'll need to find your own way back. I have a meeting soon. I'll see you here tomorrow." With that, he faded into nothing.

James made his way back to central campus. He met up with Lloyd, Carissa, and Azalea outside of the torn down tower. The fifth-years were making slow progress. The top of the tower was laying on its side nearby while they worked to repair the foundation. It didn't seem possible they would finish by Friday, but James had learned to stop questioning what people could do here. They watched it for a while and chatted.

"Look what I made!" Lloyd pulled out a tiny figurine made of some kind of ceramic material and showed James. It looked like a piano but was hard to make out. James could clearly see Azalea and Carissa had already been shown.

James forced his expression to match the excitement Lloyd was expecting, "That's amazing! Is that a piano? If only you could make a big one to play. I still want to hear your talent!"

Lloyd was overjoyed. "Nobody else could tell!" Carissa and Azalea glared at James for showing them up. "Professor Wagner said by the end of the lesson I might be able to make it into a sound box. It's going to take a lot of work, but I'm going to do it!"

Azalea piped up, "You could make it into a tiny, fully functioning piano too! I just made this," she said, holding up a bowl with a wobbly side, "cause we stuck to the assignment."

James laughed, "What about you, Carissa?"

Carissa held up a plate that looked a few years old. "If I could just get the edges to curve up, it would be perfect. I'm still working on it."

"The lesson is over. I'm sure we'll get plenty of time to work on it next time," Azalea said.

"I need to work on the next assignment in the next lesson. If I fall behind by a day, I'll never catch up." As she talked, Carissa concentrated on the plate. James saw a tiny droop as the plate's surface dematerialized.

"Did you get anything out of your lessons with Flynn?" Azalea asked.

"No trophies. It was honestly pretty fun, though. I'm not allowed to do anything when I'm not in his line of sight, which just means I'm looking forward to next time."

"What's it like?" she asked, her full attention toward James.

"For most of the lesson, he attacked me with stuff and made me defend myself. There was a tree, rock, and some water. The rest of the lesson I spent attacking him. It was a good back and forth!" He laughed at their bewildered looks. "He said it's pointless to learn control in a stress-free environment." Azalea looked worried.

"I can't believe you attacked the Provost," Lloyd said. "What's the coolest thing you did?"

James thought for a minute, "It has to be the icicle. I threw a small icicle at him. It was cool because it's the only one that actually hit him. He got pretty angry about it and said something about a sore memory. In the end, he brushed it off like it was nothing."

"You actually managed to hit the Provost?" Azalea asked, moving closer. "That's impressive."

They chatted back and forth about lessons and the upcoming labors for several hours. Seeing a tower being built right in front of them was the best dinner and a show they could've asked for. The construction sped up in the evening, when more people gathered around to watch it happen. In the time they sat there, the outside of the tower was starting to be built. The walls grew full of stone and several recruits followed behind with different styles of artwork, complementing the vines of light and elemental chaos that echoed through campus.

Carissa was the first to retire for the night. She was exhausted after spending the entire time improving her plate. The edges were curved up enough for it to now be considered a bowl, but she wasn't satisfied. Lloyd called it soon after. He tended to wake up earlier than the rest of them, the downfall of being elderly for so long, as James liked to tell him.

Eventually, it was just James and Azalea. They sat in silence for a while, staring at the construction.

"What was Alisa like?" Azalea asked.

James was taken aback. It took a moment for him to collect his thoughts. "She was... We were great together."

"How so?"

"Have you ever had somebody in your life that you only really noticed when you were apart from them?" He shook his head. "Not like you don't notice them. Like, when they're with you, you feel whole. It's only when you're apart, when that part of you is gone, that you really notice it was there to begin with."

Azalea smiled, "My sister. We were twins, and from the moment of birth we never left each other's

184

side. Eventually we had to because, you know, life. But I really felt like myself around her."

James nodded, "Exactly. Except for us it was death. But that's the same for everybody," he shrugged.

"Do you think you'll find that other half of yourself again?" She didn't look at him as she asked.

"It's possible, I guess. What was it Wagner said about cherishing what's passed and blah blah?"

"That's crap. It's easy to say when you've died five times. It's harder to actually do it."

"Do you think you will?"

"What?" Azalea asked. "Find another sister? I'm sure I'll probably have a sister in my next life." James saw her looked down at her ring finger where a tan line had recently replaced her wedding ring.

With her obviously avoiding the topic, he didn't want to pry. Instead, James talked about his uncle, Hugo, and mother. Turns out, both of them had overprotective but very loving mothers. It was nice to share these things after they had passed. Toricane may feel like, and actually be, an entirely different world, but the memories were still precious to James. Some relationships might feel like they're over, but the people remained with him.

Toricane

Pushing Up Fresh Daisies

"Hello, and welcome to the first labor of the year!" Chloe started her speech with the same enthusiasm as the initial announcement. She stood on a stage in the main hall while people ate their breakfast. Everybody was there for the announcement; breakfast was just a perk. "It's finally here. The professors have a great time creating these challenges for you all, and we can't wait to see how you handle them. As you know, today is the first-years' time to shine.

"Because of the hunting aspect of this labor, we have decided it will be done in the forests just outside the city. Professor Ruskin and I have sectioned off a piece of the forest for today. So, watch out. If you're not paying attention, you will run directly into the barrier we've put up. Are you ready?!"

Cheers erupted from around her. "Everybody get your medallions and meet at the gates of town in an hour! No wandering around."

Since waking up that morning the first-years had stuck to their groups. It wasn't a game to them. This was a competition. James, Azalea, Lloyd and Carissa had the same mindset. They snuck quickly back to Volition Tower, avoiding classmates.

"I feel like we're at a disadvantage," Lloyd said, as they made their way back.

"Why?" Carissa asked.

"Well, for starters, that one team gets five players, since we have an extra classmate. On top of that, James can't use his abilities, which would come in handy." James couldn't help but feeling like both of these were directly his fault.

"Actually," James corrected him, "Flynn will be watching the whole thing with the rest of the academy. He guaranteed an eye would always be on me. I think you could do it without me, though. You've come a long way!"

Azalea swiped her hand an inch from her hair and made the wind blow it back confidently. "I think we've done pretty well for ourselves. Lloyd, your piano alone is

188

detailed enough that even Wagner was impressed. Plus, you're in teleportation, which I hear is really hard. How is it coming, by the way?"

Lloyd puffed out his chest, "I can now successfully teleport a bunny across a room."

"They don't teach you how to teleport yourself?" James asked.

"That comes way later. I was disappointed at first, but the amount of times I've accidentally teleported half a bunny has made me rethink that." Carissa's face winced. "Don't worry," he said, "Chloe's husband repairs them immediately. He says they're just manifestations and can't actually feel pain."

"You call him Chloe's husband?" Azalea laughed.

"The whole Professor Ruskin and Professor Ruskin thing gets a little confusing. He told us to just call him whatever we want."

"So you call him...?" James fished for more.

"Nothing." They all laughed. "I just say 'hey, you' or 'Professor.' It's worked pretty well up to now."

"Now it's falling apart, since they'll both be here," James mocked.

"They will? How many people will actually be watching us?" Carissa worriedly asked.

James seemed to be the only one with any information about the game. Having Flynn as his instructor was a lot like gossiping with a police officer. He gets the inside scoop, but he's not sure how much he should actually know. "Everybody! Flynn said they're creating a glass viewing pavilion above the forest to watch with. It's high up, but the floor is basically a giant magnifying glass. So, they'll be able to see everything."

Azalea smiled, "I'm just imagining groups of people striding along above us looking directly at their feet and running into each other over and over." James and Carissa laughed. Lloyd didn't respond. He was having trouble processing the fact that they would be watched the entire time. "They're going to have to pick groups to track and just run alongside them from above."

Azalea looked over at James, "I bet we'll have a big group following us after your fiasco with the main tower." James looked down, but she continued, "It just means we'll have more of a reason to win. With your abilities, we'll also be more able."

Azalea smiled at him but noticed Lloyd's nerves started to kick in. "Hey, Lloyd, just do your best. You'll be fine." He nodded and gulped in some air.

The walk through town brought back memories of their first week. As they walked through the border between campus and city, their old residential tower came into view, followed by the Mesopotamian

190

restaurant. The group went to the other side of the street to avoid any familiar smells. They saw Barley and his books. The first-years all waved at him. Barley's smile spread and his hand jerked back and forth, excited to see them again.

As the gates neared, they saw Chloe and her husband, Edgar, chatting at the exit. Everybody seemed to be arriving at the same time. She motioned toward the worker nearby and the gate lowered. Even after all this time in Toricane, watching a thirty-foot tall gate form out of a solid wall and lower was astonishing. It bridged the pit they had seen coming in their first day. The recruits made their way across and gathered near the forest's edge.

"Everybody who will be spectating, get on the platform." Chloe called out as she gestured toward a large panel of glass lying flat on the ground. As the professors and students hopped on the panel, the transparent floor raised farther than James could see and carried them off. "As for the rest of you, here is what you will be hunting."

She pulled a mouse out of her pocket. It was a tiny, stone mouse, not unlike those James had seen in Flynn's office. The first-years looked around at each other, confused. One recruit spoke up. "A mouse, Professor? Couldn't we have done that on campus?"

Gary asked. There were nods of agreement from the crowd.

Choe smirked and threw the mouse at Gary as hard as she could. He flinched, but it seemed to disappear just before hitting him. He searched himself and found a large stone tarantula on his shoulder.

"Ah!" he screamed. Gary smacked the spider off by instinct. It flew through the air, morphed into a bat, and glided back to Chloe. The creature hung upside down, gripping Chloe's outstretched finger, and stared at the recruits.

"As you can see, Gary, it's not a mouse. It's obviously a bat," she laughed at the bewildered looks on the faces of the first-years. "I'll be taking this little guy up with me and you can make your way into the forest. I'll release him in a few minutes."

"Wait," Lloyd said, "what else can it do?"

Chloe looked at him, amused, "Well, where would the fun be in me telling you that?"

Without another word, Chloe stepped on a smaller glass platform with the rest of the instructors and flew up to the viewing pavilion above. The first-years were left on the ground, unsure of what to do next. Azalea tapped on each of the other three's shoulders and motioned toward a nearby tree big enough to hide them behind it. They stealthily made their way away from the crowd. When they were sure nobody could see them, Azalea started planning.

"We need to remain unseen by the rest of them. Our movements will give away our strategy."

James was confused, "We have a strategy? I thought it was just *'find the thing'* then *'kill or capture the thing'.*"

Azalea held in a laugh, "Yes, that's essentially the plan, but, if we remain unseen while we track, we will have the advantage in finding it first."

"Seems like you've done this before," James said, not sure if he should be impressed or worried.

"A few times. Just don't be seen and do what you can to find the thing, basically. It's better if we split into two groups. How are your telepathy lessons going?" she asked James and Lloyd.

Lloyd and James look at each other, waiting for the other to answer. Neither wanted to admit they weren't going well. James pipped up, "Not great. I think we could both send each other messages, as long as the line was kept open, so to speak."

"That's plenty," she said. "What about scrying?"

James felt like his programs were being picked on and he didn't want to keep admitting their difficulty, so he yielded to Carissa. "We can only scry objects so far," she stated. None of them had noticed until now, Carissa was listening intensely to the plan Azalea was laying out.

Azalea was confused, "So you...see what the rock sees?"

"Not exactly," Carissa explained. "We can feel where it is in relation to us."

"Perfect!" she said. "We--"

James cut her off, excited to have figured it out, "We each hold onto something of each other's. Me and Lloyd can communicate if we find something, and the other group scries the object to track them down."

Azalea smiled at him, "Exactly. So, Lloyd and Carissa, go to the right side of the forest. If you see the barrier, come back toward the center. We want to cover as much ground as possible. Try not to be seen. Me and James will make our way around the left side. If you run into another group, stay only long enough to learn what they know."

Carissa nodded with purpose. Lloyd held his hand out. It took the rest of them a second to understand what he was doing. They all laughed a bit and put their hands on top of his. "Team Volition," Lloyd said quietly.

"Team Volition," they all repeated in a low tone. Their hands shot into the air. The game was on. Azalea and James made their way, tree by tree, to the left side of

194

the forest. They passed a couple groups wandering around, chatting loudly. As far as he could tell, nobody had seen the animal yet.

James got preoccupied watching his step and, when he looked to the side, there was no Azalea. He panicked, looking around, but didn't see anybody. *How is this possible?* he asked himself. Then, he felt a stick jab into his side.

"Watch your six. Somebody could sneak up on you," she laughed.

"I thought that's what you were for," he snickered and turned around. She was closer than he had anticipated, holding the stick into his ribs and looking up at him. Just a few inches away, she didn't move. James cleared his throat uncomfortably and took a step back.

"I knew you were there," he lied casually. "I just wasn't expecting you to literally stab me in the back."

As Azalea was about to respond, James held his hand up for her to stop. He felt a message coming through from Lloyd. James heard, *'Snake!'* as if it was yelled into his ear. He flinched and messaged back asking if it was a real snake or the stone animal. Again at yelling volume, *'Real snake!'*

"Never mind," he told Azalea. "Lloyd saw a snake, a real one. He seemed pretty scared. I wonder if we should be on the lookout for dangerous animals."

"I'm sure we're okay. We have medical supervision," she said, pointing into the sky where they were being watched.

They continued on for another half hour without seeing much. As their adrenaline wore off, they slowed down. Eventually, Azalea and James found the boundary on the left side. Chloe didn't make it easy to see. It was a solid barrier to the touch, but the only visual clue was a slight blur to their line of sight when looking through it.

Azalea suggested they head in the opposite direction from the boundary. They were likely to cover the most inner area that way. James agreed, but before they could head that way, there was a noise coming down following the side of the wall. It sounded like one of their classmates running, sprinting really. It was coming toward them from the entrance into the forest. James pulled both of them behind a nearby tree, squeezing in so as not to be seen. Celia ran by right after they took cover. Her speed and form looked every bit the Olympian she once claimed to be. It still wasn't fast enough.

James watched as a full-grown bear ran after her from about fifty feet back. This was the animal they had been looking for, made of pure stone. It hauled down the side of the arena. Azalea and James looked at each other and nodded before running after it. Neither of them knew what they were going to do if they caught it, but that was for them to figure out later. James sent a quick message to Lloyd about a stone bear heading deeper into the forest and heard an affirmative response.

"They're on their way," he said as the two of them started running. Azalea was slightly faster than James but slowed herself to stick together. With all the trees and wild vines, it was difficult to get up to full speed. They couldn't see the bear but heard its massive paws hitting the ground ahead of them. The two of them ran until they were exhausted then kept running. The bear's steps faded ahead of them, out of earshot. They kept running, pushing ahead, hoping for a sign of the bear.

James pushed just ahead of Azalea, looking for any sign that a monstrous animal went down the path they were on. He was exhausted and about to give up, but the trees opened up in front of him. There was a clearing ahead, open field for a few hundred feet. The only thing he saw, other than rock and grass, was a stone structure roughly a hundred feet ahead that sloped down into the ground.

As James slowed down, Azalea ran past him, toward the opening. She yelled, "It could be a den," as she passed. He took a big huff of air and ran after her. Azalea made it to the entrance but didn't stop. James couldn't see into it, but it looked like a destroyed building from the outside.

"I don't think this is a den!" he yelled after her. He watched as Azalea flew through the air out of the entrance and landed several yards away on her back. As his gaze followed her trajectory, he saw out of the side of his eye the exterior of the structure forming into a large stone golem. It charged at her.

Azalea didn't get up. James' mind jumped to the worst conclusion. He wanted to run to her, but there wasn't time. The stone golem stood at least three or four times James' height and leapt toward Azalea with a hand made of stone, ready to strike. James flung his hand out like he was throwing a frisbee, a hidden instinct guiding him.

A disc of light and darkness, each bumping off the other in a spinning ripple of poorly crafted interconnectivity, erupted just past his open hand. It spiraled toward Azalea, expanding as it traveled. Just as the golem brought its massive fist down to strike her, the disc lengthened to cover her body and took the full force of the blow. Light from the disc flowed into Azalea. Darkness gripped the golem's arm like a squid that had found its prey.

James watched as the darkness enveloped the golem's fist, turning it to sand. The golem seemed unphased by the loss of its limb and, before James could react, went in for an attack with its other hand. The fist came down directly on Azalea, and translucent light pulsated out of her body, breaking the stone golem's fist in half. As James looked at her, he could see her eyes open, leaving him some hope.

James' hands pushed forward to attack the golem. The ground broke beneath his feet as he looked at the rock monster before him. He felt heat from the air infiltrate his skin. It intensified as a barrage of compacted lava needles were carved from the broken earth below and flew toward his enemy. From above, a shower of water turned the needles back to stone, which abruptly fell on the ground.

He looked up to see Flynn falling straight down toward the golem, hand outstretched as if physically pulling himself to go faster. He allowed the full force of his descent to impact the rock. The golem was pulverized with a puff of dust and gravel blocking James' view. When it fell, Flynn was standing over a pile of motionless rocks.

"Are you two alright?!" he quickly asked, as a few other professors landed.

James ran to Azalea. She sat up as he got there, not a scratch on her. "Yeah, I'm okay," she said, in shock at what had just happened. He let out of sigh of relief. "Was that not the animal?" she asked.

After seeing they were both fine, Flynn laughed, "No, that was not the animal. You two went through the barrier just before the clearing, when you were running. I'm guessing James broke through without realizing it, and the barrier didn't heal in time for Azalea." He scratched his head in frustration. "You should not have been able to come this way." Chloe and Edgar walked over to examine Azalea while he talked.

"So, what was that?" James asked, also frustrated.

"The golem was protection. This," Flynn said, pointing toward the entrance, "is not a den. It's an old battlefield that has been buried and memorialized. There's a barrier just inside that Azalea hit. It threw her back and triggered the defenses."

"Was that thing going to kill me?" Azalea asked, waving off the help being offered to her.

Chloe responded, "Yes, it was. Anybody allowed out here knows not to go in that memorial. You look fine to me. I think the light James produced healed you after the fall." She looked at James with a mixed expression of worried and impressed. "You two are going to sit out the rest of the labor. If Lloyd or Carissa win, you can join them in their victory."

Azalea was about to protest, but Wagner, who had been uncharacteristically quiet, interrupted, "I agree. Get on the platform. We'll take you up. This place isn't as safe as we would like." James and Azalea didn't argue after that. When Wagner tells James to get on the

200

platform, there was no compromise in his eyes. James avoided eye contact with Wagner as he obeyed.

"The first labor doesn't get you much anyway," Edgar reassured them. "Each of the first few just give you advantages on the final labor. It's the fourth one that really counts."

They got on the platform, too shocked to consider Edgar's comment, and Flynn guided it to the pavilion above. As they ascended, James was thinking back to what just happened. It was so fast he didn't really have a chance to think. "What was that thing I made, the disc?" he asked nobody in particular.

Flynn answered, "Something you should not know how to do." He paused before adding, "Something that most likely saved Azalea's life. We'll talk about it during our next lesson." James, who normally would've been excited to learn about his abilities, didn't like the tone Flynn used. It sounded more like a scolding than an affirmation.

The rest of the trip was silent. Azalea was still in shock. She normally scanned the environment as she moved. Now, Azalea stood motionless on the platform. Her face was pale, as if the light she absorbed had temporarily lightened her blood.

James and Azalea separated from the professors as soon as they reached the pavilion above the forest. It was nothing like they had imagined earlier. The transparent floor didn't just magnify, It zoomed in on the recruits. If James looked to his right, he could see every group on that side of the forest. If he looked to his left, every group on that side was in sight. The voices of each group seemed to feed directly into James' head when he looked at them.

After a few minutes of this, James and Azalea were dialed in on Lloyd and Carissa, putting the whole incident in the past. They pointed out the animal, which was now a butterfly, and wondered how anybody was going to find it. James made sure to tell Lloyd they were out of commission, so he didn't keep tracking them, but hoped that didn't put a damper on them. Right now, James noticed Carissa was attempting to use her scrying to locate various objects around the forest and see if they were moving. It was an easy way to track other groups.

After wandering around to watch the rest of the groups, Azalea walked to James side. She seemed uncomfortable, which was unusual for her. "James," she started, not finishing her thoughts.

"Something wrong?"

"No. Not at all." She took a deep breath. "I just wanted to say thank you."

"Oh," James was caught off guard. "Don't mention it. I know you would've done the same thing for me."

"You're right. We would both do that for each other." They went back to watching Lloyd and Carissa spying on another group. James could feel a stiffness in the air that pulled his attention toward Azalea, regardless of his friends below. He hadn't noticed it there before and didn't know why it appeared now.

He wanted to comment on it, to allow the thickness of the air between them to fall. Before he could, Azalea spit out, "Have dinner with me," almost in one word.

James was flustered. He wasn't sure how to respond. His immediate thought went to Alisa. He hadn't considered dating in Toricane before. He thought that ended when you got married. James wasn't married anymore. Technically, he was dead.

As if reading his thoughts, Azalea kept going, "We both had significant others. That doesn't mean everything ends when you lose them. Let's have an evening, here in Toricane, just the two of us."

He didn't know what to say. As if instinctually, he replied, "Okay. Yes." James wasn't sure if he made the right call, but it didn't feel particularly wrong. The tension in the air settled into a knot in the pit of his stomach.

"This weekend," she said.

"This weekend," he replied. They both smiled and looked back down at their friends, who were nowhere near the animal. It had taken the form of a monkey and was swinging through trees. Some recruits had taken to making weapons and walking through the forest like hunter-gatherers. Others were still examining every branch, looking for a mouse or spider. This hunt was going to take a while. Azalea grabbed James' hand while they watched. *The longer it takes, the better*, James thought.

"I hate to say it," Azalea started, allowing James to take his thoughts away from their hands, "but I don't see us winning this one. Our plan isn't really working without all four of us down there."

James let out a deep breath he didn't realize he had been holding in. She was giving him an out to just talk about the hunt, and he was going to take it. "I don't know about that. I liked Carissa's idea of scrying the objects to find other teams."

"It was a good idea. It just didn't really work. I also don't think this plan is going to play out well."

James looked down to find Lloyd attempting to capture the construct by transporting a bunny into a nearby trap. "I don't think a stone manifestation needs to eat." They both laughed and let the competition of it fade away, leaving the enjoyment with them.

James pointed to one person not far from Lloyd's trap. "Where is the rest of his team?"

"I saw him separate from them," she pointed at three different people scattered around the forest. James couldn't think of their names off the top of his head. "Not too long ago. No idea what they're doing, though."

"Oh!" James remembered, "I did see them planning during Carissa's rock scrying exploration. They are using basically the same idea, just bigger. They're trying to create a telepathic web around the forest. If it works, they'll know where every living object is, based on the movements between each other."

"Seems too convoluted," Azalea critiqued. "They're trying to catch an animal, not plan battle strategy." After a few minutes of silence, Azalea pointed James' attention toward the west barrier. "Did you see that?"

"What is it?" James asked, searching around the forest. It took a moment to find because she wasn't looking at the forest floor. Up in a tree, one first-year had been knocked out by one of the rock-weighted nets

Gary's group had put up all over the forest. "Oh, I wonder if they're okay."

"I'm sure she will be." As Azalea spoke, James looked toward Gary to find his group making a continuous line of the same traps throughout the middle section of the forest.

"They're going to get so many of the recruits with those traps. Do you think they know?" James saw Chloe falling head-first through the air, straight toward the unconscious, trapped victim. James continued, "I'm guessing they know Chloe will come help.

"Yeah, it's still no excuse. They're purposely hurting everybody just to win a recruit game," Azalea complained.

"A game?" James questioned, "It seemed like more than that. Didn't they describe this as a training exercise?"

"Scare tactic." Azalea bluntly stated. "You heard Edgar, on the platform. He basically said this one doesn't really matter. Unless these things actually get dangerous, it's still a game."

James had to agree. It did seem more like a game than training, but they hadn't learned much at this point. Not being able to actually use their abilities, it would've been difficult for anybody to train in the ways Azalea seemed to want. As their programs progressed, James fully expected the labors to live up to their hype.

James and Azalea spent the remainder of their day watching the different teams. The winning strategy also ended up being the most obnoxious, Gary's. Even Chloe, a notoriously enthusiastic announcer, wasn't excited to declare the winner. Her face gave away the irritation of such carelessness in their strategy. She told them to start preparing now. The next labor would be a couple weeks after their winter holiday.

The next few days of games flew by. They used the same animal but increased its violent tendencies and transformation capabilities each day. By the end, the fifth-years were facing creatures the recruits had only heard in myths. Of the many, James recognized a hydra, chimera, sprite, and even, at one point, the ghost of a cyclops. It made a charging bear look tame.

It really made James think about the things he had yet to see in Toricane. The creativity in the academy's design was astonishing but could make James forget about everything else that was possible. There weren't creatures being created every day or people throwing lightning bolts, which went right through the ghostly cyclops and almost hit the platform they were standing on. It was the first time he had realized the only limitation was his imagination. It was exhilarating.

Carissa could be found sitting on the platform asking rapid fire questions to her Book of Knowledge, trying to figure out what the advanced years were doing. She wanted to learn as much as she could during the week. Lloyd was running around, excited to be out of danger's way, trying to imitate them. Azalea and James didn't leave each other's side, not that there was much room or reason to do so. Instead, they spent their week dissecting the strategies of the older recruits, looking forward to using them.

Nothing to Scry Home About

During the week of the first labor, a few of the late programs still made the recruits attend. James had Luck and Scrying this week. Luck went by quickly, though. Azalea and he played blackjack without looking at their cards. She won. James found it irritating to lose in that program. He couldn't blame it on luck, because that was the entire point. But neither he nor Azalea understood that yet.

Scrying was a different story. The night of the last labor was also the first time recruits were asked to scry on another person, which took the entire group by surprise. Until now, they were told to stick with objects, else they could cause damage to themselves or the person they were scrying. After that scare tactic in the first couple months, the professor suddenly thought they were ready.

It's what James had been waiting for since signing up for the program. Finally, he might be able to see Alisa. His heart fluttered, palms became sweaty, in anticipation of seeing Alisa again. She wouldn't be able to see him, but he could see his wife for the first time since their wedding. *Ex-wife*, James corrected himself.

Azalea went through his mind. *I'm sure Azalea would understand if I just checked in on her*, he thought. He had to see Alisa, after all this time. He had to know how she was doing, if she was okay.

"Settle down, first-years," Professor Braddock said, after explaining what they would be doing. "I know it's exciting. Just keep in mind, you may *not* do this to anybody who has not given you permission. In the same way that telepaths can detect an invasion into their brain, once you develop this skill, you will be able to detect somebody trying to scry you. That means there will be no scrying unless you've been told it's okay."

The group nodded excitedly and quieted down. "Okay, then partner up. Take turns attempting to scry each other. Remember, it's just like scrying an object, except, in this case, your senses will be equal to theirs.

What they feel, see, hear, you will also. You will know your partner has successfully scried when their eyes change." After several confused looks, she added, "You'll see what I mean."

Carissa turned to James. He wasn't ready to move on and raised his hand. "Professor, is it possible to scry people on Earth." His curiosity didn't allow for side-stepping the question. He wanted to know exactly that, nothing else.

Braddock nodded in understanding, "Yes, that's always a tough subject. It is possible, but I don't recommend it. While there aren't rules specifically prohibiting it, you're still invading the most intimate privacy somebody has. You're invading all of their senses and there's no way to ask for permission first. It's a hard line to walk. Like I said, it is possible, but once you do it, there's no going back."

The excitement in the room dialed back after his comment. Everybody had loved ones they wanted to check in on but never thought of it as an invasion. James turned toward Carissa and saw her giving him a look of disappointment. "Alisa?" she asked.

"I just want to check in on her, make sure she's okay."

She shook her head, "You know it wouldn't stop there."

"There's not anybody you want to just give a quick look at, one last time?" James asked.

"I'm not going to. I'm dead. There's no going back, so I'm not going to put myself through that," she said bluntly.

James didn't like this conversation. "Do you want to try first?"

Carissa nodded, "Take this deck of cards. I'm going to close my eyes and see if I can read the cards you pick out. We'll practice a little magic trick for Lloyd and Azalea."

He mumbled under his breath in disagreement but took the cards regardless. "Sounds fun," he dryly stated.

She closed her eyes and drifted into one of her intense concentrations. It was funny to watch, but James knew better than to laugh and interrupt. Before he knew it, James felt a small pang in his mind. It didn't feel wrong but uncomfortable. It was a type of vulnerability he hadn't experienced before. He allowed it to continue without pushing back.

James pulled out a card from the deck. "Hang on," Carissa said. "I felt you pull a card out, but I haven't quite figured out the vision thing."

He looked at her, squinting her eyes closed and also trying to see. James laughed, "Try opening your eyes."

She opened them, and James took a surprised step back. They were his eyes. Carissa had solid brown eyes. He was sure of it. When he looked now, sparkling blue eyes replaced the dark brown, just like his. He was standing in front of a carnival funhouse mirror. Almost immediately, her eyes turned back to brown as she lost focus.

"Woah, that was intense. I opened my eyes and saw myself through your eyes. Did I have your eyes?"

"Yeah, that was freaky," he replied.

"Give me another go! I wasn't expecting that. You made me lose concentration." She closed her eyes for a moment before opening them. He saw his open eyes reflected back at him again. James decided it was best to not look at them. It probably made the experience weirder for her, and it was not pleasant for him.

"What card am I holding up?"

"Ace of spades. Now, it's three of clubs. Now, seven of diamonds. Now, king of hearts. I think I have a hold of this. You give it a go."

James handed her the deck of cards and closed his eyes. She got it so fast; he wanted to beat that. He thought of Carissa standing right beside him and being able to see through her eyes. He tried to concentrate on a single thought, out of the multitude flowing through his head. He needed to find the one that would lead to Alisa. Carissa. Definitely, Carissa. The one thought that would lead to Carissa.

Suddenly, James felt fabric running through his hands. His hands had been at his side. In the blink of an eye, they were out in front of him, combing through something. He smelled old wood and perfume. He recognized that perfume and opened his eyes. James was staring at a sky blue wedding dress. It hung in a closet and had blood stains. His hands looked smaller than normal. He didn't have a wedding ring on.

James realized he was in the bedroom of their home. He closed the closet door and started walking back through the house. Then, he felt a sharp pain on his face. He was back in the group. Everybody was staring at him. His cheek hurt really bad. He looked at Carissa and realized she had just slapped him.

"Sorry, I wasn't concentrating well and got lost. I kind of forgot where I was for a moment there," he admitted.

She gave him a worried look, "Just try again." The rest of the group eyed them curiously and went back to their scrying.

He closed his eyes again and thought, more firmly this time, "Carissa."

James opened his eyes and saw them looking back at him. Carissa started pulling cards out of the deck and he recalled them perfectly. His mind was in it, but his heart was back scrying Alisa. He wanted to do it again. The first time was an accident, but some accidents don't just happen accidentally. *Rather elegant how simple and random it is,* he thought, quoting Daniel's words to himself.

* * * * * *

Once both of them completed the assignment, the professor let them go for the day. Carissa joined Lloyd for dinner and talked about the latest labor. James went back to the Volition Tower to get ready for his date. He was fairly nervous, having only been on a first date with one person, the same person he'd just spied on.

When James got to his room, he started putting together what he wanted to wear. He opened the closet and for a split second saw that blood-stained dress taunting him. He couldn't tell if it was his imagination or the scrying. Either way, it was horrid. He ignored the unpleasantness and ruffled through his clothes for much longer than necessary before grabbing his only nice outfit.

216

What are we going to talk about? Where are we going to go that's not surrounded by people we know? How is this going to work? James' brain was not into getting ready, even though there wasn't much he actually had to do. It's just nerves, he told himself. We just saw a week's worth of monsters and fighting. There's plenty to talk about.

He took several deep breaths and collected himself. *What did Alisa and I do on our first date?* James closed his eyes, laid on his bed, and thought back to that day so long ago now.

Alisa snuck away from her house for a night. They had spent hours wandering the countryside, chatting about anything and everything. Neither of them knew the other outside of school but felt something worth pursuing. Typically couples in his town would have dates that were more like chaperoned discussions at the woman's house. Their date was more unusual. It didn't take long for their nightly walks to become a pattern.

In a field on the edge of town, several miles from either of their houses, without light to guide them, James and Alisa would meet under the biggest tree, their tree. James knew to meet her every night under that single weeping willow. It started out as a getaway from their houses and ended up feeling like much more than that for both of them.

Without fail, she would be there at his side. It was never talked about outside of the date, for fear of being caught. There was also no need or want to discuss it. The day was just a necessary step James took before a night spent under that weeping willow.

His mind wandered further, trying to imagine what she was doing right now, probably just getting home from the factory. She would be so lonely. Suddenly, he felt his hands moving. He was talking to somebody, gesturing at them. James opened his eyes and saw his mother, Mariam, sitting in a chair across from him. He saw Alisa's hands gesturing in front of him. He realized what happened but didn't stop it. James let himself drift into the scry.

He could feel the couch cushion under him, see his mother listening to Alisa, and smell that same perfume he'd grown used to. He couldn't hear them, though. It was like watching a mute film. He concentrated on hearing the words, but nothing came. After a few tries, he just let himself watch the scene playout in front of him. He couldn't see Alisa. Though, being present with her felt like enough.

He watched their conversation and also looked around her peripherals. The house looked just as he had expected. When he died, they had just bought it. Now, there were decorations everywhere. Furniture lined the room, although he recognized most of it as donations from his family. Then, he took a good look at his mother. She looked happy. He hoped Alisa looked just as happy.

Suddenly, there was a repeated, loud rap at the door. His scry broke immediately. *Crap! How long was I out?* he thought as he jumped off his bed. "I'm almost ready, just one second!" he called out.

"No rush!" he heard Azalea say through the door.

James made the final touches, running a hand through his hair and straightening wrinkles out of his shirt. He walked to the door and took a preparatory breath. The door opened to an Azalea he had not expected; one he had not seen to this point.

Azalea, as James knew her, had always been about functionality. She typically wore jeans and a shirt, nothing extravagant. She let her hair fall wherever it wanted, not taking the meaningless time to fix it any certain way. She refused to wear makeup, just like in life, finding it unnecessary to everyday life. Truly, she never needed any of it.

A different Azalea was standing at his door now. She wore a simple, conservative dress that hugged her frame and matched the green tint in her eyes. The long brown hair that usually fell for convenience, now had a soft curl to it that framed her face. She smiled up at him.

He was suddenly self-conscious about the nicest outfit in his closet.

"Wow, you look amazing."

"Surprised?" she laughed.

"Yes," he said, immediately realizing what came out of his mouth. "I mean, no...I...You just usually...You always look great."

She watched him stumble through his words and a snort came out of her laughter. "You can stop now. Your stammer tells me everything. You ready to go?"

He nodded and cleared his throat, "I'm ready! You know, I don't think I've heard you laugh that hard since we first got here. Everything's been so hectic; it'll be nice to have an evening away from everybody." He closed the door behind him, and they headed down the stairs.

"Definitely! That's why I've found a spot on the very edge of campus we can go. It's a bit of a journey though." As they walked out of Volition Tower, Lloyd and Carissa, who were heading back from the main hall, waved at them. "We'll be back in a little bit!" Azalea called out.

"Don't worry about us!" Lloyd said as they passed. "Apparently, one of the fifth-years is throwing a party tonight to celebrate the end of the first labor. We'll see you for breakfast tomorrow."

"I hope it's not the one who threw a lightning bolt at us," James said after they passed. "I can't believe how close that came before Wagner shot it down."

"In his defense, what else do you throw at a ghost cyclops?"

"A ghost net, obviously." He said, matter-of-factly.

They both laughed and kept talking about the different monsters and what they would have done. Azalea thought she could have taken the animal down as a hydra. "Everybody knows you burn the heads after you cut them off," she said. James commented that it was much harder to burn stone. The two of them went back and forth about which captures were the best, who the professors went easy on, and if there were any new tricks they could do now, since they'd seen them performed.

Before they knew it, the spot Azalea had picked out was right in front of them. As far as James could tell, it was a normal patch of grass, just like every patch of grass they passed on the way. "It's perfect," he said.

She chuckled and pulled a small white box out from behind one of her curls. "I had some help making this for tonight." Azalea placed the box on the ground and stepped back several yards. James copied her movements, not sure what to expect.

As if from nothing, the box unfolded itself over and over until a small platform was built. From the platform, a small table and two chairs rose. Colors vined through them as they came to life. The platform extended outwards to their left and then rose straight up into a small wall.

"You made this?!" James let out.

"Maybe more like supervised." Azalea made her way to the table. "Okay, so I didn't do it at all. I did a favor for Professor Wagner a while back, and, in return, I asked him to make me this."

"This is incredible!" James was really taken away. He had no idea how she even thought that up. Before sitting down, Azalea grabbed his shoulder for support and tiptoed up to kiss his cheek. "What was that for?" he asked, honestly curious what any of this was for.

"For saving my life."

They both took a seat at the table, but James paused. "Is that what all this is for?"

"No," she shook her head at him, "just the kiss. This," she motioned toward everything around her, "is because we are in Toricane. I'm embracing it, and you should too! If I can make a tiny box that unfolds into a portable date, I'm going to. If I can materialize a dress around myself, why wouldn't I?"

He had to admit, it was a good point, and the dress looked great. "You're right. I'm just not used to

222

this. So, with the world at our fingertips, what's for dinner?"

She smiled and lifted the cover off the platter. "Mesopotamian food."

James chuckled, "No coffee, then?"

"No coffee, but there are sixty varieties of beer. It's good to know the world's first civilization really had their priorities straight." She grabbed some fish and bread to put on the plate.

"I guess it is fitting. I figured out the other day Toricane is kind of this world's first civilization. Before that, there were just tribes."

"What happened to the tribes?" she asked.

"I don't know. Flynn tends to tell me bits and pieces of lessons, usually in diluted allegories. For all I know, by tribes and civilizations he could've been referring to beer and coffee."

"Well, you two do spend plenty of time together. You must know him at least a little bit by now."

James thought about it, "The only thing I know about him is that he was probably a Roman warrior, which is pretty cool. He has all this armor and weaponry around his office."

Azalea looked disappointed, "What about Daniel? Has he told you anything about him?"

"Every time I bring him up, Flynn says the lesson is over. It's a good way to get out of training but not helpful for much else."

They sat in silence and ate for a moment, until James noticed black ink start to form on the wall. "What's going on there?" he asked, pointing to it.

"Oh! I almost forgot. It's dinner and a movie. Wagner told me he did this thing with our memories. I didn't fully understand what he was talking about. He said it's our life highlights. Something about telepathy and memory. It's all nonsense to me." She seemed nervous about it.

"Our life highlights? This is going to be fun; I know almost nothing about yours." He started to get nervous too, thinking about his wedding. *Is that a highlight or a low point? Maybe a little of both.* "Anything I should know first?" he asked.

"You should probably know I was married," she stated.

"Was he a spy too?"

"No, he didn't know I was a spy." She sighed, "He died because of it. Heavy first date topic, right?"

At the mention of her husband, James felt a pang of guilt for scrying Alisa. Then the guilt turned into pity when he learned Azalea's husband had died. It didn't seem like she wanted to dwell on the topic, so he gave

224

her a way out. "It's all behind us. Otherwise, we wouldn't be able to watch it like a movie." He gestured to the wall as it started.

Different colors started soaking through the wall. The first memory was one of James' early birthdays. It was the last birthday he ever had with his dad. The whole family gathered around to celebrate.

"Ah, I remember that. My dad got me this really cool gun."

Azalea laughed, "He gave you a gun? You had to have been like 10."

"It was more of something I would come to learn how to use. Something he could teach me to do." James stared at the screen, mesmerized by the image of his father.

The scene changed. An image of one of Azalea's birthdays came on the screen. She was surrounded by a twin sister, her mother, and father. It looked like an intimate gathering, only for family.

"I got a similar gift at this birthday. It was a necklace, a locket, that was passed down to me from my mom. Well, technically me and my sister shared it." A slight frown appeared on her face. "I do wish I had it on me when I died."

"They always said you can't take it with you. The memory of it is still there. What was in the locket?" He tried to pry without invading.

"It was a picture of my grandmother. When my mother died, I put a picture of her in there. I guess my sister has it now."

On the screen, her mother handed the locket over, a small golden circle with a silver chain. Next, it showed Azalea sitting on the beach. She was concentrating on talking to James and didn't notice her memory was on the screen. In the memory, she looked so peaceful sitting there, watching the sunrise.

James pointed it out to her, "When was that? It looks like it's just you there."

Azalea looked over at it, "You know, I can't remember." She thought about it for a moment, really thinking back. "Are you sure that's not your memory?"

"That's definitely you on the beach," James chuckled.

"I've never done that. I mean, I've been to the beach, but never during a sunrise. This isn't me."

James thought she was joking, then something clicked. It was a sunset, not sunrise. He looked at the beach and immediately lifted his hand to melt the wall away, along with any image on it. Nothing happened. "Make it go away. Make it stop!"

226

She was confused, "I don't know how to make it stop. The box will pack itself up when we leave it."

"Then, let's leave it. Now." He got up and grabbed her hand, pulling her along.

She went along, not really understanding why. "What's going on?"

"Every time Daniel gets brought up; I see that same beach at sunset. So, it's time to leave."

Hearing Daniel mentioned, she immediately left the platform. "You're right. Time to go." She stepped off it and turned around, expecting to see it refold. Instead, the platform stayed exactly in place. The image of her on the beach faded and a white wall sat blank.

James wasn't going to be patient. "Let's just go. I'll come get this tomorrow. We can find something else to do for the rest of the evening."

"Just give it a second. I'm sure it'll work," Azalea responded, pulling him to a stop.

They both stood there and watched as the wall that had previously been showing a beach soaked black ink through it. Immediately recognizable handwriting appeared, taking up the entire wall, '𝔜our first mission is almost here -𝔇aniel.'

James talked to the wall, not sure exactly how he was supposed to respond to the message. "Mission? You haven't told me anything about a mission." Azalea stood in silence.

The ink reformed: 'On the day of the winter holiday, you will break into the main office.'

"Why would I do that?" he mocked the wall. It had been a while since James heard from Daniel. Time had come with the harnessing of his abilities and a new confidence.

'Shall I remind you.'

James' leg started to throb. It was so unexpected; he fell to the ground in agony. It felt like the bone was being ripped in half, but his confidence stood strong. "No. I'm not doing your bidding. You wouldn't break my leg. You need me to walk."

The pain halted. James stood up triumphantly, feeling like he could take on the world. The writing morphed again, 'You're right, I wouldn't break your leg.'

Just after he finished reading that line, James' right middle finger felt like a hammer crushed it. Not only did he feel it, he saw the impact cause blood to rush toward the break. The bone was crushed. He screamed out in agony.

'Choose your next words carefully.'

James took a second to himself. He tried to collect his thoughts and push the pain to one side of his brain. Azalea, who had been trying to comfort him, responded to the words, "He'll do it! Just stop!"

'𝔜𝔬𝔲 𝔟𝔬𝔱𝔥 𝔴𝔦𝔩𝔩.'

These words gave her pause. She stepped up to the platform. "We both will. What do you need in the main office?"

'𝔍𝔞𝔪𝔢𝔰 𝔴𝔦𝔩𝔩 𝔨𝔢𝔢𝔭 𝔱𝔥𝔞𝔱 𝔱𝔬 𝔥𝔦𝔪𝔰𝔢𝔩𝔣. 𝔅𝔯𝔢𝔞𝔨 𝔞 𝔣𝔦𝔫𝔤𝔢𝔯. – 𝔇𝔞𝔫𝔦𝔢𝔩 𝔐𝔠ℭ𝔩𝔲𝔯𝔢'

The words dematerialized and mixed with more colors that soaked through. The wall turned back into the beach. This time Daniel stood in the sand, waving at them. James appeared on the beach next to him, cupping his broken finger. Daniel pointed at him and laughed, then took another finger and broke it. The image melted, and the portable date packed itself up.

James, who had been expecting another of his fingers to break, winced in anticipation, but no extra pain came his way. Azalea looked at him in understanding, "That guy has some sort of twisted sense of humor."

The adrenaline from his finger break was starting to level out, allowing him to concentrate past the pain. "Why did you offer yourself up?"

"James, if he can actually break your finger, what stops him from killing you for fun?"

"He needs me for something," he said, confident that Daniel wouldn't kill him.

"What if you stopped being helpful or fun for him?"

James nodded in understanding. The only thing stopping Daniel was his subordination. "He said both of us, but there's no reason for you to get caught. We've broke in before. This time, I'll do it alone."

Azalea laughed as she examined his finger, "We both know that's not happening. I was going with you before he told me to. We need to get you to somebody that can help with your hand."

He nodded, "I'm sorry about the date."

"Daniel's fault, not yours," she shook it off like it was nothing. "Plus," she smiled up at him, "it just means we need a redo. Let's get you to Chloe. I've seen her use the self-manipulation stuff to heal before."

"What if she asks questions?"

"Then, you fell down some stairs. We'll figure it out." Azalea wanted to go to Wagner but knew she would have to wait to tell him what happened tonight. She also considered going to Flynn. He would be able to heal it no problem, but he would ask a lot more questions than anybody else. Chloe was always kind to them, no matter what. She would heal first, ask questions later.

Azalea told him to take a deep breath and reset the finger. It wasn't the worst date she'd been on. Definitely one of the more eventful ones. She wanted to be in the moment, but her mind kept drifting to her next meeting with Wagner. It needed to be soon, like tonight. Daniel breaking James' finger was a new level of worrisome. She would need to find an excuse to call it a night.

Daniel just made their lives much more complicated. But for Azalea it was more of the same. It wasn't necessarily a sense of joy Azalea felt at the prospect of having a mission to go on but one of purpose. She wanted to believe her actions were to protect James, but, in reality, being as close to the battle as she could made this place feel like home to her. Deep down, she thought she needed to make the dates perfect because, ultimately, she didn't deserve it.

Sowing Dragon's Teeth

The next couple months went by without any signs from Daniel. Both James and Azalea got more nervous as Winter approached. James was afraid of getting caught. His Book of Knowledge said the punishment for breaking into the head office was to be sent back to Earth early. Just when he had started building a life here, Daniel came in and destroyed it. Either he did what Daniel said and risked getting sent back to Earth or he refused and suffered more torturing and possibly death, which also meant getting sent back to Earth.

James did want to go back to Earth, in some ways. He wanted to see Alisa, to live the life he felt he was meant to. But things were different now. Even if getting

232

'sent back to Earth' meant he could see Alisa, which James knew not to be the case, Alisa looked happy again, and James was happy here. Leaving would mean abandoning Azalea with Daniel. He needed to sort this out before he could leave.

James thought he and Azalea were in the same boat, but she had an entirely different set of concerns that he was unaware of. Daniel had made it clear; she was now a part of his plans. Plans that Darius still could not determine. Azalea's mission, as given to her by Darius, was to go along with whatever schemes he had until they could get enough information to take Daniel down. It meant lying to everybody except a professor she could only meet in secret, indefinitely.

On the flip side, it was nice to know they wouldn't hear from Daniel again until the Winter Holiday. They had time to relax into their lives in Toricane and act like a couple of regular recruits. Carissa and Lloyd became their homing beacon for normal, talking about assignments and what the next labor was going to be. They also convinced James and Azalea to redo their date, without the interruption. They were, rightfully, frightened by Daniel's appearance, but, as Lloyd pointed out, there was no point in stopping their death because of it.

"What's the point of fighting back if you can't live?" Lloyd asked, to the surprise of the other three.

James shrugged, "I mean, when you say it so simply, it seems obvious."

"I say," Lloyd interrupted him, gathering steam as he talked, "we have a party. A Winter Holiday party."

Azalea laughed, "Why would we throw a party on the same day James and I are going to rob the main office?"

Lloyd hesitated, so Carissa jumped in, "It would be a good alibi!"

James and Azalea looked at each other hesitantly. James said, "I guess it's not going to take all day." Lloyd and Carissa smiled in anticipation of the party.

Lloyd went on to suggest exchanging presents, eating too much food and spending way too long decorating, the normal Earth things. So, when programs let out for the break and snow most likely made by Flynn littered the ground, they started decorating what came to be called Winter Tower, a building Chloe enthusiastically made for them.

Other than the tower itself everything was done by the four of them. The group could've asked for help from some older recruits, saving them days of work and lots of effort, but it wouldn't have been the same. Instead, they spent their days making large ice sculptures, evergreen trees, and ornaments. Most of what they could do was the forming of different materials, which was not-detail oriented work. This left James with the coloring and final touches.

The training with Flynn really helped him understand how to use concentration to aim and control his powers. This ornament decoration, while it seemed like a mundane task, was actually something supervised by Flynn. It was a great learning experience to know how to manipulate smaller and delicate things. Flynn allowed him time off from his usual attack style of learning to dive into this lesson in control.

After his lessons, James would take the decorations to the others to place. The tower started to look so nice that, to the great surprise of James, other first-years volunteered to help. After a week of preparation, the tower looked like one big decoration. They had evergreen trees as landscaping outside and a big star on top of the tower. A few days before the Winter Holiday, they came back to a huge banner hanging from it, telling everybody to come join them. Nobody knew who made it, but it was a huge success.

What started out as a group of friends having a get together, turned into an academy-wide Winter party. They told everybody to bring handmade presents to exchange, which meant the whole campus was electric with people attempting to show off their new skills. As an added bonus, nobody would be allowed in without an ugly sweater of some kind.

Everybody prepared for the party in their own way. Lloyd and Carissa made sure there were plenty of drinks and food. James' and Azalea's planning, however, was quite a bit different. Using their books of knowledge, they found layouts of the main office and memorized everywhere Daniel could possibly need them to go. It was difficult without knowing what they would be looking for, but security was pretty consistent all over. The only room with an increased presence was a basement room. The book couldn't list what the room stored. They assumed that's where they would be going.

The day before the Winter holiday, they were having an argument about Daniel's prize's location. "It's obviously going to be in the most guarded place, the only place we can't see on a map," Azalea explained.

"We don't even know what 'it' is. How do we know for sure?" James was skeptical about the whole thing. He couldn't walk into the main office without a for sure plan.

James pointed at his book, where a map of the main office had been depicted for the last hour. As his index finger went to the page, an inscription appeared, '𝕿𝖍𝖎𝖘 𝖎𝖘 𝖜𝖍𝖆𝖙 𝖜𝖊 𝖓𝖊𝖊𝖉. 𝕽𝖊𝖕𝖑𝖆𝖈𝖊 𝖎𝖙 𝖜𝖎𝖙𝖍 𝖙𝖍𝖊 𝖕𝖊𝖓, 𝖜𝖍𝖎𝖈𝖍 𝖜𝖎𝖑𝖑 𝖗𝖊𝖕𝖑𝖎𝖈𝖆𝖙𝖊 𝖙𝖍𝖊 𝖔𝖇𝖏𝖊𝖈𝖙.'

Below those words was a dagger. Nothing about it seemed out of the ordinary to him, but, keeping within Daniel's rules, he shielded the book from Azalea.

"I know what we are stealing," James corrected himself. "It's going to be in the bottom level, unless there's an armory of some sort." Azalea was still staring at her book, and a look of despair came over her face. James didn't understand her expression, "You had to assume it was going to be something dangerous."

"It's not that," she waved off whatever they would need to steal, knowing he wouldn't be able to tell her. "There's increased security on that day... Why would he have us do it specifically on the Winter Holiday?"

"Well, not exactly," James had seen that earlier. "It's kind of like they replace the decrease in people at the office with an increase in booby traps. It's just going to be a lot harder to physically get there. Avoiding detection might be easier."

"That's not exactly a comfort, but maybe we can use it to our advantage. You seem to just walk through whatever barrier gets put up, so maybe you can do that when we come across one," she suggested.

"Well, let's not rely on that. We don't know if it's going to work. You seem pretty cool about the fact that what we are stealing would be found in an armory," James wanted to make sure she actually heard him.

"Whatever we stole was going to be dangerous." She was more interested in the security. "Maybe this is the reason you can walk through barriers so easily. It could be for this purpose." Azalea looked at him and saw a puffy-eyed, exhausted James. He wasn't used to the late nights and secrecy. She kicked herself for not thinking of how overwhelming this would be for him. "We've been at this for a while. Let's finish later." She shut the book and went over to a drawer in her room. "We'll have time tonight to think about it, while we're tossing and turning. Right now, I have your holiday present!"

James rubbed his hands together in anticipation. "A day early, huh?"

"Tomorrow's going to be so busy with the party and all the illegal, stealing and breaking and entering fun stuff. I figured today would be better." She pulled a small round object out of her pocket. It looked similar to the marble James took from Flynn's office. This marble, being a glowing ball of light, seemed to be somewhat the opposite of his. "I've been doing some research on what you did against the stone golem. The light and dark disc thing that I still don't really understand. I couldn't find anything on the darkness, but I did find something for light."

He took it and twirled it between his fingers It looked like a ball of pure light. The light was bright, but not blinding. He could stare at it without pain, but no matter how long he stared, the light covered up its center

238

and most of his hand down through his wrist. "What is it?"

"It's light," she said. He looked at her, confused. "The information on it isn't specific. It's all vague nonsense, spouting metaphors about goodness being individualistic and the eye of the beholder stuff. I'm not sure it'll actually be useful. It's more of a keepsake than anything else."

He was still twirling it, trying to find the end and beginning. It seemed to just go on forever. "It's amazing! I love it!" The ball of light took him back to that first labor. He hadn't been able to replicate the darkness or light since then. He had tried multiple times. It was so pure and instinctual, though. Flynn refused to show him how to do it, always saying unhelpful stuff like, 'light and darkness are a part of us all' and 'darkness is simply the absence of light.'

James got so preoccupied looking at the light, he didn't notice Azalea sitting on the bed, excited to see her present. He snapped out of it and put a finger up, "Be right back." James had been excited about the gift since their first date. He walked to his room to grab her gift; a replica locket Azalea's mother gave her before she died. He had realized on their first date that was something Azalea was missing from her life and was happy he had the ability to make it. Putting it in his pocket, James notices an inscription on an open page in his book.

He recognized it immediately. He stuffed the locket his in pocket, not wanting to taint the joy he was feeling with any dread to come. Leaning over his bed, '𝕴𝖙'𝖘 𝖙𝖎𝖒𝖊.'

"No, it's not time," he called out to the book. "Holiday is tomorrow."

He started to walk out but the inscription changed. It said, '𝕲𝖔 𝖓𝖔𝖜. 𝕴 𝖜𝖔𝖓'𝖙 𝖘𝖆𝖞 𝖎𝖙 𝖆𝖌𝖆𝖎𝖓. 𝕹𝖔𝖇𝖔𝖉𝖞 𝖘𝖊𝖊𝖘 𝖜𝖍𝖆𝖙 𝖞𝖔𝖚 𝖘𝖙𝖊𝖆𝖑 𝖇𝖚𝖙 𝖞𝖔𝖚.'

James grabbed the pen and stormed out of his room. He threw open Azalea's door. "We have to do it now."

Her smile reverted to confusion, "We still have a whole day. Plus, we can't go into the city overnight."

"Daniel says now." By his tone, she could tell this wasn't negotiable.

"I'm getting tired of his jokes," she replied. "Give me five minutes. I'll meet you downstairs."

Accelerating the timeline threw them off, but there was no way around it. The little preparation they had would have to make do. They both grabbed some medallions Azalea acquired and, within five minutes, were both downstairs, ready to take off. The barrier to the city was about to close for the night, so there was no time to tell anybody.

240

"This seems unnecessarily risky," Azalea said, as they made their way to the outskirts of campus. "Did he say why now?"

"Does he usually give a reason?" James asked. "Let's just get in and out as quickly as possible. Maybe we can stay in the tower we were in our first week here. That could be fun!"

"Yeah, I just wish we could've told Lloyd and Carissa." Really, she wanted to tell Wagner. She was expecting him to watch over the mission. His oversight is what gave her a sense of calm. Without that safety net, it was just her and James venturing into the unknown.

They slipped through the barrier between the academy and the city then made their way around the border, to the main office. Azalea pushed her hand out toward campus but was pushed back by an unseen force. "Looks like we made it just in time."

"Just in time to get locked out," he replied.

The sunset in front of them, barely seen through the city's many buildings, made the city look dark and desolate. James could tell the light was bright outside the city walls, shining for a lush, green forest, but the city blocked that view with shadows upon shadows of buildings too tall for their purpose. Everybody was home for the holiday or off celebrating with friends. They were in their homes filled with animated veins of light, just like Lloyd and Carissa, leaving James and Azalea in the dark.

If all went to plan, they would only see a few people the whole time they were here. Azalea had refused to allow James the optimism of not seeing anybody. Of course, the plan was for tomorrow. They couldn't know what the main office would look like tonight.

"Ready?" James asked, as they stood in front of the small, white entrance to the main office.

"As ready as I'm going to be," her voice shook. She would have been confident tomorrow, when Wagner knew they were gone. Now, her plan B was gone. Regardless, she needed to do this; it needed to be done, so nothing was going to stop her.

"What happened to all the confidence and excitement about breaking the rules?" he mocked.

She shook her head. It was fun with a safety net. "It's just nerves. I'll be good once we get there. Follow my lead. I'll get you to the room and wait for you to retrieve whatever it is. You remember what we need to steal?"

"Yes," James begrudgingly said. He wanted to tell her. "Let's go."

Azalea stepped through the building and found her footing a few seconds later. She looked around to find a deserted entrance. *Easy enough*, she thought. They made their way through the maze of identical, grey-scale walls and rooms until they reached the stairs. The stairs didn't go down far enough for their needs, but they were able to get to the floor just above their objective.

They stepped into a room near the stairs. It had only moderate cover from the hallway, but it was the best they could get. Luckily, and strangely, neither of them had heard anybody in the building, so Azalea felt safe, for now. Her official job was to stand and wait until James returned. Her unofficial job was to wait for something to go wrong and deal with it.

Azalea looked back at James, "You ready for what we practiced? Remember, any damage you make needs to be rebuilt exactly. This is a stealth mission. I'll be waiting here to help you back up."

James had a rather simple objective, on the surface at least. As he stood in the room, he dematerialized the floor underneath his feet to create a hole large enough for him to squeeze through. After the initial wince of pain from the fall, which he mitigated by partially liquefying the landing pad, he stood up ten feet down, on the floor below. Around him was nothing but complete darkness. The light from above didn't make it past the newly melted floor.

He called quietly up to Azalea, "All good but I can't see a thing." No response. *Dammit*, he thought, *there must be a barrier in the hole I fell through.* James squinted, trying to see anything in the pitch-blackness he dropped into. Nothing. He could see up through the hole above him, which contrasted with darkness to make it more difficult to see.

He got an idea. James pulled out the light marble Azalea gave him earlier. *That was lucky.* Light reflected out from the marble, showing a few feet all around, but nothing further. It wasn't as much help as he expected. Knowing what to do, he sighed and focused on the marble for a moment. It broke it in half.

A pang of guilt invaded him knowing he had only received this gift hours before, and, already, he was destroying it, on purpose. *Azalea would understand. It's for the mission.* The light poured out and floated in every direction, like it was floating through empty space.

In his mind's eye, James pictured grabbing ahold of the light and controlling it. This took a few tries. It wasn't like the typical elements he was used to manipulating. James had no idea how Azalea made this, but he was immensely impressed. The light slowly reacted to his presence and rose to the ceiling, spreading out like liquid light above him. It still wasn't bright enough. Having control of the light allowed him to search the area much faster, so it was better than nothing.

244

The most active thing he found was thick dust floating through the air. It looked like nobody had been down here in years. He walked around the small room, expecting to see something, anything, but only saw a straight, empty expanse of stairs filled with the same dust instead. The stairs in front of him went quite a bit farther down into another, much larger, single room, which James had no other choice than to explore.

It looked different down here, with more primitive stonework than anywhere he had seen in Toricane, but there was still a lack of any signs or hidden areas to look at. The rocks looked to be put in by hand, given the sloppy work. Along with that, the ceiling stood taller than he could see, not wanting the light to leave too far from his side.

He ran his hand down the side of the wall and felt it pull back from the unexpected presence, before returning to its resting position. It seemed to curve, an odd thing for a wall, but the curve was slight. James made his way to the other end of the room and hit another wall. It was a dead end. The only way out of this empty room was the staircase he came down. He sighed in exasperation. Azalea wouldn't be able to stay there forever. He needed to figure this out quick.

James went to the center of the room and decided to try a trick Flynn taught him. His eyes closed and he, through a mixture of telepathy and scrying, felt around the room for anything of note. It was a purely mind-centered ability that James wasn't particularly skilled at since it used more finesse than strength. The technique felt odd to James, feeling the room without using his sense of touch.

He extended out his presence and didn't let walls interfere, simply feeling the pulse of everything surrounding him. As Flynn explained to him, every object vibrates at its own frequency, flexing and contracting, and, by interacting and interpreting an oscillation, it's possible to identify the object's origin. The difficult part is separating the waves of vibration, feeling each part of a room instead of the room itself.

He called on those lessons now to speed up the exploration of a dark expanse. The stone, dirt, and rock ran deep beneath his feet. He separated, in his mind, the dirt from rock and concrete. Above him was an expanse of air, followed by more stone and the main office. He blocked those frequencies out, feeling the room, everything of importance to him in this moment.

Some things were more easily recognizable. In his lessons, he could tell the difference between fire and water easily. Wind and rain were slightly harder to decipher. Cold was almost indistinguishable from ice, just as fire was from heat. There was one thing, however, that was discernible from everything else. It was impossible to miss. He saw that in the room with him and opened his eyes. He saw life. He felt the multitude of different organs it requires to operate life all vibrating on a single frequency, expanding and contracting together with the beating of a heart and the inhalation of lungs.

The light around him flew toward that feeling. His adrenaline kicked in hard. The light hit the curved wall to his right. James realized immediately that this wasn't a wall. Something was alive and sleeping. The retraction he felt when he touched the wall wasn't some ability imbedded in it. This was the reaction skin had when touched unexpectedly.

The light flowed up, around the being. It went twenty feet in the air before curving toward, what James believed to be, the side of the room he needed to get to. He took a few deep breaths. *It's asleep,* he thought. With that thought, he closed his eyes and tried to feel the other side of the room. On the other side of the monstrosity, he felt a dark presence. Not life. Pure darkness, not unlike Flynn's marble, which was currently tucked away in his pocket. That had to be what he was looking for.

Why can't it just be a snatch and run mission. Not wanting to wake the creature, a seemingly stone monstrosity that expanded farther in any direction than James could comfortably send his light, he tried to think of anything that could get him across in one piece. His heartbeat with a ferocity that clouded his mind. The adrenaline of standing so close to this creature was giving James tunnel vision.

He knew concentration was the key. James took a few deep breaths to calm himself. *I could fly,* he thought. He'd seen Flynn do it several times but had never attempted it himself. James wasn't sure how it worked but was sure he could do it. *It can't be that hard.*

The easiest way, it seemed to James, was to rip out a huge chunk of floor and hold on for dear life as he maneuvered this large chunk across the room. Though the sound of That would most definitely wake the creature. Instead, he concentrated on his clothing. His shoes would fly upward; the shirt would be his balancing piece; his pants would steer him; the light would guide him. *Moving four things independently under the stress of death. What could go wrong?*

James picked himself up by his bootstraps and started to slowly levitate. It was good he couldn't see far below, keeping the light close to himself, since the height would've startled him. He ascended to the top of the creature, a continued stone appearance, and started to make his way forward. From a bird's eye view, he could see the creature curled up, sleeping like a dog, but still couldn't make out what it was.

The sheer size of it caused James to panic. He rose as high up as he needed and started to make his

248

way forward. In fear, he accidentally pulled his shoe out in front, throwing it across the room. He had forgotten to pull the rest of himself forward too and lost balance. It was too much.

The combination of pulling forward and holding up, while also balancing, threw him off. His feet flew out from under him. He fell twenty feet to the ground. An uncontrollable scream escaped James' mouth. He couldn't see how far he was going to fall, only a few feet below as the light fell with him. The panic and fear escalated. Tunnel vision accompanied the rise in his heart rate, and he forgot about the massive creature in front of him for a moment. His only thought, only fear was for his life.

James' screams echoed around the room as his ankle snapped on the stone floor. The curved wall in front of him let out a groan, and he felt it stir. He couldn't stand on both feet. Unless he could hobble around this monster without it noticing, he didn't see an easy way out.

James pulled the light toward himself. The whites of two eyes followed it. He stopped it immediately. The light sat just in front of the creature's eyes, each as big as a person and sitting on a long neck. The wall got up from its lying place. Its head came in closer to the light, looking around for the noise. James flew the light across the room as a distraction and saw an outstretched wing unfurling, getting ready to attack the light.

* * * * * *

A hundred feet above him, Azalea was getting anxious. She didn't know how long this would take but wished he would hurry up. She looked down into the hole but couldn't see anything. There was no confirmation from James that he was okay and no way of knowing where he was. Azalea felt lost and unsure of herself for the first time since her arrival to Toricane. There was no way she was leaving until he came back, but that could be an hour for all she knew.

She stood staring at the hole, worrying for his safety when she heard two people walking down the hallway. They were quickly approaching the room she was hiding in. She panicked and started to hide behind the wall, hoping they wouldn't see, but realized there was a huge hole in the floor. She quickly concentrated on the hole and stretched the concrete floor next to it, covering the empty space, collapsing the darkness where James was now trapped. She got as small as possible against the wall.

They walked by, voices echoing through the hall, "It's Winter's Eve. I can't believe they have us working tonight," the first one, a feminine, loud voice complained.

The other, a squeaky masculine voice, responded with, "I'm not happy about it either. What I don't get is why we have to stay here through tomorrow. Apparently, there's going to be an intruder. That's crazy. First, why would there be an intruder here? Second, why would we know about it?" Azalea heart started racing, *how do they know?*

"None of it makes sense. We have plenty of defenses to stop any intruder that would come in here, but we still have to be the one to arrest them. I say set up some extra traps and call it good."

They continued walking through the hall, paying more attention to each other than their surroundings. Azalea needed to get out of here fast. Not only was she a sitting duck, she was an expected duck. *Wagner*, she thought. That's the only person she told. There was no way James told anybody. It was the only explanation. Why would Wagner betray her like that? He was supposed to be her safety net.

He would get questioned about that later, right now she needed a better place to hide. Azalea reopened the floor, and she held her breath before jumping into the hole. Expecting to fall into darkness, she was surprised when her feet planted firmly on top of the hole. There was nothing below her, just black. Still, she didn't go anywhere. It must be a barrier. There was no other explanation. James had gone through it without even realizing. She sighed and went back to her hiding place, waiting for the guards to make another round.

* * * * * *

Far below her, James was experiencing something he never had before, the feeling of intense fear and helplessness. His ankle gave out, and he had momentarily distracted the creature with light. This couldn't work for long. A creature that lives in darkness would have no trouble seeing him. The distraction was just that, a distraction.

He rammed the light from wall to wall, making sure to keep it far from himself. The creature's wings expanded from one side of the room to the other as it leapt and glided toward the light, attempting to catch it. From the little glimpses James could make out, he knew this was no stone golem. It wasn't some abstraction that materialized out of earth. This was a living, breathing animal and not one he wanted to trifle with.

As James continued to throw the light from one end of the room to the other, he started to break the concrete beneath him. With every step the creatures made, a pounding would echo across the room, giving him the opportunity to crack the floor without being noticed. He didn't dare move during this process; in case the monster could see him. Eventually, the rock underneath him released its grip on the floor and allowed him to lift it up.

252

James slowly levitated, not rushing for fear of another failure. He floated through the air, more graceful than before but still wobbly. The platform he lay on rose to the ceiling, far from the creature, and the light followed upward, on the other side of the room.

The creature's body extended further with each bound across the room. James concentrated on it for a moment, wanting to understand the gravity of his situation without sacrificing the light, and let the platform float stationary in the air. He felt the vibrations of stone scales popping into action after being unused for a long rest. It's body, being bigger than the room, couldn't fully be utilized. James felt a strange pity for the isolated beast put in a cage to guard the one thing he was going to steal.

Its jaw reached up and would have eaten the light, had James not quickly retreated from his inner thoughts and thrown it out of the way. This happened several more times as he slowly made his way to the other side of the room. At one particularly large throw of the light, James grasped a small portion of it with his mind and separated it from the group. That small piece of glowing, gravity-less light was placed in his pocket, in case the monster ate his only method for sight.

James descended against the side of the far wall, feeling out for the pull of darkness he felt before, not just an absence of light but the source of its absence. He felt its presence near the floor, but the concentration took him away from his game of fetch with the creature for too long. He opened his eyes just in time to see it bite and swallow the light. His heart dropped. He couldn't see. There was no way of knowing where the creature was.

Suddenly, his heart leapt back up. The light shined through the monsters body as it floated, as if unaffected by gravity. He could see it again. Now though, as the light surrounded the interior of the creature, he could make it out completely. It stood fifty feet tall and walked from one side of the expansive room to the other in two strides. The wings couldn't expand all the way out, as they were too wide for the confines of the room.

What he suspected to be a completely stone monster after feeling the wall when he entered the room, ended up as a dragon with rock hard scales. The stone craftsmanship he'd seen as a wall before was only due to the length of its stationary captivity, not a showing of its true nature. Its scales now gleamed with a white glow from the light it swallowed, as did the large face that turned and noticed a small light it had yet to grab: the piece in James' pocket. In this moment, James felt like the room wasn't a hiding place for anything. It was a cage for this monster, and he was the food.

He sat up on the stone slab, having just reached the darkness he detected before. Using every bit of courage he could muster, James looked away from the

254

dragon as it took its first step toward him. Without fully being able to see what he was grabbing, James reached out and took the object.

He felt the dragon's jaw only feet behind him. With the flick of a wrist, James and his platform were thrown toward the stairs on the other side of the room. He turned and saw razor sharp teeth looking to eat. The stone wasn't moving fast enough. He was being thrown through the air, away from the teeth, but the dragon took one step and made up the distance in a heartbeat. James looked at his hand and saw a dagger. The dagger he came here to get. The one he saw a picture of in his book.

He thrust the knife out toward the dragon. It was only six inches long but felt powerful in his hand. Darkness seemed to filter itself through the dagger. The stone fell toward the floor as he lost concentration. The knife sliced the bottom of the dragon's jaw.

It screamed out in pain as James fell and the stone platform shattered against the floor. He couldn't see what damage the knife did because darkness seemed to flow from the injury. It snuffed out every bit of light in the creature's system, going from its jaw through the tail and wings. It was pitch black again. James heard the dragon fall heavy on the ground, moaning in pain. He took out the small piece of light left and sent it floating around the dragon.

He knew it was still alive from the grunts and heavy breathing but wanted to see for himself. Having broken his ankle and now shattered his ability to escape, James needed to know how much danger he was in. He wanted to take a minute down on the floor to collect his breath and calm himself. After the sheer force of will he exerted in the last few minutes, his breathing was painfully fast, body sore from the injuries.

The dragon's jaw, where the dagger cut it, had completely turned black. A large piece of the dragon's throat fell off. No blood stained the ground or came from the wound, Instead, a black crust formed over it. The dragon, seeing light revolving around, started to sit up.

Without giving it a second look, James broke a slab of stone off underneath him and grabbed on with both hands. One more minute of exertion and he could relax. Before the creature had fully stood up, James was up the stairs and into the room where he'd started. He heard the dragon roar from down below but knew it couldn't fit up the stairs. He was safe, for now.

James took a second. He'd never done anything near that dangerous before, or even wanted to. *Daniel*, he thought with hatred. This was his fault. What kind of person makes somebody go through this? *Somebody evil.* There was no going back on that now. James was surer than he'd ever been; Daniel was evil.

256

He formed the stone beneath him into a chair-like device that he could sit in as he floated through the air. It took much more focus and control than walking, but he wouldn't be doing any of that in the near future, not with his broken ankle.

Before he could leave, there was one more thing to do. Fearing for his life, James spent time the last couple months mastering one trick, something to hide the dagger from prying eyes. Having read about ways to hide things in his Book of Knowledge, he came across a complex trick to open a pocket dimension. If he did it wrong, the dagger could be lost forever.

He'd lost dozens of rocks attempting to get it right. The dimension wouldn't be bigger than his hand but should be able to fit the dagger inside. It would stay there either until he got it back out or he lost the dimension. Given that James still had trouble navigating campus, his chances of finding the same pocket dimension again were not huge. Regardless, he put the dagger into the pocket, Hopefully, Luck would pay off.

He floated up through the hole and found Azalea stretched out against the wall. She motioned for him to get against the wall, quickly. As quietly as possible, he glided his chair to her side just as she closed the hole. They waited several moments. Two guards passed by.

After they passed, she pointed to his chair, "What's going on with that? Did you get a souvenir?"

James couldn't tell if she was joking or being serious, so he pulled up his pant leg. "I wouldn't want a souvenir to that place, even if I had the time to grab it. Let's get out of here, fast."

She nodded and looked down the hall. She needed to focus on escaping stealthily and would interrogate later. The coast was clear. They followed the same stairs up to the entrance and out of the white building. Once they were out, Azalea turned to James and started questioning him, "What happened? Why did it take so long? Why are you in a chair?"

Before James could answer, a shadow emerged from behind the building. Neither of them saw the figure. It moved without sound. The cloak it wore, pure shadow, extended with an aura of umbra. As soon as James opened his mouth, the cloaked figure reached out its hands. Both of them fell to the ground unconscious, James with a smack on the stone beneath him. The figure looked around, but nobody was there to hear as James and Azalea were dragged away.

Ignorance is Bliss, Knowledge is Helpful

James appeared in his living room, talking to his mom about working at the factory. This really cute guy kept asking him out, and he was venting about it. The venting was just a cover, though. Really, he didn't feel like he should want to date somebody else. Not this soon after the wedding. Should he even date at all? It wasn't something he needed to think about six months ago. But, now, everybody was encouraging him to get back out there.

Wait. This didn't make any sense. James didn't work at the factory. There was no cute guy asking him out. He tried to move but noticed he wasn't in control of

259

those functions. He realized he was scrying. When did this happen? What was this about a cute guy asking out Alisa?

Before he could get any more information, James was awakened abruptly. It took him a second to adjust to his new surroundings. He moved his head, to make sure it was his own. It was his, with an added throbbing that wasn't there before. The chair under him was wooden, much more comfortable than the stone he'd been sitting on. His leg was propped up on a table. Professor Wagner was messing with his ankle.

James winced from the added pressure on his broken ankle. He started to reach out and move Wagner back, but it faded quickly, feeling better by the second. He realized the abrupt awakening was due to Wagner resetting his ankle. "Some warning next time!"

"I figured it would be easier while you were passed out," he replied, without looking over.

"Wait, how did I get here?"

"Azalea brought you into my office, then ran off. She said something about your other friends, Lloyd and Carissa." His voice maintained a low, irritated tone.

James relaxed. He didn't remember anything, but at least Wagner didn't know.

"I know you were off academy grounds tonight. What were you doing that got your ankle broken?"

260

Wagner asked. He finished working on the ankle and let it rest on his desk, as he moved to rest in his chair.

After dealing with a dragon, James' heart didn't feel like it could take much more anxiety. Surprisingly to him, a lie came out smoothly, "Me and Azalea thought it would be romantic to spend Holiday Eve in the city. We were planning to stay in town for the night and mess with our abilities some. I tried to show off and fly. It didn't work out, as you can see," he said, pointing to his injury. "I must've passed out from the pain."

Wagner looked him over for a second before responding, "Be more careful next time. If you're going to do something that dangerous, be around somebody who can catch you." He motioned toward James' ankle. White bandages appeared in a spiral around his ankle, tightening it and holding it in place. James was unclear why Wagner didn't just fix the ankle, but, more than that, he wanted to get out of the office. "You should be able to walk around okay with that. I'll keep an eye on it and let you know when to take it off."

It was clear, that was the end of the conversation. James got up and slowly walked out. He wanted to get out of the situation as quickly as possible, but the boot was going to take some getting used to.

"One more thing, James. Don't tell Flynn you left campus, and don't do it again. There will be consequences next time." James nodded and left the office. He made his way toward Winter Tower. That's where Lloyd and Carissa would be. Maybe that's where Azalea headed.

* * * * * *

Azalea was hiding around the corner from Wagner's office and watched as James hobbled away. As soon as he left, she strode in and took a seat. "Did you get it, whatever it is?"

"No," Wagner replied. "He didn't have it. Daniel must've shown him a way to hide it." His tone had gone from irritation to anger as soon as she stepped into the room. "What happened to doing it tomorrow? I almost didn't know you were gone!"

"Daniel contacted James at the last minute. We had no choice."

He nodded. "Where did you go to get the item? I might be able to narrow it down."

Azalea's instincts from her time as a spy kicked in as she recalled the mission with surgical precision. "We went to the west side of the main office, down the stairs to the bottom floor, and James dropped below that in a room near the stairway. I tried to follow, but there was some sort of barrier blocking me from dropping below the floor."

"There are labyrinths of different artifacts down there," he said, shaking his head. "The only way James

262

could've found anything is if Daniel somehow led him right to it. He might not even know." They both sat in silent frustration for a moment. "His first big move and we miss everything that matters!"

"What happened to James down there?" Azalea asked.

He shrugged his shoulders, "Honestly, I have no idea. I've set up some of the defenses down there but not all of them. When somebody puts an item down there to be guarded, they also set up the protection." Wagner thought for a second. "His excuse was that he was showing off to you. He said he tried to fly, and it didn't pan out well. That would match his injuries."

"You questioned him?" Azalea laughed, "He's a terrible liar."

He chuckled, "Yes, he is. I just wanted it to seem believable. I also told him you took him to my office for help. So, good luck coming up with a story."

She rolled her eyes, "I'll see if I can get any information out of him, without being suspicious. I have a feeling it's not going to take long for Daniel to contact us again."

"Us?" he asked.

"Yeah...it wasn't just James he told to go on this mission. I was there when he told James to do it. Daniel broke his finger because he refused, then laughed about

263

it. I had to speak up, say something." She looked down, disappointed in herself for getting involved.

"You did the right thing. He has some sick sense of humor. It could've gotten a lot worse. Just be careful. Don't take anything James gives you. It could be a trap to connect with you, like Daniel is with James."

"You want me to refuse to take any holiday gifts he gives me?" Azalea gave him a doubtful look.

"Yes," he stated simply. "Now, go to your Winter party before it gets suspicious. I think it's nearly light outside. You were passed out for a while."

She nodded, said, "I'll see you there," and walked out.

Azalea walked out toward Winter Tower. It didn't take long to see James hobbling along. He didn't make it far. She trailed him for a while, not wanting to give away the direction she came from. About halfway, he ducked into a nearby tower. *Strange.* Azalea followed him. Just inside an archway that led straight through the interior, she saw him sitting on a bench with his eyes wide open. At first, she kept her distance, not wanting to be seen. Then she saw bright brown eyes staring forward. Those were not James' eyes.

She walked in the building and looked closer at them. They weren't recognizable eyes. Curious, but not wanting to interfere, she pulled up a chair and sat beside him. It wasn't more than a few minutes before he came out of it. She put her hand on his leg, letting him know she was there.

James jumped back in his seat, "Woah, when did you get there?"

"I came back to get you and saw you walk into the tower. What were you scrying?" She asked, trying to change the subject. "Something to do with Daniel?"

"No. Nothing like that," he said. James was visibly uncomfortable. "When I passed out earlier, I dream-scried Alisa. I just needed to go back in and make sure she was okay."

Her hand retreated off James' leg. "Oh. I see. So, not Daniel. Have you done this before?" Anger started to seep into her mind, an emotion she typically lets loose but, in this case, may need to suppress.

"No, of course not. Curiosity got the best of me after the dream."

James was a poor liar. Azalea could see right through him. The only problem was, she couldn't get angry or upset. She needed to stay close to James, to protect him, even if he was scrying his widow. Getting angry would mean storming off, and James had information she needed now. Right now, the mission was more important than her feelings.

She composed herself before continuing. Azalea needed to be believably upset but also supportive. "I would scry my husband, if I could," she truthfully said. "I don't blame you, but I don't like it. Just tell me if it happens again, okay?"

He nodded, "Of course. I won't do it again, voluntarily."

Another lie, Azalea pushed the anger down further. Azalea decided it was best to change the subject. "So, what happened to your ankle?"

"Oh, I tried to fly over this dragon that was guarding what we needed to steal." As soon as James finished the sentence, he felt like he got punched in the face. The force of it knocked him to the ground.

"If I'm not supposed to say something, you should really give me a heads up!" he shouted at nobody.

Azalea didn't feel bad for him. She kind of wanted him to get punched in the face after his scrying endeavors. This was just karma. Regardless, she bent down to make sure he was okay. A bruise started to cover the side of his face. This might have been a bit much for karma's sake. "Maybe this is just another injury from the flying accident," she said.

Ignorance is Bliss, Knowledge is Helpful

"I seem to be getting in accidents a lot this year. That might get suspicious!" he, again, shouted at nothing.

She looked at him sympathetically, "Let's get to the party. It should be starting soon." She pushed the anger down and allowed empathy to prosper, at least as much as she could.

They made their way to the party in silence for a while. They could both feel the tension between them that grew with the length of the walk. James' boot made a walk through the campus feel like a marathon. It was slow but still easier than a floating chair.

"I almost forgot because of everything that happened. I have your present," James said. He stopped and pulled out the locket from his pocket. It was the same locket her mother gave her.

A little piece of light came out with it. James grabbed it and stuffed it in his pocket before adding, "By the way, that light you gave me saved my life. Most of it got...," he paused looking for a word he was allowed to say, "destroyed, but I have a little bit of it left."

Azalea looked at the locket and some of the anger left. That locket almost never left her neck in life and now she could have it here. Then, Wagner's words popped into her head. She couldn't accept any gifts from

James. It could be a trap. It didn't feel like a trap, but, knowing Daniel, he could've done something to it.

In an attempt to push down the affection she felt toward James for such a personal and intimate gift, she let the anger resurface. "You should give it to your wife." The look of hurt on James' face was mirrored in Azalea's. She stormed off toward Winter Tower, leaving James to waddle behind with the locket outstretched in his hand. She didn't look back at him.

At the party, Azalea found Wagner as soon as she could. He was chatting with Chloe about the next labor, preparing to make an announcement. "Professor Wagner, could I talk to you for a minute?"

"Of course!" He turned to Chloe, "It sounds great. Just don't give away anything. I want them to be surprised." Chloe nodded and walked toward her husband.

"This isn't a safe place, Azalea. Is James here?" Wager said, as he looked around the room.

"It will take James a bit to get here in that boot. What's with the boot anyway? Couldn't you have just healed his ankle?"

"Yeah. I'm sure one of the other professors will. I just wanted to slow Daniel down as much as I could. What's so urgent?" he asked.

Quickly, Azalea described what James told her. "This information has to be valuable. Daniel basically smashed in his face for telling me. You'll see. The bruises are already showing." Wagner waited, impatiently, for her to get to the point. "James said he injured himself trying to fly over a dragon."

Wagner's face went white. "What else did he say? Did he get the object? How did he get out alive?"

Azalea was confused but spilled any information she had. "As far as I know, he got it. I don't know how he got out alive. He said something about using light, but I didn't get any more information."

"I need you to get more information!" His eyes flashed red, hand grabbing her shoulder, "Now! That thing he stole was the dagger I stabbed in Daniel's back. It was his dagger."

Azalea had seen the dagger but didn't know its significance. "I can't get more information. We aren't on speaking terms right now. What's so important about this dagger?"

Wagner took a quick breath, "It destroys. It's pure destruction."

"That doesn't make sense. If his big plan was to destroy, he could've used James on the first day here. Why wait and go through the trouble of getting the dagger?"

"I don't know. I think it's time I had a pointed conversation with Flynn." He concentrated on Azalea for a moment to get a feel for her emotional state. "Look, I don't care what kind of squabble you and James got into. He could do anything with this dagger. We need to find it now, and we need to figure out his plan." With that, Wagner stormed off.

Azalea wondered around aimlessly in the tower. The whole campus showed up, so there were plenty of areas to hide from her friends. She would see them later in the day. She would make up with James. Right now, being alone was nice.

As Azalea made her way through the crowd, Chloe got up on the stage to start her announcement. "Quiet down. Quiet down. I have a little announcement to make about the second labor!"

Everybody in the tower went silent. Since the first labor, people had been anxiously waiting for more news. She continued, "As we pass this celebration for our halfway point, the labors are going to come quickly. The professors have decided we want to get them done sooner rather than later. The winning team's mission will take most of the rest of your year in Toricane.

"In light of that fact, the second labor will start tomorrow, followed by the third and fourth each week after. Everybody meet on the west side of campus tomorrow morning. And don't ask me, you'll get no spoilers!" Cheers erupted in the town. Then, murmurs circulated. Everybody was speculating on what could possibly happen at this labor. Nobody had the slightest clue, making speculation useless and more fun.

Azalea noticed Carissa motioning in the midst crowd. She sighed and walked over. James stood next to Lloyd, talking about what happened to his ankle. Carissa questioned Azalea about it, too. That's when she realized they made it. The two of them robbed Toricane and came out with a dagger. Better phrased, James came out with a dagger; Azalea came out with resentment and a lack of information.

She would make up with him tonight, as part of the job. It was necessary. She found it hard to distinguish whether their relationship was for purpose or for them. Even when she first asked him out, it wasn't completely for either reason. Throughout the months they'd spent together, that complexity hadn't lessened, but she enjoyed it regardless. Now, she felt disconnected from it. Either way, *motivations don't matter*, she thought. *The end result is the same.*

Playing with Fire

The weekend went by fast. Everybody was preparing for the labor. They still didn't know what it was, so preparation was difficult. Over the weekend, it was announced to non-scryers that they would be getting speed lessons on it. So, that's where Azalea and Lloyd spent the majority of their weekend and could confidently assume it was for the labor. The professor was very specific about what they learn by Monday. Somehow, that still didn't give any good information away.

When the day finally arrived, the entire campus was gathered around a vast structure with stands around the side and a hollow middle, much like the Colosseum One difference between it and the Roman Colosseum was a constant swirl of elements around the hollowed interior. It created a dangerous border between the stands and anybody in the ring. James could only assume Flynn was the main creator, with all his Roman armor and weapons.

The recruits and professors made their way into the stands. James scanned the professors and noticed a few missing. He noted in particular Wagner wasn't there to stare at him uncomfortably. James had an entire other set of concerns to worry about without Wagner. The first-years were getting scared looking down at the swirl of elemental chaos that awaited them. Lloyd was the first to voice his concerns, "Are we going down there?"

Chloe answered, "Not exactly. We have built suits that will go down in your stead."

"Suits?" James asked.

"Yes, suits," she said as a bunch of manakin-looking bodies came into sight. "We've created these as scrying suits. You'll be sitting in the stands. When you scry into your suit, its body will change into yours. It will be an almost identical match. The insides, however, will still just be made of wood."

Gary laughed, "You couldn't make them out of something a bit stronger?"

"Oh, we could have," she smiled. "That would ruin the fun. These suits are going to be used for you to battle it out down below. We'll be throwing some fun stuff at you from the elemental swirl. Last person, or team, standing wins."

Carissa was mortified, "This is barbaric."

Chloe laughed, "You can feel free to not join them. It will simply count as a forfeit on your behalf."

She got defensive, "I'm not forfeiting. I'll fight." Carissa was not one to back down from a challenge from a professor, regardless of where the lecture hall was.

"Just watch out. You will be very flammable. I recommend, if you catch on fire, to stop the scry. You can't feel pain in these suits, but it will be unpleasant nonetheless." She motioned for them to step toward their suits. "It will start when you're all in the arena. Good luck!" Chloe walked to sit with the other professors, all preparing their challenges for the students.

The first-years each stepped up to a suit. Groups chatted for a moment, strategizing, before they started the scry. James looked at Azalea and smiled, "Any ideas?" He was trying to test the waters, to check if she was still mad.

Surprisingly, she smiled warmly back, "Yeah, don't die." James was glad to be on talking terms with her, but the quick turnaround from the tension at their last encounter didn't add up.

"Good advice for anybody!" Lloyd added in.

"Good luck, guys," Carissa chimed.

James stepped up to his suit and concentrated on scrying it. He wasn't sure exactly what to expect, but it was relatively easy to do. The professors must have made the suits specifically for scrying. Usually James' body would feel constricted, unable to move until he woke up. Now, he could freely move his suit around, seeing and hearing everything around it.

The suit was unusually light and flexible. Students jumped around, getting used to the feeling and their capabilities. James pulled metal from the elemental storm in front of them and created himself a sword and shield, in the typical Roman fashion. First-years around him copied, to varying degrees of success. Azalea was the only one to create a unique weapon. She carried a crossbow.

James attempted to ask her how she made something so complex, but nothing came out. He felt around his mouth and realized it was made of wood. The suit may look like him, but the inside was all wooden. This meant the only way to communicate was through telepathy, something only he and Lloyd knew how to do.

He reached out to Lloyd, 'Telepathy is going to be the way to go here. Do you think it's okay if we send them messages and read their thoughts back to us?'

Lloyd hesitated before responding, 'I don't really see another option. I'll contact Carissa. You get Azalea.'

He turned toward Azalea, 'Hey, we can't talk in these. Is it okay if I read your outermost thoughts, so we can communicate? Just nod or shake your head.'

On the other side of her, Carissa was nodding to both Lloyd and James. Azalea's eyes got wide. She froze in place. James started to get worried she was losing control of the suit but eventually got a nod. He reached out to all three of them and said, *'Let's get going.'*

The other teams were making their way down to the arena already, many making hand gestures back and forth. The elemental storm opened up to allow them through. It was a chaos of recruits trying to understand what they'd gotten themselves into, with almost no fighting knowledge or experience. The only one of them who had used their abilities in a fight was James. Even he didn't feel prepared for whatever this was.

They were corralled into the bottom level. Flynn stood up to make an announcement. "Students, there are but two rules. First, if you leave your suits, you are not allowed back in them. Second, last man standing wins. You may fight amongst each other, but I don't recommend it." A devious smile appeared on his face, indicating to James that he would enjoy some intergroup fighting. "We will be throwing challenges at you in waves.

My suggestion is to survive as long as possible, as a team."

Flynn sat down and the first-years pulled their weapons up. Each group stood off from the others, in constant watch of an attack. Nobody attacked, though. Everybody waited for the first wave. They wanted to know what they were up against. James, Carissa, Lloyd, and Azalea stood in a circle near the outer edge. James faced the elemental chaos. Lloyd stood more toward the other teams.

Flynn raised his hand. Out of the elemental chaos walked five iron rhinos, one for each team. The rhinos, however, didn't discriminate on who they took down. They immediately charged forward from their creation to the closest person. Several people were taken by surprise and flung several yards through the area. One recruit almost evaded the attack, but their arm got ripped off by a horn. It would've been unpleasant to see, but the arm broke off like a branch, reminding James he wasn't in any real danger.

A rhino came out of the chaos right in front of James and started charging. He would have had time to dodge out of the way but no way to tell his friends in time. He put up his shield as the others looked around to find their closest rhino. At James' command, the shield's metal shot out in every direction and buried itself several feet in the ground, encircling them in steel.

The charging rhino's horn went through the shield, but it stumbled and took off in a tangential direction.

The metal retreated; the shield vanished, and James fell to his knees. That was exhausting. '*Everybody okay?*' he sent out. Everybody nodded in return and turned toward another rhino that was charging toward them.

Azalea shot a crossbow bolt toward the rhino, but it ricocheted off. Carissa and Lloyd squared up, preparing to stab as it ran by. James was still recovering from the shield and couldn't get out of the way in time. Azalea grabbed him and threw his light wooden body to the side. Lloyd and Carissa confused it by each stepping to one side, making it choose a direction. It couldn't, instead heading straight back toward Azalea. Luckily, both swords buried deep in its underside. The rhino went down.

Lloyd called out to them, 'The underside is soft. Don't try to hit them anywhere else.'

The four of them lined up and waited for another to come their way. Around them, several first-years had been injured badly enough that they couldn't move, causing them to stop scrying. In total, the first wave wiped out five of the first-years. James' group kept with the same strategy, one that worked. They confused one more rhino by making it choose between two directions at the last second, then collectively stabbed its underside.

During the battle, Azalea looked at James and pointed to her head. James read her thoughts, '*Try to do the smallest amount you can. Conserve energy. There's no telling how long this battle will take.*' He nodded in return but was caught off guard by something he detected in her thoughts, anger. It was unexpected. He didn't know if the anger was directed toward him or somebody else. Either way, he couldn't let it be a distraction.

The rhinos were down, and the first-years looked wildly around, waiting for some bigger, worse threat. Chloe stood up and the iron from the rhinos rose from the ground, mixing back with the elemental chaos. She twisted her wrist around. Balls of spinning fire gathered from the chaos and started circling the arena.

James thought fast. *Something small.* He looked around to see other groups forming walls of water around themselves. *Too big. Keep it small.* The fireballs, each as large as James, seemed to overheat and spit parts of themselves into the air, raining embers down on the arena. Azalea put her hands in the air. Wind blew the embers away from them, toward the other groups. Lloyd started throwing water from the elemental storm at the swirls. The speed they spun at caused the water to bounce off.

He needed to get water inside the fire. *Grenade,* he realized. James started pulling water from the elemental swirl and packed it as tight as he could into a ball. He formed a crossbow bolt and attached the waterball to it. Azalea took it without hesitation and fired directly at the nearest ball of fire, while Lloyd and Carissa kept the embers away.

The speed of the bolt allowed it to penetrate the fire. James held the water's shape until he was sure it was inside, then he released. The water shot out of every opening inside the ball and steam poured out. The ball exploded, and fire rained down on the arena. Several recruits caught on fire and went lifeless. A group nearby them saw this strategy and replicated it, causing more fire to come down on everybody's heads.

Trails of embers and smoke ran across the stadium. Carissa and Lloyd were blasting air over their heads in an attempt to keep it circulating toward the other teams. James looked over to see the state of his teammates and noticed an ember had gotten loose. He pulled a stream of water from the storm, but it was too late. The ember landed on Carissa. She didn't notice as her back started smoking. The water James pulled came crashing into her, knocking her down. It didn't work. The fire had spread unnaturally fast; it was like pointing a water hose at a tree burning from the inside.

Without Carissa's help, Lloyd couldn't keep out the fire. A bolt of flame came down, smiting him on the spot. Carissa, who was smoking and slowly turning to ash, tried to pull him out of the way. Instead, her legs gave out. She fell on the ground. Carissa stopped the scry, leaving Azalea and James to fend for themselves.

People started to mimic James' water bolt, leading to a bunch of fire raining down on everybody. Regardless of collateral damage, it did work. The fire storms faded. The ash blew away. There were six people left.

Chloe looked disappointed her fire got taken out so quickly and sat down sullenly. Edgar was next to stand. He raised his hand. A swarm of light came out of nowhere. Each creature had a ball of light in its center with wings like a bat.

As the six of them looked at the bats, the creatures disappeared. Not all at once, but one-by-one the bats disappeared and reappeared across the stadium. *Teleportation,* James thought. He called out to the Azalea, *'Back to back. They're teleporting.'* Again, as he talked to her, anger swelled up in her head. It was hard not to dwell on but this was not the time. These creatures needed their full attention.

The bats had a way of teleporting above you and dive bombing in herds, which was fairly predictable, as far as teleporting bats go. Their method of killing was far more surprising. The groups saw it first within ten seconds of the bats appearing. A small cluster of them targeted a lone recruit in the middle of the arena. She threw up a shield of water, leftover from the last wave, but it didn't slow them down. They dove through the water like it was air and into her torso.

Once the bat entered her suit, shadows seemed to expand from her extremities, accumulating light at the location of impact. The light was being sucked out of her suit, leaving only darkness. It spread throughout her body as she became immobilized. The four remaining recruits looked horrified in her direction. Without true features, they looked like dolls who had only just realized they weren't real.

James had some experience with light and darkness, but Azalea was the only one out of them who had researched and actually created any. James looked at her and she pointed to her head, '*That gave me an idea. Light is just the absence of darkness and vice-versa. Try pulling the light and darkness apart in the air.*'

James reached his hand up and concentrated on that one idea. Nothing happened. He shook his head at her and saw a swarm of bats coming their direction. He threw steel daggers at them from the chaos, which went straight through their bodies. A tornado formed around them; the bats curled their wings in and dove through. The air around them froze; their light melted the ice as they flew.

Just as James was running out of ideas, Azalea turned around. Her hands were surrounding a ball of intermingling light and darkness. It swirled together, trying to combine, but she didn't let it. She pulled the light out and threw it into the elemental chaos. As the bats descended, she flung the darkness toward James. It created a familiar disc shape in front of him that the bats crashed into it and disintegrated.

Azalea didn't have time to protect herself. She threw everything into that disc of darkness. A small swarm deviated from the pack and dove into her. They created a glow, like a lantern, on her chest. Darkness crawled down from her fingertips as the light grew brighter. Once the light had finished accumulating, the bats escaped through her back. Azalea was motionless; her body fell. She stopped the scry, leaving James to fend for himself.

By this time, it was James and two others remaining: Gary was one of them and the other was a sweet girl James didn't talk to often by the name of Melia. James thought for a moment about simply letting the bats defeat them while he defended himself with the darkness. The bats had other plans. Seeing the darkness in his hands, they attacked.

The bats teleported in every direction around him. The ball of shadow in his hands needed to form into something helpful pretty quick. As they dive bombed, he threw his hands up and the darkness surrounded him like a bubble, creating a pitch black encasement. He saw light crashing into its exterior like stars in the sky blinking in and out of existence as the bubble shrunk. Just as it almost caved in on him, the stars stopped appearing.

He let the bubble down. With some darkness left in his grasp, he saw the bats were gone. They were somehow attracted to the darkness, like a bug to light. Every last bat had died in the attempt. Edgar did not look pleased. James could tell by the murmurs, that trick was meant to leave only one person standing. They talked amongst each other for a moment, letting the contestants gather their breath. The others had only survived by constantly dodging the bats. They were exhausted.

Professor Wagner, who James was seeing for the first time today, walked over and chatted with the other professors. He got the affirmative and raised his hand. The ground rumbled. All three recruits in the arena did not want to know what was about to come from under the ground, and their faces showed it.

The ground split. A hole opened up in the center and, for a moment, everything was still. Then, James heard a familiar groan come from below. His heart sank and fear blossomed from it. Before anybody else could react, he ran from the hole. There was nowhere to go. The elemental chaos surrounded him. Then, he remembered something comforting. *This is just a suit.*

Playing with Fire

When he turned back around, a dragon flew up through the opening. James wanted to see its face. What happened to all the damage? The dragon flew too fast for him to see. It darted out of the ground and expanded its wings completely. The only thing James could see was black. The color of the dragon was utter and complete darkness, the exact same color he held in his hands.

It glided in the air before diving down and smashing into the newly reformed ground. The dragon's jaw had a long white scar that stretched down and expanded on its chest in veins of pure white pulsating against the darkness that covered the dragon. The white and black of its body bounced off each other independent of its movement, either fighting for control or attempting to merge. It's eyes searched the arena for signs of life, finding three nearby. They didn't stop at just anybody though. The eyes rested firmly on James: the one to give it the scar; the one that fed darkness through it.

Every professor except Wagner looked frightened by the dragon's presence. Flynn stood up, about to throw something, but Wagner stopped him. He motioned for Flynn to sit down. He hesitantly complied. The recruits, confused by the commotion, were worried too.

Everybody's eyes were on the dragon. The dragon's eyes were resting straight on James. Gary forged a sword that flew directly at the dragon. It hit with a thud and bounced off. Melia formed fire and ice in her hand, swirling them around, ready to strike. As the dragon walked toward James, its tail whipped around and smacked her, causing the elements to release randomly through the air. Her arm broke off from the blow.

The dragon took another step closer and rocked the colosseum. James needed something to defend himself. He didn't think it would stop at the suit. The look in its eye said it was ready to take him out for good. He looked down at the darkness he held and remembered the distractions in the main office. James separated the darkness into a hundred tiny marbles of void. He then scattered them across the arena, concentrating on the area between himself and the dragon.

Annoyed, the dragon tilted its body sideways and swung its wing across the stadium, absorbing the darkness. It's wings expanded out, allowing it to glide around the area toward James. Both front feet came forward with claws as long as his body. James threw his hands in the air. A forcefield extended out, knocking back the claws. He threw that forcefield into the air, attempting to punch the dragon. Instead, the dragon opened its mouth, swallowing the forcefield whole. It's teeth came down on James. His scry came to an end.

James, knowing he was back in his body, hid behind the nearest post, not wanting the dragon to recognize him. Azalea came out from the stands, confused. "You're okay, James. The battle's over."

"Already? I just lost!"

"Well," she said sarcastically, "it's a dragon. It immediately killed the other two. I think Gary survived longer, but it was so fast, I'm not sure. You okay?"

"No!" he said in a hushed voice. "That's the dragon. I gave it that scar. It's pissed at me."

She frowned, "It did look like it was out to get you. Maybe you should stay here. I'll tell you when it's gone." As she walked off, James thought he might've seen a smile but had to be mistaken.

He stood there, too afraid to move. The fear of death was the only thing that kept him going at the main office. He didn't want to even see the dragon again. He didn't need to. Its eyes beating down on him from so high up was an image that would never leave his mind. They were black bloodshot eyes with scales surrounding them and giant teeth not too far below.

A few minutes went by before Azalea came back. "You're good to come out. The boogeyman is gone."

He didn't care about the sarcasm. "Where did they put it?"

"Wagner let it go out into the forests outside Toricane. I'm sure you'll never see it again." Her face was blank, but she did enjoy this. It was funny to see him so scared when everybody else was cheering in the stands. There might've been a small part of her that felt bad and wanted to comfort him. She would get to that part later.

He laughed, "Yeah. Except when you say, 'you'll never see it again,' it's bound to happen."

She pulled his hand over to join the others. "If that happens, I'll be right there with you, I'm sure."

Realizing the dragon was gone, he calmed his heartbeat. "Hey," he said, "you sacrificed yourself for me back there. Thank you."

She blushed, "It's just a game."

"It felt very real for a game."

She agreed. The professors were having fun with it. The recruits, on the other hand, were scared out of their minds. *Sure,* James thought, *it was a cool experience to think back on, and they were never actually in danger, probably.* They were just realizing how crazy things can get here in a day. The boundary between sane and insane varied dramatically between recruits and professors. What's a game to some is life and death for others.

James couldn't rationalize the way the professors treated them in the labors versus lectures. They went to join Lloyd and Carissa, who were discussing what they

288

could've done differently and how they could've won. Everybody's adrenaline was still spiked. They were talking about it like a true battle, exactly what it felt like to them. James felt differently, like it was all too much.

He interrupted their conversation, "I'll be back in a minute. I'm going to talk to Flynn." Azalea gave him a strange look, but the conversation only stopped for a moment before they jumped right back in.

The professors sat nearby, and Flynn sat several rows above them, supervising the entire event. He walked over and took a seat beside Flynn.

Before James could speak, Flynn questioned, "I figured you would want to be discussing the dragon with your friends. Why come visit a professor? Was the labor more than you anticipated?" Flynn didn't look over at James, holding his gaze toward the center of the arena.

James looked vacantly in the same direction, not wanting to make eye contact when he broached the subject. "I don't understand the point of these labors."

"You question the violence of them?"

James was still shaken by the dragon and was having trouble calming his mind, but he felt this conversation was important. "Kind of. I understand why there's violence in training, just like the lessons you give me. But I haven't heard of a reason for the labors, for the training. Are there attacks on the city? Why do we have walls thirty feet high around Toricane?"

"You battle iron rhinos, pure fire, light, and a dragon without ever actually having to fear for your life, and instead of talking with your friends about the magnificence of it, you question why?"

"Yes. Why?"

Flynn looked over at him, amused. James didn't want it to be true, but the fear he felt still laid apparent on his face. "Do you want to hear something you can't learn in those books my city is so intent on fixating on?"

"Your city?" James asked, ignored by Flynn.

"There were four people who had a hand in the creation of those books. I am the sole survivor."

James took his moment of pause to ask, "What do the books have to do with-"

"About a century ago, there was a divide between the four of us. Fendrel, or who you know as The Founder, was on my side, along with much of the city. After long battles and loss, I came out alive with the chance to start anew. That's when I built those walls, The Fortress of Toricane. This part of the world was uninhabited at the time. I built everything from the ground up."

This was more information than James had ever gotten out of him. He was looking to push his luck. "So, you have us train in case those people come attack?"

"Those people are dead, all of them. I train you because there are more people out there that want what Toricane has, and they will eventually strike; it's just a matter of time." Flynn's expression was stone.

"Why don't you tell everybody that?" James asked, also not understanding why he was being told.

"Do you know the story of Hansel and Gretel?"

"Of course," James answered. "Everybody knows that story. The siblings get lured in by a candy house and almost get eaten."

Flynn nodded. "Yes, but before that, they leave breadcrumbs throughout the forest, so they won't be lost. The breadcrumbs get eaten by birds, which causes them to come upon the house."

James thought back to the story he'd learned. "I never really understood what the point of that part was. Why include that they left breadcrumbs if they were only going to get eaten?"

"It's a cautionary tale. The siblings thought they could venture out into the forest by themselves, aided only by breadcrumbs, and not get lost or taken. In reality, having only this small amount of information about their world, they were bound to get lost."

James hated when he talked in circles. It meant he had to find the point. "So, you're saying it would have been better if they had no information at all?" He was starting to think there was a reason Flynn never talked about Daniel. He specifically avoided it.

"Assuming the father never sent them away, wouldn't the children have been safer in his hands, not wandering the forest where anybody could find them?"

"Yes, but-"

"And isn't it the father's duty to keep them from wandering, getting sucked in by witches who offer them treats?"

"At some point, the father has to let them go," James countered.

Flynn smiled, "Only when they learn not to wander the forest. That's why I don't leave breadcrumbs. That's why you have to trust me. There are witches out there who wait for those that lose their way."

James didn't feel like he'd gotten his question answered, but Flynn stood up and walked out of the arena, followed by some of the other professors. James walked over to Azalea, Lloyd, and Carissa, who were still talking about the fire storm, how it got to Carissa. He allowed himself to get absorbed into the talk. There was a portion of him that did find the battle amazing, and the creatures fascinating, but that was masked by his inability to understand how or why Toricane operated the way it did.

After some time of discussion, Chloe announced Gary was the winner, for the second time. Everybody shuffled off. The older recruits were talking about how crazy the dragon was. Most of the first-years would be practicing their skills in any free time they had the next few weeks, making sure the surprise of today didn't happen again.

Lloyd and Carissa went to get lunch, but James needed to rest. He had never been more exhausted in his life, or death. Azalea went with him, feeling the need to comfort him after the dragon. It wasn't necessary, but she was still trying to get over the scrying Alisa incident. She'd concluded that wasn't going to happen until they actually talked about it. Before the next labor started up, she needed to do just that.

They headed back to Volition Tower and walked into James' room, expecting to lounge the rest of the night. Instead, they walked into a completely trashed bedroom that once resembled James'. His nightstand was broken to pieces. The bed was turned over. Parts of his wall had even been ripped apart. Everything in the closet was on the floor. Somebody was looking for something.

Alarm bells started ringing in James' head, literal ones. He cupped his head in his hands. "Daniel, stop. I know, this is alarming." The bells got significantly louder, then shut off.

"I know I haven't been in your room in a while, but this isn't how it normally looks right?" Azalea asked.

James laughed, "No, it's not torn apart, usually. We need to find my book. Daniel wants to chat. I doubt that's what they were looking for."

The two of them searched around his room and found it under his overturned bed. On the first page was a large inscription: '𝕳𝖊 𝖐𝖓𝖔𝖜𝖘. 𝕴𝖙'𝖘 𝖙𝖎𝖒𝖊 𝖋𝖔𝖗 𝖞𝖔𝖚𝖗 𝖘𝖊𝖈𝖔𝖓𝖉 𝖒𝖎𝖘𝖘𝖎𝖔𝖓. 𝕿𝖍𝖊𝖗𝖊 𝖜𝖎𝖑𝖑 𝖇𝖊 𝖙𝖍𝖗𝖊𝖊. 𝖄𝖔𝖚 𝖙𝖜𝖔, 𝖌𝖔 𝖙𝖔 𝖙𝖍𝖊 𝖗𝖚𝖎𝖓𝖘 𝖔𝖚𝖙𝖘𝖎𝖉𝖊 𝖙𝖍𝖊 𝖈𝖎𝖙𝖞, 𝖙𝖍𝖊 𝖔𝖓𝖊𝖘 𝖞𝖔𝖚 𝖊𝖓𝖈𝖔𝖚𝖓𝖙𝖊𝖗𝖊𝖉 𝖜𝖎𝖙𝖍 𝖙𝖍𝖊 𝖘𝖙𝖔𝖓𝖊 𝖌𝖔𝖑𝖊𝖒. 𝕭𝖗𝖊𝖆𝖐 𝖎𝖓. 𝕴 𝖜𝖎𝖑𝖑 𝖑𝖊𝖆𝖉 𝖞𝖔𝖚 𝖙𝖔 𝖙𝖍𝖊 𝖔𝖇𝖏𝖊𝖈𝖙. 𝕯𝖔 𝖎𝖙 𝖇𝖊𝖋𝖔𝖗𝖊 𝖙𝖍𝖊 𝖓𝖊𝖝𝖙 𝖑𝖆𝖇𝖔𝖗.'

Azalea finished reading first. "We've become his errand boys," she mocked.

"What is the point of all this? Am I getting anything out of it? Are you just going to kill me when I'm done?" James asked, in desperation. Every time he started to feel like one of the first-years, he gets pulled back into this. "Death here means going back to Earth. Maybe it's time I do that," he threatened.

The inscription on the page changed, '𝖄𝖔𝖚 𝖓𝖊𝖊𝖉 𝖒𝖔𝖗𝖊 𝖒𝖔𝖙𝖎𝖛𝖆𝖙𝖎𝖔𝖓?'

James' vision went black. He opened his eyes and knew immediately where he was. This had happened enough times now, he was starting to recognize the feeling of scrying. He was looking through Alisa's eyes. He thought back to Azalea standing right beside him and tried to pull out of it but couldn't.

Alisa was making dinner, nothing fancy. She didn't know how to make anything fancy. This looked like soup and bread. There was also wine. *That's weird. Alisa only drinks on special occasions,* he thought. He wanted to look around but could only see what she saw. When Alisa turned around, he did see what the occasion was. A guy sat at her table. She was making him dinner. This was a date.

Suddenly, Daniel appeared behind the man. He looked exactly the same as the first time James saw him. The limp was pronounced and the suit one of a kind. His smile looked exactly the same, but it felt different. All the pain he had inflicted seemed to make it twist into one of mischief. It was just as wide, just as white. The only difference was that he now knew what this man was capable of doing.

James wanted to speak but couldn't use Alisa's mouth. He wanted to warn her to run but couldn't. He couldn't even hear their conversation, but he could hear Daniel clearly say, "They can't see me, only you can. However, I wouldn't want you to make the mistake of thinking I'm not here. I'm just as much here as I was the day you died. The day I killed you.

"I told you randomness is elegant. That's true. Choosing you was as random as a stranger flipping a coin. There was no rhyme or reason you got picked. There was a reason you got killed, and if you don't do what I want, there will be a similar reason everybody you love on Earth dies."

He smiled from ear to ear knowing James wanted to respond. "The great thing about living so many lives on Earth is the number of loved ones you accumulate over the years. I have access to all of them."

Daniel pulled out a chair and sat down. Neither of them seemed to notice. "If you don't do what I want, not only will I kill Alisa, and you, I will also kill everybody you love in your next life and the lives after that. I will allow you to get close to those people and take them from you. You will have no idea why your life is cursed, except when you die and have to live with the knowledge that every death you experienced was on your hands.

"Knowing that, you might want to just end it all, kill yourself and get it over with, but think it through. If you do that, you'll live another life that much sooner, creating new connections with people I can attack. I have given you two more missions. Fulfill those and I will not kill you. Oh, one more thing. To die trying is to fail. Capeesh?"

296

His bedroom came back into view. James fell to his knees. Azalea bent down to his level, "What happened? Are you okay?"

He looked at her in desperation and replied, "We have two more missions to do."

Toricane

Life and Death...and Light

"It's time," Azalea told James.

The third labor was to start the following day. Luckily for them, it was in the forest again, so they would more easily be able to get back to the city after their mission. Unlucky for them, it was in the forest again, where a dragon, one that had some sort of vendetta against James, had just been sent. The plan was to camp in the ruins, inside and away from danger, then attempt to blend into the crowd when the labor came in the morning.

The book had less information on the ruins than the main office, but they spent more time preparing.

Azalea spent the week learning to teleport and honing her light and darkness abilities. They seemed to come in handy anytime something went wrong. James even gave her the marble from Flynn, to figure out more about it. All she knew was the darkness in that marble was older than anything she could conjure up. They were 'as different to each other as an ocean is to a bird.'

James spent his week learning everything about where they would be going. As far as he could tell, their journey would be short. It was only a mile or so inside of the forest. He couldn't find, however, anything about the inside of the ruins. There was no layout or description. His book couldn't even tell him what battle was fought there.

"Are you ready?" he asked.

"As ready as I'm going to be." They gathered their bags and started heading toward the city. "Any idea what you're looking for yet?"

James shook his head, "No. He hasn't said anything yet. If it's this important, I'm sure I'll know before we make it to the ruins."

They left in the evening, plenty of time before sunset. If anybody asked, they were just going to grab dinner in the city before heading back to campus for the night. In reality, they were walking to a remote part of the city and teleporting outside. Azalea discovered in her research that the city's border was protecting it from intruders, not people leaving. There shouldn't be anything stopping them from leaving, assuming the teleportation goes well.

The teleportation didn't need to take them far, just across the huge wall in front of them. She closed her eyes and felt the air change around her. When she opened them, they were both already across.

"That was much more painless than I expected," she said.

"You're welcome!" he laughed as they made their way into the forest. He got out the book for a map. "We should just need to go straight ahead for about a mile. It's getting pretty dark out. Any way you could get a light going?"

She nodded and focused on a point just above her fingertips. She separated the light and darkness in that area and a tiny, solid white light appeared above them like a candle flickering in the wind. Below it sat the darkness, giving a contrast to the light. It expanded to cover her hand. "Keep an eye out. We have no way of knowing what's out here, and this light's going to be like a beacon."

They made their way through the dense forest, wary of any animals spying on them. It was fairly uneventful until they got within sight of the ruins. James heard flapping of humongous wings in the distance.

"Shut off the light!"

"We won't be able to see," Azalea argued.

James threw his hands over the light, covering it from view. "Do you hear those wings? I know for a fact that dragon is attracted to light. It's like a dog chasing a ball."

"How could you possibly know that?" she asked, still holding the light out.

"That's how I survived it the first time."

She put out the light and laughed, "You survived by playing fetch with a dragon?"

"Yeah, it worked pretty well. I'm thinking it has a bit of a grudge against me now, though." James quickened his pace and made his way to the entrance of the ruins. "So, let's get in here before he finds us." The dragon's wings beat against the sky above. It was coming in their direction but was quite a way off at the moment.

"How are we supposed to get in there? I know you can just go through the barrier, but I can't," Azalea asked. "I really don't want to be here when the dragon shows up. Fetch can only work for so long."

"Maybe Daniel has some instructions," he said while opening his book. There was an inscription on the front page, '𝔘𝔰𝔢 𝔱𝔥𝔢 𝔡𝔞𝔤𝔤𝔢𝔯 𝔱𝔬 𝔠𝔲𝔱 𝔱𝔥𝔢 𝔟𝔞𝔯𝔯𝔦𝔢𝔯. 𝔍𝔱 𝔴𝔦𝔩𝔩 𝔞𝔠𝔱𝔦𝔳𝔞𝔱𝔢 𝔱𝔥𝔢 𝔡𝔢𝔣𝔢𝔫𝔰𝔢𝔰. 𝔊𝔬 𝔦𝔫𝔰𝔦𝔡𝔢 𝔞𝔫𝔡 𝔤𝔢𝔱 𝔞 𝔯𝔢𝔡 𝔠𝔯𝔶𝔰𝔱𝔞𝔩. 𝔖𝔲𝔯𝔳𝔦𝔳𝔢. 𝔒𝔫𝔩𝔶 𝔶𝔬𝔲 𝔴𝔦𝔩𝔩 𝔰𝔢𝔢 𝔱𝔥𝔢 𝔠𝔯𝔶𝔰𝔱𝔞𝔩. 𝔎𝔢𝔢𝔭 𝔦𝔱 𝔥𝔦𝔡𝔡𝔢𝔫. 𝔍 𝔴𝔦𝔩𝔩 𝔥𝔞𝔳𝔢 𝔪𝔬𝔯𝔢 𝔦𝔫𝔰𝔱𝔯𝔲𝔠𝔱𝔦𝔬𝔫𝔰 𝔱𝔬𝔪𝔬𝔯𝔯𝔬𝔴.' A picture of a pulsating red crystal was below the inscription. As soon as Azalea tried to look at the book, it faded away.

"He's always so cryptic," James complained. "It would be much easier if I could just tell you what we were doing. Apparently, though, you can see this now." He closed his eyes and reached out, attempting to get access to the pocket dimension he created. It took a few tries, but he eventually felt something open in front of him. He reached in and pulled the dagger out.

"What is that?" Azalea asked, trying to seem surprised by the dagger. Really, she was just asking about the hiding place.

"I'm not sure. I can tell you it's powerful. This is what gave that dragon it's scar and turned it black."

She went wide-eyed, "And you keep it laying around?"

"Not exactly," he defended. "It's a pocket dimension. Unless somebody knows exactly where I've stored it, there's no way they can take it. Daniel said I needed to hide it, so I found the best possible hiding place."

Azalea wished there was a way for her to contact Professor Wagner. He needed to know as soon as possible. Unfortunately, she wouldn't see him until after the next trial. "Yeah, nobody would find it there, not even by tearing apart your room."

"Daniel says we need to cut through the barrier with this knife. It's still going to activate the golem. Could you summon up some of that darkness? It worked so well last time."

"Yeah, I got it," she said.

"Just, quickly. The dragon seems pretty close," he said, getting nervous.

She nodded and started to reform her candle from before. The light expanded out, but she threw it away and left the darkness in her hand. The light evaporated as it flew away from them, like smoke into the air. "Ready."

James used the dagger to feel his way into the entrance. It sliced through the barrier. He ran the blade down, destroying the invisible force field blocking their pathway. The archway around him came to life as a stone golem. It looked like somebody had healed it since the last time. Azalea threw the glob of darkness at its torso.

Before the golem could fully form, it's body turned to ash. It's arms and legs formed and laid on the ground, trying unsuccessfully to run and attack. Azalea stepped around them and walked behind James into the ruins.

James saw past her into the ruins. The stone entryway seemed to be something of a misdirection. Inside was a completely different structure. It looked like somebody took a battlefield and built a roof on top of it. The forest was completely preserved underground, along with the bodies. Every piece of armor and weaponry was in the same spot as when this battle ended.

James felt a chill go down his spine when he looked at the bodies. The feeling was akin to being the last one standing after a battle. He had an inkling of survivor's guilt, even though this battle had been fought long before James' arrival. He wondered if this is what it would've been like had he been drafted. Although, in that scenario, he could have been the one on the ground. He forced himself to focus on something else.

"What do you think that's for?" James asked. He pointed toward the web of light that encompassed the entirety of its interior. It ran along the floor, through every body and piece of equipment. It looked like a spider's web. If that's what he was looking at, James did not want to see the spider. He chose his steps carefully.

"My guess," Azalea started, "it's preserving everything. These bodies would be long decomposed, and they look recently dead. This is a tomb. People have always tried to preserve the dead and create great places for them to rest. I guess, here you can do that."

Azalea's facial expression didn't reveal much, but James found it hard to believe she wasn't affected by the scene. He'd learned that when she seemed the most calm, her mind was racing the fastest. They walked through the battlefield, making sure not to step on anybody. "I'm sorry about this," James said.

"About what?" Azalea asked, confused.

"I got you involved. If we hadn't gone on that date, you wouldn't be here, putting your life at risk." James looked at the ground, delicately stepping over a sword.

"I'm putting my life at risk because your loved ones are in the same position, including Alisa."

She'd never said Alisa's name before. It took James by surprise. "That's really not fair to you. We should be able to just have a relationship without you defending my ex."

"Your wife," she sourly corrected.

He looked at her, "My ex."

She eyed James, "And the scrying?"

"Aside from Daniel forcing it on me, I haven't scried her since. She's not my wife anymore. I'm dead. I

306

still don't want to see her die, but he didn't just threaten her. He threatened the people I love. That includes you."

That gave her pause. He wasn't lying. James continued forward to the end of the chamber. She hesitantly followed, spending as much brain power on her steps. "I think I found something," he said. "Don't come over here. You can't see it. It looks like all the webs of light are running through it. I'm not sure what's going to happen if I take it."

"Wait, don't take it, yet." Behind a mound of rock and through a plate of glass, Azalea saw two people she had not expected. One of them was wearing a ruby-red cape and the other was a woman in robes. "This is dangerous. These two," she pointed toward them, "are The Founder and The Destroyer."

James walked toward them and spied through the glass, "I guess that's why they get their own separate container." He looked at the founder, "Hey, Flynn has the same cape hanging in his office. He wouldn't tell me much about it, always talking in riddles and side-stepping my questions."

"I don't know what's going to happen if we take it and break the chain. Any ideas?"

He thought about it. "Well, Daniel's instructions just after taking the... loot were, 'survive,' so I would prepare for a fight."

She laughed, "We can't take them on. There have to be hundreds of them!"

"He wouldn't have brought us here for no reason. There has to be a way to disrupt the web. Try introducing some darkness into it."

"You want me to desecrate a battlefield that has been memorialized?" she was baffled.

"No, I don't want you to. I need you to," he stated calmly.

She bent down and ran her hand across one web of light, inserting darkness into it. The darkness caused that part of the web to disperse. It was quickly replaced by another string of light. "This isn't working. Try the dagger." James took the dagger and cut a web. It severed but was immediately replaced.

He grew impatient of tiptoeing. "I'm going to take the thing, and we can just run."

Azalea grabbed him, "Run by what? We don't know what's going to happen."

He grabbed her hand and put the dagger in it. "Stand by me while I take it. I'll stuff it in the pocket dimension, and we can face whatever comes next, together, just like you said." An alarm started going off in James' head when he handed her the dagger. "I know what I'm doing Daniel. She won't see it. We'll survive. I'll take the dagger back when we escape. Good enough for you?" The alarm subsided.

Azalea took the dagger and nodded, "Let's do this."

They positioned themselves at the end of the chamber, by the crystal. James opened the pocket dimension and quickly stuffed the crystal into it, then turned around. He saw the light from the crystal sever and retract back into the ruins. The web that ran through the battlefield soaked into its surroundings. The only light that remained unbroken was circulating in the glass case with the Founder and Destroyer.

Within a few seconds of the connection being disrupted, the soldiers on the ground started to stand. They grabbed the weapons nearby and stood at attention. They looked normal except for their eyes. Each soldier's eyes were stark white and gleaming with the same glow as the light web.

"We can't take on this many people with abilities," Azalea said.

"I'm not so sure they have abilities. They're dead. This is just the light reanimating them."

"Okay, I'll rephrase. We can't take on this many people."

James pushed his hands out in front of him and a shockwave rippled through the cavern, knocking most of the soldiers to their knees. He imagined the closest one being pulled toward them and the image came true. "Use the dagger! Now!"

The soldier was pulled forward, toward Azalea's outstretched hand. The dagger shoved into his chest. All light in his eyes turned black, and his body fell to the ground. She reminded herself, *he was already dead. It was just a trick.* "One down. One hundred to go," she managed to get out as she ripped the dagger back out of the dead soldier's chest.

"We just need to lead them outside. I have an idea." As James spoke, he picked up the dead man's sword and threw it into another's torso. It didn't seem to faze him. "Normal attacks aren't affecting them. We need a bigger, dark weapon."

"Where are we going to get that?" Azalea panted, as she sliced the throat of another dead man that came after her.

"Follow me, and cover behind me." Every soldier in the room had gotten back up and was starting to run at them. James put his hands together with all the force he could muster and spread them, forcing the air in the room to separate down the middle with the force of a tornado.

Bodies flew through the air but got back up almost immediately after hitting the ground. As they made their way down the center, James continued to throw rocks and water at the soldiers, forcing them back. Azalea killed the stragglers with the dagger. One got a hand on James. Azalea threw the dagger, piercing the shoulder of the undead warrior, drawing the light from its animated form. She was left defenseless. James backhanded the air, throwing several soldiers back that were closing in, which gave her just enough time to retrieve it.

They were both exhausted by the time they made it to the entrance. James wanted to lay on the ground and give up, but something told him these soldiers weren't going to stop at the ruins. As Azalea made her way out, James threw his hands up, creating a wall of wind at the entrance. The soldiers beat at it, trying to get through.

"I'm not going to be able to hold this for long. Throw light into the air."

"Are you trying to get us caught?!" she yelled back.

"Just do it! Then, run for cover."

Azalea created an orb of white energy and threw it high up into the air. She heard something move off in the distance. It was the dragon. *Why would he want the dragon here?* she thought. Without hesitation, she ran out of the clearing and hid behind a tree nearby, dagger at the ready.

James stood strong, trying to withstand the increasing force coming from the pileup of people on the other end of his wind wall. The moonlight, which he had been using to see, disappeared. Looking up, he saw wings expanded far above them and Azalea's ball of light being eaten. A silhouette of the massive creature turned toward the commotion below. Its eyes beat down on them. The dragon dove straight down.

The first soldier broke through his barrier, forcing James to release it. An onslaught of weapons came James' direction.

Heavy claws dug into the broken ground. A roar erupted. Just as James was hoping, the dragon scanned the clearing and saw hundreds of gleaming white eyes. Unexpected to James, they didn't seem to notice the dragon. James was their only target.

Outside of the clearing, Azalea looked on at the scene in horror. She held the dagger at the ready. The ground shook from the force of landing. The dragon got closer. The dagger seemed to draw her toward it. Unsure

312

why, she moved out from behind the tree and pointed the dagger toward the group of charging soldiers.

Regardless of how much James threw them across the clearing or stabbed them with weapons, they got back up and ran at him. He was about to faint from exhaustion. There were too many of them. He needed help.

The dragon turned its head from James and attacked the glowing eyes. As it absorbed the light, its black body seemed to pulsate. It's claws dug into the nearest bodies and sucked the light out. It bit down on several, and James saw light flow toward it's chest. The white scar grew.

Within a couple minutes, the dragon had finished off every last one. The only person standing was James. Now he was going to have to deal with the downside of calling a dragon to his side: *How do I survive a dragon?* He ran. When he turned around, Azalea stood there, pointing the dagger into the sky.

"What are you doing?!" he screamed. "Run!"

"Stop! It's leaving. It just wanted the light."

He heard the whoosh of wings against wind. The dragon flew into the air and took off. "Why? How? Why did it leave?" he stuttered through his lack of breath.

Azalea thought about mentioning the dagger, then realized Daniel would be listening. "I have no idea! We got lucky. Maybe it was only attracted to the light. It didn't care about anything else." James didn't care enough about why it left. It did. That's all that mattered. She continued, "We need to clean this place up before tomorrow. The professors could see it."

He sat down against the tree. "We will. Just give me a few minutes to rest. That was too much." James started to close his eyes.

"Thank you."

"What? I think we're past the whole, 'saving each other's lives,' thing," he said, with his eyes closed.

"Not for that." She walked off toward the ruins. James was left remembering before the battle happened. He loved her, and he said it. *That's better than no response, I guess,* he thought. James' eyes wouldn't open. He stopped trying. Quickly afterwards, he drifted off.

He appeared in a garden. James instinctually recognized the scry. He was looking through Alisa's eyes again. There was no need to stop it. The scry felt like a dream, just more realistic. It was relaxing to see his home back on Earth, to see a garden. His head turned, and he saw another man, the same man from the table last time, digging up a plant next to him.

He couldn't hear them talk but also didn't want to. James only wanted to see his home again. Everything looked so different on Earth. The buildings were plain. The landscape flat and uneventful. People were ordinary. There were no surprises, and nothing ever really changed. He missed that. The ornate towers and creatures he couldn't imagine in his wildest dreams were becoming normal.

The stakes seemed higher in Toricane. Knowing about both places and the limited number of lives he had made it a constant struggle to achieve more. Life could be altered with the flick of somebody's wrist. On Earth, it was different. Life only seemed hard because he was so close to it. It was an optical illusion. Life was easy.

In life, he could only live and die. Those were the ends and beginnings of his time. Everything between was a way to make that life more enjoyable, for himself and those around him. He wasn't preparing for anything. There's no trial for his eternal existence, as far as James knew. He could just live to the fullest extent he was able before the end came. He made Earth too complicated.

James envied this man in front of him. Yes, he wished he could be there with Alisa, no question. That wasn't why, though. He envied this man because of the smile on his face. It was a carefree, loving smile. James wanted to have that smile on his own face. Maybe he was being too hard on himself. Somebody could be looking at him from wherever comes after Toricane and saying the same thing. It was all about perspective.

The Rat Race

James woke up to Azalea shaking him, "It's time to get out of here." He was still sitting against the tree from the night before.

"We need to clean everything up!" he sat up quickly, looking for the bodies.

"It's taken care of. You were too tired to do anything, so I got all the bodies back inside. I even created a sort of net of light. It's not as advanced as what was there before, but it may fool somebody at first glance. Do you think you could create a forcefield at the entrance?"

316

He stood up nodding, still exhausted. His voice was bleak, "I'll give it my best shot." He almost forgot, "I should probably take the dagger back."

Azalea looked disappointed at the prospect of giving it up. Regardless, she handed it back to him. James took it and asked, "Did you get any sleep last night?"

She shrugged, "I'll sleep when we're not under the threat of a dragon eating us, among whatever else is out here."

James went over to the entrance and found that, while the dagger had destroyed most of the barrier, some of it remained. He stretched it out to cover the entire entrance. It wouldn't work as effectively but should still be believable. The grounds looked good as new. James was impressed. She even managed to fix the ground where the dragon landed.

"That should be good enough. Ready to head out? I'm sure the labor starts soon." James started walking toward the forest entrance.

"Yeah! Shouldn't you check with Daniel this morning?"

James gave her a strange look and frowned, "I guess I should."

He opened the book to find an inscription ready to read. '𝕻𝖔𝖚 𝖉𝖎𝖉𝖓'𝖙 𝖉𝖎𝖊! 𝕿𝖍𝖆𝖙'𝖘 𝖊𝖝𝖈𝖎𝖙𝖎𝖓𝖌 𝖓𝖊𝖜𝖘! 𝕵𝖚𝖘𝖙 𝖔𝖓𝖊 𝖒𝖔𝖗𝖊 𝖒𝖎𝖘𝖘𝖎𝖔𝖓 𝖙𝖔 𝖌𝖔, 𝖙𝖍𝖊𝖓 𝕵'𝖑𝖑 𝖌𝖊𝖙 𝖙𝖔 𝖒𝖊𝖊𝖙 𝖕𝖔𝖚 𝖎𝖓 𝖕𝖊𝖗𝖘𝖔𝖓! 𝕮𝖍𝖊𝖈𝖐 𝖇𝖆𝖈𝖐 𝖔𝖓𝖈𝖊 𝖙𝖍𝖊 𝖑𝖆𝖇𝖔𝖗 𝖘𝖙𝖆𝖗𝖙𝖘.'

James froze. *Meet in person.* Somehow, Daniel was going to come back. James thought he just wanted destruction and mayhem, maybe some murder. Him coming into this world would be worse than any of that. What was he planning to do, overpower the entire academy? Could he do that?

He wanted to tell Azalea so badly. He looked at her, face completely white. She rushed over, "What is it?!"

Then, he thought back to his dream the night before. He thought of Alisa and the new person in her life. They were so happy. He couldn't ruin that. He closed the book, "It's nothing! Let's go. It looks like we'll be done with Daniel's missions by the end of the day." He wanted to say more but knew that was a bad choice.

They saw the forest's entrance and a group gathering on the other side of the trees. A few hundred more feet, they would be in the clear and out of the forest. Azalea went into a panic. She hadn't had the chance to talk to Professor Wagner. She needed to buy time. Something to stall. When they got to the edge of the forest, recruits were starting to gather around. There was a large jumble of them near the forest's edge. James

318

and Azalea slipped in and walked over to Lloyd and Carissa.

"How'd it go?" Lloyd asked.

"We're alive. It wasn't easy," James replied.

Carissa joined in, "How much more of this is he going to make you do? It's only a matter of time before you get caught." The crowd of recruits were crowding around, waiting for the labor to start.

"Give them some credit. I bet they've gotten used to evading the law by now." He smiled toward Carissa. James realized that all the time he and Azalea spent together was drawing Lloyd and Carissa closer. They hadn't all spent a ton of time together over the last couple months, aside from the Winter party.

James was going to dive into the story of the memorial, but Chloe stood up on a pedestal and started making announcements. They would have to catch up later. "We have exciting news. You won't be just doing one labor today. We have moved up the schedule. First-years," she looked in their direction, "you will be completing the third labor this morning, followed by the last labor after lunch. Conserve your energy." There were several gasps and murmurs of disbelief.

James was already exhausted. This was just worse news. He needed to sleep for the next three days before he could be fully recovered from the night before. She continued, "The third labor will be a race. Other professors are in the forest right now working on creating the intricacies of it."

Azalea and James looked at each other with wide eyes, glad to have missed them. "Your objective is to find this," she held up a flag that read '𝔜𝔢𝔞𝔯 𝔒𝔫𝔢' on it, "which will be used in the fourth, and final, labor.

"The winning team of these labors will be venturing into the forest as a diplomatic mission for nearby tribes. There are untold dangers that await, but I have faith, you can surpass them! We are unsure how many tribes live out in these forests, but there are others, some of which aren't quite as civilized. We want you to initiate a discussion with them. Some will be peaceful, others will not."

With that, she stepped down from her pedestal and showed each group to their starting points. They were allowed to start anywhere, but she recommended not starting directly adjacent to the other teams.

Once the starting points were established, branches shrunk, allowing passage in front of James. To the side, and seemingly everywhere else around him, vines thickened; bushes grew; thorns became sharper. The forest became dangerous before his eyes, manifesting a new fear in the first-years, all except James and Azalea who were too exhausted to panic. "We'll be waiting for you at the finish line. Good luck."

320

The professors flew past on their platform over the forest, and first-years made their way into the forest. Azalea pulled James back, "Hang on. I want to try something." He was confused. "Do you have that marble on you?"

"Yeah," he pulled out a solid black marble. "Why?"

Without saying anything, she took it from him. "I need the dagger. We're going to win this labor."

After a couple tries, James pulled the dagger out and handed it to her. "What's going on? The labor is hardly a priority. I need to check and see what Daniel wants."

She didn't reply. Azalea took the dagger and focused for a moment on the marble before stabbing it. Black ooze shot out, which she caught in midair and formed into a ball in her hands. She gave the dagger back to James as the ooze turned into a powdery substance. Without warning, she blew the dust on him.

"What are you doing?" he asked, knowing she didn't know much about the marble's interior.

"Carissa," she called out. Carissa came over, questioning why James was covered in a cloud of black. "Try to scry James."

"Wh—"

"Just do it! Quickly!" she interrupted.

Carissa gave her a dirty look and closed her eyes. "He's not here." She opened her eyes and locked in on James. "It's like he's not there."

A smile spread across Azalea's face. "James, open your book."

He was still confused but followed her command. On the first page, writing was furiously being added and fading away. '𝔚𝔥𝔢𝔯𝔢 𝔡𝔦𝔡 𝔶𝔬𝔲 𝔤𝔬? 𝔚𝔯𝔦𝔱𝔢 𝔟𝔞𝔠𝔨 𝔱𝔬 𝔪𝔢! 𝔑𝔬𝔴! 𝔗𝔥𝔦𝔰 𝔦𝔰 𝔫𝔬𝔱 𝔣𝔲𝔫𝔫𝔶! 𝔒𝔫𝔩𝔶 𝔍 𝔡𝔬 𝔭𝔯𝔞𝔫𝔨𝔰.'

The smile widened and Azalea looked at James with hopefulness in her heart for the first time in months. "James, I have so much to tell you."

"Am I hidden from him? How did you do that?" James was skeptical that he was actually going by unwatched.

"I didn't know for sure. It was just an idea I had after I used the dagger last night. I'm not even sure how long it's going to last. For now, you're hidden." The smile reached her eyes and she kissed him. They parted and information started pouring out of her mouth. "Professor Wagner and I have been collaborating about you in secret. We've been trying to figure out Daniel's plan. We need to tell him everything that's happened since we left campus!"

Her mind shifted, "What did we steal from the ruins? What is Daniel planning? Tell me everything!"

Learning he was hidden from view was the best thing James had heard all year. Happiness warmed him. The world looked lighter. Then, it faded, "You've been a double agent all year?"

Azalea just realized how that might sound. It wasn't important right now. "James, we can talk about that later. It's not as bad as it seems. Tell me what Daniel's plan is."

Carissa and Lloyd gathered around him in anticipation. They had only heard snippets of the whole story all year and were looking for something more concrete.

He nodded to Azalea. That wasn't the issue right now. "All I know is he's planning on coming here. He said, after this next mission, we would be meeting in person. We stole a crystal from the ruins. He hasn't told me how it's going to happen or what the crystal is or anything."

Azalea was frustrated, "We need to get to the end of the maze and find Professor Wagner before this wears off," she said, motioning toward James. "Chloe said they would be at the finish line."

She started to run off, but James grabbed her arm. "Azalea, if I don't do this, he's going to kill everybody I love. It doesn't matter if *Professor Wagner* knows. It's too late."

"Just give me the time it takes for this to wear off. Maybe he can think up something to get rid of Daniel for good."

James wasn't convinced, but he owed Azalea that much. "Okay. When this wears off, if he hasn't solved it, I'm following through."

She didn't like that one bit. "Fair is fair. We need to get through this maze."

They took off from the entrance. Azalea barked orders as they went, "Lloyd, feel out with your mind around corners. Tell us if we're going to run into anything alive. Carissa, keep track of our path in your book. James keep your head on a swivel. You're our defense."

Lloyd and Carissa took their assignments seriously. Lloyd kept his mind ten feet ahead of wherever they were, feeling out for possible attacks. Carissa helped him by showing on a map that she was creating on the fly where their next step would be. The two of them moved like a well-oiled machine.

They ran through the first section of forest, a small path with vines scratching them as they passed. There weren't any forks in the road yet. The four of them ran for several minutes before Carissa stopped them. "We aren't going anywhere. We've been running in circles since we came in."

Azalea was annoyed, "How do we fix this?"

"Well," Carissa explained, "there is a point at the far end where it looks like there should be a different path to go down. Let's go check it out." It wasn't too far down the path from where they were. The circle they were running in was small. "Right here," she said, pointing at a large tree.

Azalea examined it, "I don't see anything strange about it, but there's definitely not going to be any getting around it. The brush is too thick. I can't even see where it opens up. James, could you try chopping it down?"

He nodded and felt out at the tree. Just as he was about to manifest several large axes, he felt a heartbeat inside the tree. "It's alive," he said. "Give me a second." James reached out with his mind, attempting to communicate telepathically. He just gave a simple request, '*Could you move?*'

The tree spoke back to him, 'I'm a tree. How am I supposed to move?'

'Is this a riddle?' he asked. There was no response. 'Move or I will move you.'

The tree rustled and branches came down at them like whips. "What did you do?" Lloyd asked.

"I threatened it!" he yelled back.

"Why did you threaten a tree?!" Came from both Lloyd and Carissa.

"It wouldn't move!" James grabbed a large boulder and held it over the top of them. The branches rebounded off.

Azalea leapt out, manifesting an axe to hit the tree with. "I don't think trees can move. That might not be its fault."

James followed suit. He created a swarm of sharpened steel that circled their heads, chopping off invading limbs. "I thought it was just being difficult."

After a few minutes of this, Azalea whittled enough off that they were able to squeeze by the tree. A new path opened up on the other side that they ran down to avoid the branches. At a safe distance, Azalea spoke up, "That didn't go as well as I would've hoped."

"I don't think anybody expected a tree to attack us," James shot back.

"We just need to be more on guard. Let's go." Azalea dashed ahead, leaving them to play catchup. Depending on Carissa to keep track of where they went, Azalea took random turns at each corner. Lloyd struggled to keep concentrating on what was ahead and run, but he managed. James, still exhausted from the night before, had trouble just doing the running.

"We aren't running in circles still, are we?" She asked Carissa.

"No, we're really deep in the forest at this point. Unless, you know, they've altered the maze while we're in it or done some sort of perceptual trick. I wouldn't know how to figure that out." Azalea glared at her. "But it looks like we're doing good. We just need to keep going."

They heard a commotion ahead. Azalea ran straight toward it, followed by the rest. Another group was in the middle of a battle with a creature none of them had ever seen before. It was made out of a combination of different tree's branches all intertwined to form the shape of a human but with no distinguishable face.

The other four attacking this creature were getting nowhere. They were mostly on the defensive, slowly backing up against each whip of the branch. The creature grew with each second as limbs it passed broke of their trees and joined it's body. It's torso was a constantly shifting and morphing piece of tangled wood.

Azalea shot a look back at them, "We just need to make it to the end. It doesn't matter if we help the other groups. Just kill this thing and keep going."

James charged forward, fire burning in his hand. The other team looked at him, horrified that he might throw it toward them. Instead, he tossed it at the creature. The ball of flame hit it in the shoulder and knocked it back. He expected the fire to spread throughout its body, but Luck never seemed to pay off.

The monster detached its arm, branches entwined into several muscles. The thick cluster hit the ground and continued to burn. Limbs from a nearby tree continued to extend through its body as it fought. Roots grew up from the ground, planting it on the spot as the repairs were made. The muscle, tendon, and bone, all woven with the same wood, created a new, unharmed accessory for violence. The arm was remade in the time it took James to realize his fire didn't work.

The group looked over with an expression that said they had tried that already. Each one was holding a shield and deflecting whips from the creature while they slowly chopped away at the regenerative body. It wasn't working. The creature reached out at the closest recruit and pulled the shield away from them, inserting the shield into its own chest. Vines grew around it, cementing the shield as if it was part of the creature.

As the being reached out for another shield to incorporate into its body, James' group made their way up to the creature and Azalea shouted, "Everybody, throw fire at it on three!"

"One." James threw a forcefield in front of them, absorbing the cracks from branches. "Two." The branches extended around it and started curling themselves around Lloyd. "Three." Everybody threw their fireballs and James tossed his forcefield around the creature. Branches tried to penetrate it, giving assistance to their monster, to no avail. The branched monster withered to ash in front of their eyes.

The other team didn't stick around to celebrate. They took off down the path. "That's rude," Carissa said.

James laughed, "I don't think they really care about being nice right now. Which way do we go? For all we know, they just ran in a random direction."

Carissa looked over her notes, "I think we need to go right. We already came from the direction they went. Left, I think, goes back toward the entrance. I'm thinking the finish line is going to be deeper into the forest."

Azalea agreed, "That's a safe bet. Let's go deeper into the forest."

"Wait!" Lloyd yelled, before anybody could take off. "There's something around the corner. Be cautious."

James took the first step around the corner, putting caution to the side in favor of speed, and a rock hit him directly in the shoulder, knocking him down. Azalea ran around, hands at the ready, to see Gary standing there about to attack. "Don't attack!" she screamed out at him. Too late. Another rock came from the ground and was thrown toward Azalea. She pushed toward it with both hands. The rock split down the middle. Gary was surprised at the strength she showed. It took him a second to realize what a mistake he had made.

Azalea grabbed both halves of the rock and slung them his way. He tried to knock them away but only managed to hit one. The other slammed into his side. He was out cold. "What the hell was that?!" Azalea couldn't believe he just attacked them.

James got up, hand on his shoulder. "He really wants to win. Lloyd, can you feel out to see if his group is anywhere nearby? We should make sure he can't win this one. I'm going to tie him up."

"No, none of them are around. The group must've thought they stood a better chance by splitting up."

James wrapped vines tightly around his body. "It's a good idea, until you decide to start attacking other groups. He has to be some special kind of arrogant." James lifted his hand and the vines wrapped around a tree above pulled him farther up. "I doubt anybody will see him up there. He'll hang in the tree until this is over."

They continued down the trail, making turns as Carissa told them. After another hour, Carissa yelled out, "I've got it! I figured out the maze. There's only one possible path it could be!"

"That's great!" Azalea was ecstatic. She looked at James. "It looks like that darkness is starting to wear off. We need to hurry."

"Couldn't you just make more?" he asked.

"That stuff you found in Flynn's office wasn't just darkness. There was something more to it, something primordial. It's darkness mirrored more with the dagger than anything I could make. It wasn't anything you could pull from the air. It was created by somebody. The old world darkness kind of manipulates into whatever you want it to. I wanted it to hide you, so it did."

"It was that easy? You can just create it?" James was skeptical.

"I never said it was easy," she laughed as they started to run again. "I just said I did it. And I definitely couldn't create more. That's way beyond me. Now, come on. Let's hurry to the end!"

Carissa took the lead, and they jogged for several more minutes before coming up on a dead end. Azalea huffed, "What is this?"

"It's not a dead end!" Carissa quickly stated. "It has the same look on my map as the tree. We need to go through here."

As soon as Carissa said that, what looked like a large bird flew down and perched on the top of the bush blocking their way. James looked at it again. It had the wings and feet of an eagle. It's head looked more human, and the back end looked like that of a lion.

"A sphinx!" Lloyd shouted, excited to see one. Everybody looked around at him, confused. "You've never heard of it? It asks you riddles. If you get it right, you go past; wrong, you die." When he uttered the last word, he realized what that meant for them and started sweating.

"That's right!" the sphinx squawked. "The first riddle is solved. The correct path is found. Two more and the end is near. I ask you: what four-word admonition makes the happy person sad and sad person happy?"

"Wait, could you repeat that?" Lloyd asked.

The sphinx stayed silent. James repeated it for him. They deliberated and couldn't come to an answer. Carissa got tired of debating. She shouted out, thinking it was obvious, "This too shall pass."

The sphinx stood tall and James readied himself. It squawked, "Right you are! As all things pass, so shall

332

happiness and sadness. One riddle to pass. One wrong to die. I ask you to find the hidden word in this poem: Sir, I bear a rhyme excelling in mystic force and magic spelling. Celestial sprites elucidate. All my own striving can't relate."

Azalea moaned, "I don't have time for this! What's the answer, Carissa? Just ask your book."

"I really don't think the book's going to tell me anything," Carissa said, as she opened it. She repeated the riddle to the book. It remained empty. No answer. "Maybe that's the answer. There is no special word."

"That can't be the answer," Lloyd said. "It doesn't make any sense. The words all seem weird and out of place."

James looked at the sphinx, "Can we get another riddle? That one's a little too hard."

The sphinx didn't move. Azalea laughed, "You thought that would work?"

"I thought it was worth a try. Any ideas?"

"Yeah," she said, "I have one. Me and Carissa are going to stay here and attack this thing. You're going to use the dagger to cut through the pathway. You and Lloyd will run through and find the flag as quickly as you can. We'll hold it off."

Carissa looked worried, "I think I can solve it!" They all looked at her, waiting. She thought hard on it. "Okay, I have no idea what the answer is. Let's do it."

Azalea looked worried for the first time since the labor started. "Ready?" she asked them. They nodded. Hiding from the sphinx's view, she created a huge ball of darkness and light. She handed the light to Carissa, "We may need some healing."

James took out his dagger, and Azalea threw a huge piece of her darkness at the sphinx. It hit the sphinx in the wing, causing a large gaping hole. The human head looked down at her and charged. James used that moment to slice the dagger through brush blocking their path. It withered away and revealed a clearing just ahead with the flag on top of a pole.

He looked at Lloyd, "Run for it." They both took off toward the pole and noticed a couple others groups had also made their way to it. They were trying to knock over the pole or climb it but kept being derailed by the other teams. Looking back, he saw Azalea and Carissa struggling to keep the sphinx off them. It was giving large lacerations to Carissa's arm, while she tried to conjure a shield.

He looked around at the fights other first-years were having. *I don't have time for this.* One recruit sent a quake through the ground their way. It threatened to pull their feet out from under them.

334

Before it reached him, James threw his right hand out. A wave of opaque darkness rippled out, zapping energy from the recruits on his right side, leaving most of them on their knees. The wave dissipated as it bubbled outward through the forest.

He threw out his left hand. A blinding flash of light trapped itself in the eyes of those on his left. The recruits held their hands up to their eyes, trying to protect themselves from an energy that had already invaded their sight.

Between the two extremes, a vacuum of light and dark were created. A vibration of energy felt by everybody in the clearing echoed inward, toward James, like a tornado. The force was visible only through the sway of trees and flag, which was almost ripped off its pole. James and Lloyd were now the only two recruits standing.

James stood in place when the earthquake's ripple came through. He broke the rocks under his feet and the collection of dirt and stone exploded upwards as he flew on top of it. He ascended to the flag and ripped it off the pole, holding it up for any spectators to see. The fighting stopped. Trees around them moved back to their original positions. The maze and the creatures within it disbursed.

James quickly landed on the ground and, behind the flag, put his dagger back into the pocket dimension.

He held it up high. Chloe walked out from a tree nearby. She seemed dazed by the showing of power but didn't pause before announcing the winner. "Congratulations, James! Your team has secured the flag. That means you will be the first to start with it in the final round of capture the flag, a no rules labor that will test your strength and endurance."

A recruit nearby whose energy had been zapped by James protested, "No rules? That's going to be a blood-bath! This was bad enough!"

Chloe nodded, "Unfortunately, recruits tend to get quite involved in the labors. Keep in mind, diplomatic missions don't always end well. You may need to defend yourself on this trip. We want to know you are able to do that. Everybody, lunch is back on campus. Please, be back in a few hours for the next labor."

Every recruit in the forest looked utterly exhausted. They had given this maze their all and were now going to need to do that again later in the day. They shuffled back to the start of the forest. Carissa used the light she had to heal some of her and Azalea's wounds. "Thanks for being so quick," she said to James. "I don't think we could've lasted much longer against that sphinx. It was brutal."

Azalea looked over to thank him and frowned, "James, the darkness is starting to fade. You aren't going to have time to get back to campus."

James looked at his hands. What had been a shadow that masked his skin now only slightly obscured his vision. He could see the tone of his body coming back. It was clear that time was short.

Her frustration was apparent as she thought of a solution. "Just stay here, at the edge of the forest. Daniel can't know I know anything. I'm going to find Professor Wagner. We'll figure something out. Don't do anything until I get back! We will find a way to fix this!"

James nodded, "I'll stay here. Somebody bring me lunch, though. I haven't eaten since we went into those ruins."

"I got you!" Lloyd encouraged. "We'll be back before you know it!"

Azalea took off toward campus. She was first through the bridge and ran across town as quickly as she could. She went to the main tower, where everybody was eating lunch. There was no Professor Wagner anywhere. Flynn was close by. She ran up to him, out of breath.

"Flynn, where is Professor Wagner?" She asked hurriedly.

"Well, I'm not exactly sure, Azalea. He could be in his office or getting ready for the next labor. What's going on?"

She hesitated. Flynn was working with Wagner to stop this. She looked around, making sure Flynn was the only one who could hear. "What has he told you about Daniel?"

Flynn dropped his fork, "That's not for you to know. If you know something, you'd do better to tell me now."

"Fine," she spat out. "James is being coerced into letting Daniel free, under threat of the death of everybody he loves."

"Daniel can't do that. He's lo—"

"I don't care what you think is going on. Daniel can do that. I was able to hide James from his view only long enough to get the info. It's wearing off. When it does, Daniel will be released. James has the dagger and the crystal at the edge of the forest."

"With that he could..." Flynn's eyes flooded with darkness. He looked up at Azalea. "No. He will not be released." Flynn disappeared with a loud pop.

Seeing the anger in Flynn's eyes, she second-guessed her decision to tell him. This could only end badly. He was one of the most powerful people here and that anger was deep. *Wagner may be more powerful.*

338

She wasn't sure. Azalea ran off to find him. Whatever she had just condemned James to, she was going to fix it.

Unnecessary Evil

James stood at the edge of the forest, a tree line behind him and the city in front, watching as his friends walked back toward the academy. When they were just out of sight, his vision went dark. He couldn't hear anything or feel the air around him. He didn't know if he was still standing. His eyes opened, and he found himself in a familiar experience. Alisa was chatting with his mother. They were talking about this new guy in her life.

His mom was supportive of it. Apparently, they were great together. He had asked her to move in with him the day before, and she was mulling it over. "I just don't know. I want to. I really do. I just feel like I'm insulting James. It's been six months and I'm moving in with some other guy."

"Honey," his mom, replied, "you and James were amazing together, but you have a life to live. He's gone. It's okay that you've come to terms with that. Stop beating yourself up about it."

She looked down, "I'm sorry. It's always you I come to for advice about this stuff. It's really unfair to you. My parents are just...I don't know. It's not the same."

"Stop it," Mariam scolded. "I told you to stop beating yourself up. Yes, I lost a son but, on that same day, I gained a daughter. You need to be happy. So, you're going to move in with this nice young man, and you're going to stop thinking about James. Got it?"

"Yes, ma'am," she smiled.

The sounds of their voices softened to a whisper and Daniel appeared in the chair across from Alisa. "Nice day isn't it?" he said, looking into James' eyes. "Oh, right. You can't talk here. No worries. I'll do the talking."

He took a moment to get comfortable in his chair before sighing, "I don't know how you did it, blocking me out like that. I do know it wasn't an accident. I don't need to know why or what happened, because you're going to cut that crystal open with the dagger. That's all that really matters."

Daniel sat up in the chair. His smile gleamed. He talked slow. "Do you want to know how I know you're going to do that? It's fairly simple. Like I've told you plenty of times, randomness is elegant.

"A brain aneurysm, for instance, is one of the most random acts. I've always found it fascinating." His hand raised. James' mother fell to the ground.

James tried to move. He tried to attack Daniel. He motioned for his arms to come up and throw the house at Daniel. Nothing happened. Instead, the body he was possessing leapt to the ground and stared at his dead mother, assessing what was wrong. He could still hear Daniel speaking behind him.

James wept. He couldn't show it; he couldn't cry in this body. Every feeling of wanting to get away was blocked by the scry. He didn't want to stare at his dead mother. He just wanted to avert his eyes.

Daniel, who had come into the conversation with anger, was now back to his cheery, upbeat attitude. "That's how I know you're going to help me! We made a deal. I thought it was a fairly good deal for you. As long as you survived my missions, every loved one you had, or ever will have, can stay alive. Who doesn't want that?

"Well," he paced around the room, "I guess you don't. However, I am merciful. I will still uphold my end of the deal and not kill everybody, as long as you uphold yours. We can sweep this little mishap under the rug, maybe even laugh about it later!" The sound of his laughter made James want to jump out of his skin, quite literally.

Joy echoed out from Daniel's voice. "I can feel your anger, James. I know it's going to take some time to heal this wound between us, but I believe we can get past it. Let's work together this one last time and I'll do something else for you. I won't kill *you*. That's fantastic right?! Now, I do believe you have some company you need to attend to. Because of what I think is about to happen, I'm going to give you access to some more of my power, temporarily. Remember, your mother's dead. Use that anger!"

James was standing on the edge of the forest. His eyes were closed. A tear fell down his cheek. His mother was dead. Daniel killed her. James was about to do exactly what he wanted. There was no other way. He would release Daniel. *No other way.*

He did feel the anger Daniel told him to use. It was deep down, primal. The emotion pulled him in every direction. Daniel killed his mother, forced him to do his bidding, to lie and steal and almost die. Alisa was the only reason he continued to follow orders unquestioned. Azalea pushed him to keep going, to figure out his plan, instead of just stopping. Wagner worked with Azalea and never once helped him. But more than any of that, James caved into the man who killed him, bent to the will of a known sociopath. James was at fault here.

It was his own fault, but that didn't matter anymore. None of it mattered until the murder and pain stopped. The anger would keep building and growing until something put a stop to it. James could do just that. He could break this crystal and end it, once and for all.

James didn't care what Daniel did to this world anymore, as long as he left James alone. If Azalea wanted to play spy, she could do that with Daniel. It was all just too much, the missions, the dragon, the death, the secrets. He couldn't take it anymore. James wanted to breakdown and cry, but he couldn't until the crystal was destroyed. He would hold it together only as long as it took to break the crystal, then he could go crawl in a hole.

"James," Flynn's voice took him out of his trance, and he opened his eyes, "I'm going to need you to not make any sudden movements." He was on the defensive. James had never seen Flynn scared, or anything remotely close to how he seemed now.

"What are you doing here?" James asked. He wanted to be left alone. James wanted to complete the mission and leave, never see any of their faces again. He couldn't do that with Flynn standing there. Flynn would stop James from saving everybody.

344

"I'm here to tell you about Daniel." When James didn't make a move, Flynn's voice softened. "Do you ever wonder why the academy is built inside a fortress?" He didn't reply. The mission would be completed, regardless of what Flynn said. He just had to wait for this speech to end. He only needed a small opening.

"Before the academy existed, there was a war between those of us that thought knowledge and light were better fit for rule and those who used destruction and darkness to strike fear into their subordinates. Daniel was in the latter group."

He took a step toward James. "Back in those days, there were no fortresses or castles. Most of us lived on the beach, with some scattered throughout the forests. We built fortresses, I built Toricane, to keep death and destruction out of them. They were built to defend against Daniel."

He took another step toward James, and James took one back. "One day, there was a huge battle. One that, if you've got the crystal, you've seen. Many people died that day, including our leaders. The only ones left in charge were Daniel and I, and, with help, I took him down. Then, I got arrogant. I thought he deserved a worse fate than death. He betrayed me and deserved to be trapped in a prison, forever."

James was only half-listening. His mind was back with his mother. Flynn continued, "I thought he

345

deserved that fate because he was the worst of them. When I saw all the death he'd cause my friends and family, he laughed. He laughed right in my face as I stood with a sword above him. So, I locked him up. I told nobody. The memorial was off limits to everybody. I thought he would stay there forever in that personal prison I created for him."

James grew tired of the speech and stopped him, "Your arrogance caused this." There was no emotion in his voice. It wasn't an outcry of blame or rage built up from his mother's death. There was no defiance in his tone. This was a statement of fact. Along with it, James carried disgust for his mentor, a deep and terminal repulsion.

"Yes," Flynn admitted. "That doesn't change what needs to happen now. We put the crystal back and never touched it again." His tone indicated that it was the only viable option. He was suggesting there was nothing else that could be done.

James' rage surfaced. "He will kill every person I grow close to! Leaving well-enough alone isn't well-enough. Can you destroy the crystal? Can you kill him?"

"Destroying the crystal would only release him," Flynn explained, trying to keep calm. "There's no good way out of this. I will do my best to further disconnect him from the world. I don't know how what he's doing is possible, but I will stop it."

346

"It's too late to stop it," James said. "He's already killed me and my mother. In the time it takes me to hand you the crystal, he'll kill everybody I loved."

"So, what are you going to do, James?" Flynn took another step forward. They were close enough that James could see the dark anger in his eyes. The level tone Flynn had kept seemed like a facade at this distance. His expression gave away the hate he felt toward Daniel and, in this moment, James. Everything he said was just a way to get the crystal. James believed none of it.

"I'm going to save everybody I have and will love on Earth," James calmly explained, wanting this to end. "You locked him up. It's your job to kill him." James reached behind his back, grabbing the crystal and dagger out of the pocket dimension.

A bolt of lightning shot out from Flynn's hand and, by instinct, James dropped the crystal to defend himself. He held the dagger out in from of him to absorb the blow. The lightning hit with a force James had never experienced before, knocking him back as the crystal fell to the ground between them. The lightning had caught James off guard, but he expected the next move, Flynn went for the crystal.

A single thought echoed through James' mind: *if Flynn gets the crystal, all of this was for nothing; my entire world would mean nothing.* The rage that had been settling in the pit of his mind leapt out in pure manifestation energy. Waves of light and darkness echoed from James' body, pushing Flynn back. Flynn wanted to just pretend like the last six miserable months didn't happen. Like James' mother didn't just die in front of him. The waves intensified, and Flynn waved his hand, creating a barrier around himself.

"Let's not do this, James. It's not going to end well." James was too far gone. The anger rippled out from him with the new-found power Daniel had gifted him in the form of loss. He reached forward to stab the crystal. "No!" Flynn yelled and ripped the ground up under James, throwing him into the air. "I can't let you!" James fell back. Flynn pulled a tree out of the ground and smacked him with all the force he could muster.

James was able to break the tree around him. He picked up the shards and angled them at Flynn. "Is it so easy to kill one of your recruits?"

"You're not my recruit. You're Daniel's puppet." Flynn dematerialized the wooden shards pointed toward him, melting them into a puddle. He raised both hands, creating an elemental swarm circling around them. Flynn forced James to the ground, an iron hand around his throat. The swarm broke and beamed toward a defenseless James. Then, whoosh; the air expanded, creating a small whirlwind.

Wagner appeared in the center of it, directly in front of James, blocking the elemental storm from passing. "Stop it, Flynn! We can figure this out. You can't kill him! None of this is his fault."

"Are you a part of this too? You want Daniel released?!" Flynn's rage was echoed in the waves of elemental chaos pushing Wagner back. There was no talking him down, He was past the point of no return. "I should've known you would betray me one day, Darius, just like you did him." The storm didn't calm, only barraging Wagner further.

"No, but there's a better way! We can find a better way," Wagner shouted. James struggled against the spectral hand, trying to unlatch it from his throat.

"It's time for action, Darius! You sat and did nothing all year. You knew this would happen. You still know it will, yet you sit on your hands and do nothing!" Light was accumulating around Flynn as darkness infiltrated his body. He seemed to be filtering the light in his body out to use as a weapon, one connected to his form like an appendage.

Wagner pushed forward and the storm of elements buried themselves in the ground. He flicked his wrist and the spectral hand disappeared. "You want action?! We let Daniel go and kill him right now. We end this."

James stood up. Both he and Wagner inched toward the crystal. Flynn countered, "We took him by surprise last time and only won through random chance. We face him right now, he will win. I can't let that happen."

As they got closer to the crystal, Flynn sent out an orb of light. Wagner countered with darkness. It created a blast that sent everybody flying back. They were dazed and blinded for a second. James recovered first, being furthest from the blast, and got up to see Azalea standing in the middle. She was holding the crystal.

"Azalea toss me the crystal. I can end this right now." James held out his hand. She stood there looking back and forth between James and Wagner.

"It was never supposed to come to this. We were going to have time to figure something out," Azalea said. She didn't know what to do.

Before Flynn could react, Wagner sent him flying back. "Get the crystal! I'll hold him off," he shouted at James and took off toward Flynn.

James took a step forward, "Give me the crystal, Azalea. There was never going to be a way around this."

She held it closer to herself. "You're saving yourself from his grasp, but you're putting everyone else at risk."

"No! I'm saving everybody I love," he deflected.

350

"At the risk of everything else."

He walked toward her, hand out. "So, that's what this always was for you, a mission?" A blast of light came their direction. James waved it away.

Her face hardened. Unsure what else she could do, Azalea looked around for somewhere to hide the crystal. In desperation, she put they crystal in her shirt, keeping it away from him. "You can't have the crystal." Azalea sent a swarm of ice needles his direction. The ice melted before they reached James. She manifested a sword, which buried itself in the ground. The rock beneath him rumbled. His hand raised. It calmed.

"I'm trying to save you. Let me," he pleaded.

"You wouldn't be saving me. You would be condemning me to live a life of shame and regret. If you want this crystal, you're going to have to kill me." Her feet stayed planted firmly where they were.

James faltered. He thought back to his family on Earth. He thought about Alisa. She had an entire life left to live. He stepped within arm's reach of her. She blasted darkness at him. James grabbed it out of the air and allowed it to mix with light as it floated away. "I don't want to fight you," he said. *But I can't let you kill Alisa. She doesn't deserve that.*

A half-smile appeared as she realized where his mind was. She could always read him like a book.

Azalea saw him grip the dagger tighter. She saw the look in his eyes telling her this was the end. There was room to run away, time to try one more manifestation. But she wouldn't die like a damsel in distress. She would stand her ground, and if James needed to destroy the crystal, he could kill her for it.

In that moment, Azalea realized she would give up her life for his, but she still couldn't give up on the mission. Her purpose was important, but, to her, he was more important. "It was never just about the mission, James. I love you."

"I'll see you in our next death, Azalea." He pushed the dagger into her chest. Between the two, he heard a crack from the crystal. Darkness spread through Azalea. Pain spread across her face, then a smile. She'd given her life for the mission. Her body went limp. Azalea's body hit the ground, but she was already gone. The darkness turned to ash. She blew away.

James knelt down next to the ash. For the second time today, he was staring at a dead loved one because of Daniel's mission. *It's over now. No more people die.*

James took a handful of ash and gripped it tight to his chest. He closed his eyes and allowed the tears to come. The rage left his mind completely. His pit of despair was empty, just like his life without Azalea. Sadness poured into it, filling it to the brim. He would see her again, but it would never be the same. "I love you too," he uttered.

"I'm so sorry." A tear landed in the ash. James half expected a miracle. He was in a world of miracles, so why couldn't one help him. Azalea could reform out of the ash. Maybe that was just a manifested clone. Somebody could bring her back.

Nothing changed. The elemental storm whipped by him and air blew past, taking the ash with it. He reached out, but it went through his fingers. He had no strength to pull it back with his abilities. All that was left of her was in his hand, clutched to his chest.

"No!" came a voice running toward him. Wagner had done his best to hold Flynn back, not realizing the consequences. When they saw Azalea, both of them ran toward James. "What did you do?"

He looked up to see Wagner screaming at him. That was fine. They could scream at him. It was over. "Only what I had to," he replied, still holding onto a fistful of ash for dear life. He looked back down, defeated.

"Forget it. It's too late," Flynn said, anger still welled up. "He's coming. You have no idea what you've done."

James couldn't believe he was being blamed for anything that happened here. His life was suffering at every turn. This was Flynn's fault. He would pay. "I would not have had to kill her, if you would've let me break it in the first place!" he shouted to Flynn. An earthquake started under Flynn's feet.

"Stop it now! We have bigger problems." James snapped out of his anger for a moment when he saw a purple slice in the world appear in front of them. The earthquake faded, and he stood in preparation. James' eyes were out of focus. He wasn't ready. *I don't want to fight.*

He heard another voice in his head. It sounded like Azalea, 'The mission isn't over. Carissa and Lloyd still need you. Daniel can't win.'

Can't they fend for themselves, he argued.

'Is that something a soldier would say? What about a spy?' Azalea's voice countered.

'You're surviving for her,' He heard his Uncle Hugo's words repeated from a memory a lifetime ago. 'When the going gets tough, when dying is the easiest option, you'll find a way to keep going.'

I'm surviving for her. He stood up taller and opened his fist, allowing the last of the ash to blow away.

"What happens now?" James asked, staring at the purple slice in the world.

Flynn responded, "Now, we die. But first, we fight." He looked at James, hate still burning in his eyes. The hate wasn't directed toward James anymore. It was meant for an old friend, one that was about to re-enter the world. His revenge was about to be complete.

Wagner pulled the sword out from his cane and added, "We kill him for good. No prison this time around."

From the slice, a man limped out. He shined a bright smile their way and took a deep breath in, "Ah, I can't remember the last time I smelled fresh air. It smells like..." he tilted his head and sniffed in loudly for effect "...ash and betrayal, just wonderful," he said, returning his gaze to the trio in front of him, his smile now steely and cold.

Flynn's hands twisted mechanically; several swords materialized and were sent in Daniel's direction. Without Daniel's speech breaking, the swords stopped in front of him and turned to face them. "It's great to be back. I have so many ideas for change! The first change is teaching you how to fight. Has the sword trick ever worked for you, Flynn?" He looked toward Wagner. "Is that my cane? You really shouldn't steal other people's things."

"It's my trophy for killing you. One that I will earn," Wagner replied.

James had enough. For the past six months, Daniel had done nothing but talk and destroy his life. He focused on a point under Daniel's feet and the ground turned into rock spikes, which were broken upon creation and added to the swords. A glob of darkness shot out from Wagner. It was stopped and mixed into the weapons Daniel accumulated. The swords and spikes turned a dark black.

Daniel continued, "I'll get my cane back, Darius." He looked toward James, "James! You did so well! I am sorry about your girlfriend. The one here, not the one on Earth. I get them mixed up sometimes. It was a noble sacrifice. Now, I told you I would not kill you, and I keep my word. So, goodbye."

James was flung into a tree, and the branches wrapped around his stomach, cementing him to it. He watched as Flynn and Wagner threw attack after attack toward Daniel. Each attack either added to his collection or seemed to not faze him. Nothing they did could affect him.

"Enough is enough," Daniel said. "I'm getting tired of your games. All these weapons are making me feel personally attacked. It's very hurtful." He raised his hands and an elemental storm followed. He pulled a collection of fire out of the storm, which turned into a wall pushing toward them. Wagner managed to roll out of the way. Flynn put a barrier of water around himself.

While they were distracted, Daniel sent the collection of swords, spikes, darkness and light he accumulated zooming toward them. Wagner took a spike to his shoulder, which buried him in the ground. As the wall of fire passed over Flynn's barrier, several dark-filled swords pierced it. Flynn saw it at the last second and pulled a metal shield from the elemental storm. It wasn't enough. One sword got through. He hit the ground.

James was stuck to the tree, doing everything he could to get loose. Nothing worked. Daniel had some sort of control over him and his powers. He was powerless. He needed to sever that connection. *The book,* he thought. James fumbled around the branches and took his book out. The book he'd signed when first arriving in Toricane.

The dagger came up in his hand and stabbed the book. Daniel looked over, feeling the connection break. He laughed, "I don't need that anymore. I'm already here. Destroy it all you want!"

Daniel turned back to his peers. Flynn wasn't moving. Wagner was struggling to get the spike out of his shoulder. "Did you really think it would be easy to defeat me? Isabel taught me so much during my time here, enough to almost win a battle with a backstabbing traitor. It's been a century since then and I've been locked away with nothing to do but find different ways to kill you.

Maybe I'll kill you both the same way I killed James' mother."

"Darius," Daniel said, standing over him, "it took me a very long time to get over your betrayal that day. I realized though, you were never on my side, were you? Always had to be the spy. You wanted to infiltrate them in secret, all by yourself, and you always managed to come back alive. One day it hit me, you were just playing double agent."

"It worked," Darius said, giving up on the spike burying him into the ground.

"Yes," he laughed, "it sure did work out for you. It gave you a century more of life, which ends today. I hope it was worth it."

It was over. James had nothing he could do. The branches wouldn't budge. The only thing he had was the dagger, but that wasn't enough. He closed his eyes. He was exhausted. His mind drifted to better days back on Earth. Easier days. His mind shifted. His body was somewhere else.

Alisa's new partner came into view. He was comforting her. They didn't know why Mariam died but would get through it together. Mariam's last wish was for her to be happy and move on, so that's what she did. Alisa told the man she'd move in with him. He was surprised by the timing but overjoyed at the news. They could start their life together away from the death and destruction.

James envied the comfort they found in each other. He thought for a split second he wanted Alisa to comfort him like that, but it wasn't true. What he really wanted was Azalea back. Yes, he would see her in the next life, but they couldn't make it work, not after he just killed her. The spying and double agent stuff was small compared to what James had done. Regardless, that's who he wanted.

He couldn't stop picturing Azalea, even when Alisa was right there. As he looked through Alisa's eyes, the scene before him slowly faded from view. He was surrounded by white; it was orientation day. James realized he was scrying his own memories.

The first memory was also the first positive experience he'd had in Toricane. A woman with soft features and flowing brown hair sat next to him. The rest of his classmates laughed when he told them he was seventeen. She put her hand on his leg and reassured him, introducing herself as Azalea.

The first labor flashed into view. Azalea smiled at him as they ran after a bear. The memory sped up to a stone golem charging her. By instinct alone, James threw a disc of light and darkness her way. The light soaked into her, saving her life. She was asking him out. The look on her face was so innocent. She stumbled through her words. How could James have ever thought it was just about the mission?

A small white box unfolded in front of them on the campus lawn. Azalea had gotten way more dressed up than James. She went out of her way to make a special date for the two of them. Daniel hurt him, and Azalea stepped out in front, offering herself up. She stood up for him. Azalea went on those missions to protect him.

She helped him break into the main office. They went to the ruins. She cleaned up the entire battlefield of dead just so he could get a few hours of sleep. She put herself in danger's way for him. She saved him from the dragon. *Wait,* James thought. The memory stopped. *She saved me from the dragon, how?*

The flow of memories slowed down. As James turned around from the swarm of soldiers, he saw Azalea pointing the dagger at them. When they were dead, she pointed the dagger at the sky, and the dragon flew away. Azalea had never mentioned anything about it. *She didn't want Daniel to know.*

He came out of the scry and opened his eyes to find he had been out for almost no time at all. Daniel still stood over Wagner, but he was about to end it. James reached for the dagger and concentrated on what was inside. He felt a heartbeat. It was a large, monstrous heart. His whole mind focused on that beating heart in the dagger. He pointed it at Daniel.

A wing beat in the distance. It wasn't enough to distract him. James needed to stall. "Hey! Daniel!"

The smile he'd grown so used to hating flashed his way. "I'm just about to finish up here. Give me one second and I'll make my way to you."

"How did he almost kill you back in the day? Aren't you more powerful than he is?" James taunted.

Daniel's grin flickered. He turned toward James, "He took a cheap shot! While my back was turned, he stabbed me with my own dagger!" The wings beat a little louder. "I had Flynn pinned, just like I have you now. There's nobody here to betray me this time. I don't need anybody else for this. After a hundred years, it's my time for revenge!"

A shadow was cast over the forest entrance. All three of them looked up to see wings stretched out across the sky. James took a chance, "You said you wouldn't kill me. If that dragon's about to land here, I'm going to need to run."

Daniel eyed him, "I've done a lot for you already...Maybe you're right. Consider this a parting gift." James' binds were released. He stood up and hid the dagger behind his back. Daniel looked up again to see the dragon diving straight toward him. He pulled the ground up creating a bubble of rock. The dragon smashed into it, causing it to fall apart. The vibrations shook the ground, and Daniel took several steps back.

The blow made him lose concentration, giving Wagner a chance to escape his bind. Once more, James pointed the dagger at Daniel. The dragon roared and went in for a bite. Daniel threw up a mix of light and darkness that were absorbed into the animal's scales. He evaded the crushing of it's jaws at the last second.

Wagner stood tall and pulled the spike out of his shoulder. James yelled out, "Attack Daniel! The dragon won't hurt you." Taking James at his word, Wagner pulled roots out of the ground and planted Daniel to the spot. The dragon took two swipes with his claws, that were barely batted away with metal fists.

Daniel looked at James, curious how he was controlling it and saw the dagger pointed at him. He stumbled back a few more steps after getting almost eaten but was hit by the dragon's tail. It knocked him to the ground. In desperation, a large forcefield shot out from his body, hitting Wagner back and momentarily stunning the dragon.

Daniel took the few seconds he had to create a ray of pure light. The light James produced had never been that bright. It came from the sky and hit directly on the dagger in his hand. The ray didn't stop and kept beating down on the dagger. When it relented, James reached down to retrieve it, only to find pieces of dark metal scattered around him.

Daniel laughed, "Good luck controlling it now!" He got up and took several swipes of light at the dragon. They were absorbed into its scales. He huffed in frustration and disappeared from sight with a loud whoosh of air.

The dragon lashed out in anger. It looked around to see both James and Wagner. Its tail came toward James. Instinctually, he pushed rock up from the ground to block the blow. The ground cracked but didn't budge. *Daniel's power...My power, it's gone,* was his last thought before the tail knocked him to the ground. His head hit a rock. Everything went black.

Toricane

The End of The Tunnel

James woke up in a bed he didn't recognize. He couldn't move. Somebody else was in the room. "Chloe."

She jumped, not expecting to hear anything. "James! Don't move. You're in a heal unit I set up on campus. Before Professor Wagner could get you out of there, the dragon really did a number on you. Most of the left side of your body was at least partially broken, along with a major concussion."

He had noticed the aching pain throughout his entire body. It felt like a building was laying on top of him. "How long until I can get out of here?"

"Oh, that's going to be a couple weeks. We can heal you pretty quick here, but it's not a miracle factory," she said.

"Where's Professor Wagner? Where's Daniel?"

She manifested a chair and sat down. "Professor Wagner is fine. I just let him know you're awake," she pointed to her head, indicating telepathy. "Nobody knows where Daniel went. He could be anywhere. We've tripled security at the border wall. That's really all we can do for now."

He sighed, "I'm sorry."

She waved off his apology, "You don't need to apologize or explain. Professor Wagner told us the dilemma he put you in. I can't say I would've reacted any differently."

"What about Flynn?" he asked.

She frowned, "Flynn didn't make it. We're not sure if he was still alive after the sword, but the dragon pretty much made sure he wasn't." Her eyes were puffy and red. She looked away from James before continuing, "He was a great man. He will be missed."

James didn't want to counter her, solely because he died. Flynn was the absolute last person he wanted to survive that attack, except maybe Daniel. "Do you have funerals here?"

"Of course," she said sternly, getting control of her emotions. "We are having a funeral for both Flynn and Azalea in a couple days. You will still be laid up here. I don't think it's best for you to be there, regardless." She paused. "We don't blame you. But it's still for the best."

He nodded in agreement. "Could you wait a bit before you tell Carissa and Lloyd that I'm awake? I just don't know what I'm going to say to them."

"I'll just tell them you need to keep resting. Which is true! You do need to rest. Go back to sleep and I'm sure Professor Wagner will be here when you wake up."

He didn't need to be told twice. James' eyes closed, and he drifted off to sleep. The next couple weeks went by in a blur. He was in and out of consciousness during the recovery. Carissa and Lloyd didn't seem to want to talk about Azalea, other than to say they couldn't wait until the four of them were together again next year. Wagner only stopped by a couple times. He wanted to make sure the connection to Daniel was truly broken.

Outside of the recovery unit, life had been somewhat normal. The fourth labor, and subsequent missions were cancelled. Flynn's job as director was offered to Wagner, who turned it down. Instead, on Wagner's suggestion, Chloe took the job. She would be running the academy from now on. Other than that, recruits went about their lives as normal, with the qualification that they stay within campus borders for the remainder of the year.

Once James was out, he returned to normal lessons. Without Daniel's powers, he was much more like a normal recruit. He performed better than the rest, only due to his experience during the last six months and the training with Flynn. He spent his evenings with Lloyd and Carissa, playing around on campus and training. It was a fun time, but Azalea never left his head.

After a few weeks, he came to a decision. It was time to go. "Professor," James entered Wagner's office one day after his lesson. "I have a question."

"What can I help you with, James?" he put down the paper being graded.

"How do you know Daniel can't contact me just like he did last time?"

"Oh, don't worry, James," he said. "I figured out how he did that. After examining it, I realized the crystal was actually a holding cell for a dimension that sat on top of Earth. I bet Flynn never even knew that's what he created. It wouldn't be possible for him to do that, without getting stuck back in that dimension."

James took a seat and nodded. "Then I want to go back."

"Back where?" Wagner was confused.

"To Earth. I want to go back early."

He was bewildered, "Why would you want to do that?"

"Professor, I killed Azalea. We can say I was in a bad position, I had no other option, or it was really Daniel, but it was me. I don't deserve to be here when she isn't." James looked down, not making eye contact with Wagner. He knew it was unusual, but the thought of staying here, enjoying himself, just wasn't right.

He would be back, and with her, so this felt more like a 'see you later' than a 'goodbye.' He wanted to illustrate his seriousness to Wagner, "I don't want to be here when she isn't."

Wagner looked at James and sighed, "I won't stop you, if that's what you want to do. You were both advanced enough to come back and start your second year here. You don't have to do that, though. You can stay here and have fun with your abilities, learn great things. I mean, James, you only have four months left. It's really not a lot of time." James' expression didn't change. "That's really what you want?" He nodded. "Okay. I'll arrange something for tomorrow."

James went back to Volition Tower and told his friends the plan. They weren't surprised. He hadn't been himself since the incident and they weren't going to try to stop him. By this time, Carissa and Lloyd had spent most of the year apart from Azalea and James. They had their own life, and James was always welcome into it but never felt like it was his.

Together, Lloyd and Carissa had built that piano Lloyd wanted all year. They spent most of their time around it, perfecting it, playing it. Lloyd was teaching Carissa the intricacies of learning to play, and she used her book to find songs they could play. They would be great without him.

James made it a point to go say bye to Chloe, also. She did try to talk him out of it, but that wasn't going to happen. He'd made up his mind.

He met Wagner at the edge of campus the next day. "Where is this going to happen?" he asked.

"In the main office. I realize you've never been there legally, so try to act like you don't belong. At the end of the year, recruits are all put in beds that are filled with light. It's a very peaceful way to go out, like falling asleep. I've arranged for a bed to be ready earlier than usual."

"What's it like, living another life?"

"Well," Wagner started, "you won't know you're living another life. It'll just be a life. The weird part is waking up here at the end. When you remember everything that happened, it's like waking up from a really long dream where you never figured out it was a dream. It's strange, but you get used to it."

"Want to make any guesses on who I'll be this time?"

Wagner laughed, "Once a soldier, always a soldier, is what I say."

"Drafted soldier," James corrected, "and I never made it there. Maybe this time I will." He laughed. "There's one more thing I don't understand."

"What's that?"

"Daniel told me that my death was random, but it wasn't chosen by him. I never understood that. He acted like somebody chose for him. Does that make sense?"

Wagner nodded, "Yes. Unfortunately, that does make sense. I didn't ever get the chance to tell you, with him listening in all the time. Just before you died, Chloe told me I should empathize with my recruits more. I thought a good way to do that would be to watch somebody's life on Earth. It was a random choice."

"So...you were watching me?"

"In a sense. I was scrying you. That was the day before you died. So, as you can imagine, I didn't see much. I did see you die. That was...unpleasant. Although, I'm sure not as unpleasant as it was for you."

Wagner was clearly uncomfortable with this topic but James was thankful he shared.

"So, random, yes. Well, it got me here, so not all bad." Wagner nodded in agreement. They walked through the entrance to the main office. "I'm guessing in my next life here, you're not going to be so lenient about illegal activities."

"That would be an accurate guess, James. I took it easy on you only because of Daniel. If you find yourself breaking in here on a regular basis, that would be an issue."

"What does this place even do?" James asked, looking around at the bland walls and people walking back and forth.

"There's lots about Toricane you have yet to learn. I think this is something I'll let you discover in your own time. For now, I'll just say, they keep things running smoothly."

James laughed, "Okay, be mysterious about it. I'll figure it out on my own."

After a few more minutes, they arrived in a room with one bed in the center. "So, I just get on the bed?" James asked.

"You just get on the bed," he confirmed.

The End of The Tunnel

He took a deep breath and got on. Wagner put his hand up to it and the bed started to glow. He looked solemnly at James, "I'll see you in a few months."

James looked back, "I'll see you in a lifetime." The light under James made him incredibly tired. He closed his eyes.

Wagner watched as James drifted off. This was the second time he'd seen James die, and somehow this one felt right. There was a sense of bitter sweetness to it. Wagner was looking forward to seeing James again next year, a happier, whole James. He stood and waited for James' breath to stop before leaving the room. He shut the door and didn't look back. It was time for lecture.

James was completely oblivious to this. Once his eyes closed, he started drifting off. His mind wandered back to his time on Earth, wondering what would become of his second. His body shifted into another's. He opened his eyes. James was seeing his home for what would most likely be the last time.

The rustic wood and smell of perfume filled his nose. Alisa was moving boxes. By the look of it, she was down to the last one. The house they bought together was emptied out. The man she was moving in with came and took the last box. Alisa looked around at the house for a moment. She remembered back to their wedding, that sad day, then realized all the good that came from the sad.

She realized, there aren't sad days, really. There are good days and bad days, but you never know what a day will bring you in the future. Looking back at the worst day she'd ever had, her wedding, didn't bring her sadness anymore. Her life brought only joy in that moment. It didn't matter how good or bad, every day led to the joy she felt right now. Alisa walked out the door. She shut it and didn't look back.

Made in the USA
Lexington, KY
14 July 2019